London, 1814

A season of secrets, scandal and seduction!

A darkly dangerous stranger is out for revenge, delivering a silken rope as his calling card. Through him, a long-forgotten scandal is reawakened. The notorious events of 1794, which saw one man murdered and another hanged for the crime, is ripe gossip in the *ton*. Was the right culprit brought to justice or is there a treacherous murderer still at large?

As the murky waters of the past are disturbed, so servants find love with roguish lords, and proper ladies fall for rebellious outcasts until, finally, the true murderer and spy is revealed.

Regency Silk & Scandal

From glittering ballrooms to a Cornish smuggler's cove; from the wilds of Scotland to a Romany camp— join with the highest and lowest in society as they find love in this thrilling new eight-book miniseries!

Louise Allen

THE LORD AND THE WAYWARD LADY

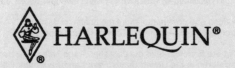

HARLEQUIN®

TORONTO • NEW YORK • LONDON
AMSTERDAM • PARIS • SYDNEY • HAMBURG
STOCKHOLM • ATHENS • TOKYO • MILAN • MADRID
PRAGUE • WARSAW • BUDAPEST • AUCKLAND

Recycling programs
for this product may
not exist in your area.

ISBN-13: 978-0-373-29596-8

THE LORD AND THE WAYWARD LADY

Copyright © 2010 by Melanie Hilton

North American Publication 2010

Printed in U.S.A.

Dear Reader,

It was a thrill to be asked to contribute to the Regency miniseries Silk & Scandal, but unlike so many things where the initial thrill wears off when reality hits, this experience just got better and better.

Not only were there five other authors to get to know—and what a joy that was—but then we had the delight of creating our Regency world with a mystery and a scandal at the heart of it. We had our own characters to discover but we also had the cast of eight books to work with, all interacting together to advance the plot or intensify the mystery.

This, the first book, introduces the Carlow family—Marcus, Honoria, Hal and Verity. Each of the siblings has a story in this series and it is Marcus, the elder son of Lord and Lady Narborough, who first realizes that the shocking secrets from his father's past have come back to haunt them all.

Interwoven with the Carlows' lives and loves are three other families along with their friends, enemies and unlikely allies. I hope you enjoy meeting them all and following them on their journey to find vengeance, redemption, the truth—and love.

But now meet Marcus, a man with a lot on his mind, and Nell, a milliner with a pistol in her reticule, and enter a world of silk and scandal.

With best wishes,

Louise

For my fellow Continuistas—
Annie, Christine, Gayle, Julia, and Margaret—
with love. What a wonderful way to meet!

Look for these novels in the Regency miniseries

Silk & Scandal

shone, the air was crisp, the fog had lifted and the

Chapter One

January 5, 1814. London

'Just look at that blue sky, guv'nor. Mornin' like this, all's right with the world and no mistake.'

'You must be in love, Dan.' Marcus Carlow, Viscount Stanegate, observed as he looped his reins and took the corner from Piccadilly into Albemarle Street at a brisk trot.

A waft of onions from behind him accompanied an indignant snort from his tiger. 'You won't find me shut up in parson's pound, guv'nor. Nah, just look at it: all crisp and sunny and fresh. A perfect day—proper lifts the spirits. Nuffin' could go wrong on a day like this.'

'After a remark like that, a superstitious man would take to his bed, order the doors to be bolted and expect disaster.' Marcus grinned, steadying the pair as they took exception to a large party proceeding along the pavement in a flurry of bandboxes and fluttering scarves.

It was a damned good day, Dan was right. The sun shone, the air was crisp, the fog had lifted and the intriguing Mrs Perdita Jensen was showing unmistakeable signs of a willingness to accept his *carte blanche*.

Yes, if one disregarded a father whose poor health was wearing down his mother's spirits, one sister whose aim in life appeared to bring him to an early grave with worry, another whose sweet innocence was equally conducive to anxiety, and a brother who, when he was not putting life and limb at risk on the battlefield, was set on becoming the wildest rake in town, then one might, indeed, believe that nothing on earth could go wrong.

Marcus contemplated the day ahead. Luncheon with the family, a meeting with Brocket, the estate manager, up from Hertfordshire with a bulging portfolio of estate business, dinner at his club and then a visit to Mrs Jensen's discreet apartments to agree terms. Calm, ordered, satisfactory and predictable, just for once.

'Take the curricle round to the mews, Dan. I won't be—' The door of the double-fronted town house burst open as a footman emerged at the run. 'Peters?'

'My lord.' The man pulled himself up at the foot of the steps. 'Lord Narborough—it looks like another heart stroke, my lord. Mr Wellow said I was to take a hack and fetch the doctor, urgently.'

'Dan, take the reins.' Marcus thrust them into the tiger's hands as the young man scrambled round and into the seat. Marcus vaulted down and pushed the footman up beside Dan. 'If Dr Rowlands isn't at home, find where he has gone and bring him.'

He took the steps two at a time and caught the closing front door. The hall was in turmoil. Richards, the youngest footman, was wringing his hands and declaring that it wasn't his fault, the young lady looked respectable enough and how was he to know she was a murdering hussy? Wellow, the butler, was demanding of Felling, the earl's elderly valet, where his lordship's drops were, and at the foot of the stairs three young women were engaged in a noisy argument.

Or, at least, Honoria, his elder sister, was arguing. Verity, the younger, was in tears. Marcus shrugged off his caped driving coat and strode across the black-and-white chequered floor to the one person who appeared to be calm. 'Miss Price, what has occurred?'

His sisters' companion turned, relief at the sight of him clear on her face. 'Lord Stanegate, thank Heavens you are returned. No, Honoria! If your mama says the young woman is to remain in the library until Lord Stanegate says what is to be done, then that is where she stays and you are not to speak to her.' She put an arm around Verity and gave her a little shake. 'Now stop crying, Verity. What good is that going to do your papa?'

'None.' Verity threw herself onto Marcus's chest. 'Marc! Papa is dying!'

'Nonsense,' he retorted with more assurance than he felt, disentangling his sister and setting her firmly on her feet. 'Verity, Honoria, go and help Felling find Papa's drops. Miss Price, where is Lord Narborough?'

'In his study, with her ladyship,' she said. 'Mrs Hoby should be up at any moment with some sweet tea.'

'Thank you.' Marcus opened the door to the study and went quietly inside. His father was stretched out on the big leather chaise, his wife seated by his side, patting his hand. Marcus stopped dead, shaken despite knowing what to expect. The earl, always in poor health, was only fifty-four, but with grey hair and stooped shoulders he

looked twenty years older. Marcus could barely recall
his father as well and active. But now, with blue lips and
his eyes closed and sunken, he looked a dying man.

'Mama?'

Lady Narborough looked up and smiled.

'Marc, I knew you would not be long. George,
here is Marc.'

The hooded lids fluttered open and Marcus let out the
breath he was holding. No, his father was not going to
die, not this time. The dark grey eyes, so like his own,
were focused and alive.

'Father, what happened?'

'Some girl…brought it. Don't know why.' His right
hand moved restlessly. Marcus knelt by the chaise,
taking his father's hand in his as his mother got up and
moved aside to give him room.

His father gripped his fingers. 'There.' He turned his
head towards the desk where a brown-paper parcel lay
undone, something heaped in its midst. 'My boy.' His
voice dropped to a whisper and Marcus leaned close to
hear. 'That old business. Hebden and Wardale. Dead and
buried…I thought.' He closed his eyes again. 'Don't
fuss. Shock, that's all… Damn this heart.'

Lady Narborough met Marcus's eyes across the room,
her own wide and questioning as he curled his fingers
around his father's wrist and felt for the pulse. 'He'll do,'
he murmured as the housekeeper came in with the tea, the
valet at her heels with the belladonna drops.

Between them, they got the earl propped up and sipping
his tea. Certain his mother was occupied, Marcus moved
to the desk and examined the parcel that had caused all the
trouble. Ordinary stout brown paper tied with string and

sealed with a blob of red wax. *The Earl of Narborough* and the address in a firm black hand, probably masculine. Marcus bent and sniffed: no perfume.

And lying in the centre, beside the knife his father had used to slash the string, a length of coiled rope. It was perhaps an inch thick and a strange colour, a mix of fine soft threads—blues, reds, yellows, white, brown and black.

Frowning, Marcus lifted it and it slithered, snakelike, in his grip. The feel as it moved was somehow alive. Silk? Then he saw the loop and the knot in the end, and recognised it. A silken rope, a luxurious halter to hang a man. The privilege, if such it could be called, accorded to a peer of the realm who was sentenced to death.

Hebden and Wardale, his father had said. One a victim, the other his murderer. Two dead men. And now, after almost twenty years, this rope delivered to their closest friend. Coincidence? He did not think so and neither, it was obvious, did his father.

With a glance to reassure himself that the earl seemed stable enough, Marcus slipped from the room. Raised female voices could be heard from the White Salon, but the hall was empty save for Wellow, on the watch for the doctor.

'Wellow, what the devil has been going on here?'

The butler tightened his lips, his face once more impassive beneath the imposing dome of his bald head. 'A young woman called—at the front door, my lord. Richards answered it. He says she appeared a lady, despite carrying a parcel, which is why he did not send her to the tradesmen's entrance. She asked to speak to his lordship, insisted that she must deliver the package into his hands.

'Richards showed her through to the study.' The butler's expression boded ill for the junior footman. 'I regret to say he has now forgotten the name he was given to announce. He left her alone with his lordship. A few moments later the young woman came out of the room, calling for help. His lordship was in a collapsed condition. I told Richards to shut her in the library and lock the door until your return, my lord, considering that the entire affair had a most irregular appearance.'

'Very wise, thank you, Wellow. I will speak to her now. Call me when the doctor arrives.'

The key was in the lock. Marcus turned it and went into the library, braced for almost anything.

The woman who turned from her contemplation of the street was tall, slender to the point of thinness and clad in a plain, dark pelisse and gown. Her bonnet was neither fashionable nor dowdy; the impression she gave was of neatness and frugality. As he came closer and noticed the tightness with which her hands were clasped before her and the rigidity of her shoulders, he realized that she was under considerable strain.

'The butler told me to wait for Lord Stanegate. Are you he?' Her voice was a surprise. Warm and mellow, like honey. Hazel eyes watched him, full of concern. Feigned?

'I am Stanegate,' he said, not troubling to blank out his feelings from either his face or voice. For whatever reason, she had made his father very ill. 'And you?'

'Miss Smith.'

Why couldn't I have thought of something more convincing? Nell stared back into the hard eyes, as dark as wet flint. He was too big, too serious, too *male*. And far too close. She locked her knees against the instinct to edge backwards as she read the anger under the control he was exerting.

'Miss *Smith?*' No, he didn't believe her. There was scepticism in the deep voice, and one corner of his mouth turned down in the reverse of a smile as he studied her face. 'Why, exactly, have you delivered a silken rope to my father?'

Nell made herself withstand the compelling dark eyes. 'Is that what it was? The parcel seemed innocuous enough. I saw no harm in it.'

'The rope looked like a snake. You are fortunate that he did not die of the shock. The earl is not a well man, his heart is weak.' There was the anger again, like fire behind the flint. A man who loved his father and was afraid for him.

'I had no idea what it contained. It was only a parcel to be delivered.' *Just let me go…*

'Indeed? You hardly look like the sort of female to be employed delivering parcels.' The viscount—she supposed that was what he was; her grasp of the ranks of nobility was escaping her under stress—folded his arms across his chest and looked her up and down. She knew what he was seeing. Shabby gentility, neatness and decency maintained by sheer willpower and a refusal to give in and allow her standards to slip.

'I am a—' *Lie,* her instincts shouted '—dressmaker. I deliver garments for fittings to clients' homes on behalf of my employer. One gentleman asked, as a favour, if she would have me deliver that parcel here. He has spent a good deal of money at the shop recently. Madame did not like to refuse such a good customer.'

'His name?' He did not seem to actually disbelieve her despite the sceptical line of that hard mouth. And it was true. Almost.

'I do not know it.'

'Really, Miss *Smith?* An excellent customer of your employer and you do not know his name?' He moved closer, just a little, just to the very edge of discomfort for her, and narrowed his eyes.

Nell lifted her chin and stared back, letting him see that she was assessing him in her turn, refusing to be cowed. Almost thirty, she guessed; six foot, give or take half an inch; fit; confident, used to getting his own way. Was that because of his station in life or his inherent qualities? All she could tell of the latter, just now, was that he was an angry man who loved his father.

'No, I do not know his real name, my lord. I know the name he gave: Salterton.'

'And how do you know that is false?'

'I assumed by the style of what he chose that he was buying items for his mistress. He spent a lot of money. Money, I deduced, that he would not want his wife to know about. I was there when he first came into the shop and I heard Madame ask him his name. He hesitated, just a fraction, and then there was something in his voice. He was lying; one can tell.'

'Indeed, one can,' Lord Stanegate said, that mobile corner of his mouth twitching up into a fleeting smile that held no humour whatsoever. Nell felt her cheeks grow hot and stared fixedly at the cabochon-ruby pin in his neckcloth. 'What does he look like?'

'I hardly saw him and I think that was deliberate on his part. I do not think even Madame has fully seen his face. He always seems to come in the evening and he wears a slouch hat, his collar is turned up. He pays in cash, not on account.

'But one can see he is dark.' She struggled for remembrance and to assemble her impressions into a coherent description. 'He is foreign perhaps, because there is something in his voice—not quite an accent, more of a lilt, although he speaks like an English gentleman. He looks fit, he moves well.' She frowned, chasing the elusive words to describe the shadowy figure. 'Like a dancer. He is not quite as tall as you and of slighter build.'

As she spoke, she realized she was letting her eyes run over the man in front of her, assessing the elegant simplicity of expensive tailoring and the fit, well-proportioned, body under it. He was dressed for driving in a dark plain coat and buckskin breeches with glossy high boots. She dragged her gaze back to the tiepin: there was something about the set of the strong jaw above the intricate folds of the neckcloth that suggested he was aware of her scrutiny and did not relish it.

'You are a good observer, Miss Smith, considering you only glimpsed him and had no reason to take an interest.' He did not believe her, but she was not going to admit that the dark man had both intrigued and repelled her from the start. He had seemed to bring danger into the frivolous feminine world of the shop. 'What is the name and direction of your employer? Doubtless she will remember even more.'

'I prefer not to give it. Madame would not be pleased if she found I had involved her in an awkward situation.' *And that, my girl, is where you get yourself when you*

*lie. I cannot tell him now, not without admitting I do not
work for a dressmaker, and then he will believe even less
of what I say.*

'And if she is displeased, what is the worst she can
do to you?' The viscount moved away a few steps and
half sat on one corner of the library table. Nell let out
her breath, then realized that he had simply moved back
to study her more closely, head to toe.

'Dismiss me.' Which would be, quite simply, a
disaster. Not, of course, that a man like this would
realize how precarious the life of a working woman
was—with no family, no other means of support.

'Hmm.' He regarded her from under level brows.
Nell had the impression that he spent rather a lot of time
frowning. 'And what can *I* do, do you suppose? I will
tell you—I can hand you in at Bow Street as an accomplice in a conspiracy to murder my father.'

'What! Murder? Why, that is simply ridiculous!' The
shock of the threat propelled her into motion, pacing
away from him in agitation. Nell came up against a
large globe on a stand and spun back to face the
viscount. 'The earl is obviously in bad health and he
must have overstrained himself getting out of his chair
or something. Conspiracy? That is nonsense. What is
there in a length of rope to harm a grown man? What is
it anyway? A curtain tie?'

'A silken rope,' he said slowly, with a weight to his
words that made her feel she should read some signifi-
cance into them. And at the back of her mind, sunk deep
in her memory, something stirred, sent out flickers of
unease as if at the recollection of a childhood nightmare.

Nell shrugged, sending the discomfort skittering back

into the darkness. Somehow, she did not want to explore that elusive thought. 'Take me to Bow Street then,' she bluffed, as though that in itself was not enough to have her instantly dismissed without a character. 'See if the magistrates think that innocently delivering a parcel justifies being locked up and abused.'

'Abused? In what way do you consider yourself abused, Miss Smith?' Lord Stanegate sat there, hands folded, apparently relaxed, looking as unthreatening as six foot of well-muscled angry man could look. 'I can ring for a cup of tea for you, while you consider your position. Or I could send for my sisters' companion, should you require a chaperone. If you are cold, the fire will be laid. Only, I will have an answer, Miss Smith. Do not underestimate me.'

'There is no danger of my doing that, my lord,' she responded, keeping her voice calm with an effort. 'I can see that you are used to getting your own way in all things and that bullying and threatening one defenceless female, however politely, is not something you will baulk at.'

'Bullying?' His eyebrows went up. 'No, this is not bullying, Miss Smith, nor threatening. I am merely setting out the inevitable consequences of your actions—or rather, your inaction.'

'Threats,' she muttered, mutinous and increasingly afraid.

'It would be threatening,' he said, getting to his feet and walking towards her as she backed away, 'if I were to force you back against the bookshelves, like this.' The back of Nell's heels hit wood and she stopped, hands spread. There was nothing behind her but unyielding leather spines.

Lord Stanegate put one hand on either side of her head and glanced at the shelves. 'Ah, the Romantic poets, how very inappropriate. Yes, if I were to trap you like this and to move very close—' he shifted until they were toe to toe, and she felt the heat of his thighs as they brushed her skirts '—and then promise to put my hands around your rather pretty neck and shake the truth out of you—now *that* would be threatening.'

Nell closed her eyes, trying to block out the closeness of him. Behind her were comforting scents from her early childhood: leather and old paper and beeswax wood polish. In front of her, sharp citrus and clean linen and leather and man. She tried to melt back into the old, familiar library smell, but there was no escape that way.

'Look at me.'

She dragged her eyes open. He had shaved very close that morning, but she could tell his beard would be as dark as his hair. There was a tiny scar nicking the left corner of his lips and they were parted just enough for her to see the edge of white, strong teeth. As she watched he caught his lower lip between them for a moment, as though in thought. Nell found herself staring at the fullness where his teeth had pressed; her breath hitched in her chest.

'Well?'

'No.' The thought of his hands on her, sliding under her chin, his fingers slipping into her hair… And the memory of Mr Harris came back to her and she shuddered, unable to stop herself, and he stepped back abruptly as though she had slapped him.

'Damn it—'

'My lord.' The butler was in the doorway. 'Dr

Rowlands is here and Lady Narborough is asking for you. She seems a little anxious, my lord.'

Nell saw, from both their faces, that *a little anxious* was a major understatement. Without a word, Lord Stanegate turned on his heel and strode out after the man. The door banged shut behind him.

Her fingers were locked tight around the edge of the shelf. She opened her hands warily, as though they were all that were keeping her on her feet, then realized that the slam of the door had not been followed by any other sound. They had not locked it again.

Where was her reticule? She ran to the sofa and found the shabby bag, her skirts swinging wildly against the upholstery as she hastened to the door. It opened under her hand, well-oiled hinges yielding without a sound. Then she was into the hall, under the shelter of the arc of the sweeping stairs.

But the butler was by the front door, giving orders to a footman; so there was no escape that way. Nell shrank back into the shadows.

'Wellow!' a clear feminine voice called from a room to the right of the front door. The footman walked briskly past Nell's hiding place and through the green baize door as the butler went to answer the call.

'Yes, Lady Honoria?'

As he went inside the room, Nell tiptoed forward, steadying herself with one hand on a side table bearing a silver salver. The second post had obviously arrived. Ears straining, Nell glanced down.

Lady Honoria Carlow read the direction on the topmost letter.

She stood transfixed. *Carlow?* That was the name

that her gentle widowed mother had spoken with such hate when her control cracked and she fell into sobbing despair. The name at the heart of the darkness in the past, the things that had happened when she was only a tiny child, the things that were never spoken of clearly, must never be asked about.

Lord Narborough's family name was Carlow? Why she must fear that family she had no idea, but they undoubtedly would know and if they found out who she was they would never believe she had acted in innocence.

Nell tiptoed across the marble, her worn shoes making virtually no sound. The door was on the latch, she opened it and was out into the busy late-morning street. A few brisk steps and she was behind the shelter of a waiting hackney carriage. She kept pace as it set off at a walk, held up by traffic, then slipped into Stafford Street. *There, I am safe,* she told herself, fighting the urge to run. *He will never find me now.*

Chapter Two

The rope was safely locked in the bottom drawer of the desk. It might as well have been in plain view on the top and hissing at him like the snake it so resembled for all the good that hiding it away did. Marcus thrust the papers that littered the desk in the library back into their folder and contemplated going into the study. But he felt uncomfortable using it when his father was in town. The older man did virtually nothing on family business these days, but even so, to commandeer his desk felt uncomfortably like stepping into his shoes.

He tried to concentrate on writing to his younger brother instead. He would say nothing of the circumstances, merely that their father had suffered an attack, but was now resting and the doctor was sanguine about a recovery, given time and care.

There was no point in agitating Lieutenant the Honourable Hal Carlow. The last they had heard, Hal was confined to his bed in Wellington's Portuguese headquarters with a nasty infection caused by a slight sabre wound in his side. His regiment, the Eleventh Light

Dragoons, had been sent back to England from the Peninsula the previous year, battered and depleted. Hal, predictably, had pulled strings to find himself some sort of attachment to another regiment out there and had promptly disappeared behind enemy lines on a mission.

Marcus could only be selfishly grateful to whoever had inflicted the wound that was keeping Hal out of trouble, although once convalescent, a bored and off-duty Lieutenant Carlow on the loose was a worrying prospect. As an officer, Marcus was frequently assured, his brother was a paragon, destined for great things and possessing the courage of a lion. Under any other circumstances he was a hell-born babe, determined, Marcus was convinced, to drive his brother to drink or the madhouse.

The sounds of a door slamming and raised voices reminded him that his other siblings were more than capable of achieving *that* without help from Hal. The redoubtable Miss Price was presumably thwarting one of Honoria's wilder schemes while attempting to preserve Verity, wide-eyed in adoration of her sister, from the sharp edge of Honoria's teasing tongue.

He tried to imagine the man strong-willed enough to take Honoria off his hands, and failed. The Season loomed ahead, full of opportunities for one sister to get into outrageous scrapes through unquenchable high spirits and the other, through sheer naïvety, to fall victim to every rake on the prowl.

The fog had descended again, blotting out the promise of the fine morning. Now, in mid-afternoon, it was thick outside the long windows, filling the room with damp gloom despite the blazing fire and the array of lamps.

That damned rope. He wanted to discuss it with his father, but the earl was sleeping. That it had something to do with that old business years ago, when his father had been hardly older than he was himself now, was beyond doubt.

Marcus looked up at the portrait that hung over the fire. Lord Narborough stared back: a virile man at the height of his powers, shoulders square, grey eyes blazing out at the watcher, wig elegant, fingers curled around the hilt of a rapier he could use as readily as he did his fine mind and quick wits.

George Carlow and his friends had faced the Revolution in France, the risk of uprising here, the justified fear of year upon year of bloody war. Close to the inner circles of government, they had existed in a hotbed of intrigue and spying, fighting not on the battlefield but amidst the familiar clubs and balls where the enemy did not wear a scarlet uniform but hid behind the facade of fashion and respectability. His father had plunged into that world of secrets and had lost his health, his peace of mind and his closest friends in the process.

Marcus folded his letter, tossed it to one side, got up and began to pace. That young woman. *Miss Smith* indeed. Was she an innocent tool of someone—her dark man—or was she involved in whatever mischief this man intended?

Instinct told him she was lying. Smith was not her name, and that was not the only falsehood. He could sense the tension in her as she answered him. And yet, he wanted to believe she was innocent of harm. That was presumably his masculine reaction to a remarkably fine pair of greenish hazel eyes, a glimpse of golden-brown hair and a voice that did provocative things at the base of his spine. Marcus frowned. He needed to listen to his brain for this, not other parts of his body.

She was too thin, he told himself. Even bundled up in that drab gown and shapeless pelisse he could tell that. He was not attracted to thin women. Marcus contemplated Mrs Jensen for a pleasurable moment. She was most definitely not thin, not where it mattered. And she would be waiting for their meeting; she had made that quite clear.

Dressmakers were not fair game for a gentleman, in any case. Miss Smith was a respectable young woman so far as chastity went, he would wager. The flare of anger and alarm in her eyes when he had stood toe to toe with her, that was surely not the reaction of a woman who would try to buy her way out of trouble with her body.

He got up and walked to the spot where they had stood so close, wondering if the faint scent of plain soap truly lingered in the air or if it was his imagination. Imagination, obviously. It was too long since he had given his last mistress her congé, tired of her petulance and constant demands. If the household was more settled, he could still go out tonight, conclude matters with the lovely Perdita. *That* would stop him thinking about Miss Smith.

Something pale clung to the folds of the sofa skirts. Marcus hunkered down to pick it up and found it was an inch of fine straw plait, a long thread dangling from it.

He pulled the bell rope. 'Peters, ask Miss Price if it would be convenient for her to spare me a moment.'

His sisters' companion came in promptly, bandbox neat, calm and collected as always. 'Marcus?' She smiled and took a seat as he resumed his. In private they had long since used first names, allies in maintaining order and decorum in the Carlow household.

'What do you make of this, Diana?' He passed her the fragment of plait and watched as she studied it.

'It is a straw plait of course. Hat straw—it is too fine for anything else.' She rubbed and flexed it between her fingers. 'English, I would say. Very good quality and an unusual plait. I have never seen anything quite like it.' She tugged the thread dangling from it and looked at him with intelligent eyes. 'Our visitor of this morning is a milliner?'

'She *said* she was a dressmaker, but it would not surprise me to know that was untrue.'

'If she is working with expensive materials such as this, then she will be with one of the better establishments. Not necessarily of the very highest rank, but good.'

'Could one narrow them down using that piece of plait?'

'I should think so.' Miss Price picked at it with her fingernail. 'It is unusual enough to be the work of one plaiter, or perhaps from a village where this is a traditional pattern. I can give you a list of establishments to try.'

'Thank you, I would be obliged. I would like to get my hands on that young woman.' Diana's fine eyebrows rose. 'And drag her off to the magistrates,' he added smoothly.

Within an hour Miss Price produced the promised list, by which time Peters had returned with Hawkins, the ex-Bow Street Runner that Marcus had found useful to employ in the past. He handed the man the piece of plait and the list. 'I want to know which of these establishments uses this plait—without arousing suspicion.'

'Aye, my lord. I'll send in my daughters, they can say they are ladies' maids, trying to track down an exclusive pattern for their mistress.' He glanced down the list and bowed himself out. 'I'll be back by this time tomorrow.'

'Who on earth is that man, Marcus?' He looked up, startled to realize that he had been so deep in thought that he had not heard his mother come in.

'Mama.' He got to his feet as she settled on the sofa in a flurry of silk skirts and held out one immaculately manicured hand to the blaze. Despite the prospect of an evening at home and frequent visits to the sick room, Lady Narborough was exquisitely attired in teal-green silk and adorned with the Carlow opals. 'An investigator. I wanted to track down the young woman who so upset Father this morning.'

'I do not understand it.' His mother turned her large dark eyes on him and he noticed with a pang the fine lines radiating from the corners. She was still a beauty, but no longer a young one, no longer so resilient. 'What on earth was in that parcel that disturbed your father so much?'

'A foolish practical joke. A cord. It appeared to be a snake. I assume Papa got up too suddenly and then, on top of that, was startled by what he thought was a reptile.' Marcus shrugged negligently. If his mother knew the true nature of the rope, she would make the connection with the past, and he had no intention of worrying her with that if he could avoid it. 'I imagine it will turn out to be one of Hal's madcap friends playing a trick on me that misfired.'

As he intended, that was enough to turn his mother's attention from the parcel to thoughts of her sons. 'Your father is fretting,' she said. 'You know how he does when he is unwell. He wants to hold his grandchildren on his knee—and soon! It is too much to hope that Hal will oblige us. Every respectable young lady has been warned against him Seasons ago. You are the heir, Marcus. It is time you found yourself a wife and settled down, set up your nursery.'

It was a subject she returned to with increasing frequency these days. Perhaps it was natural, with an ailing husband, to seek comfort in thoughts of descendants, but he saw no possibility of satisfying her in the immediate future.

There were attractive women aplenty out there and many who caught his eye, but none of them were the kind a gentleman married. What he wanted, he knew, was maturity, intelligence and wit. Breeding went without saying, for he had his name to consider. Wealth was of lesser importance; he was in the fortunate position of not having to marry for money. As for looks—well, character was more desirable, although he did not imagine his chosen bride would be exactly muffin-faced.

But where to find her? 'The Season is about to start, Mama. I'll give it serious thought, I promise.' Some young lady, fresh-faced, innocent, schooled by her mama to perfect deportment and without an original idea in her head would be the expectation for a man in his position. His heart sank.

What he wanted…green eyes, a determined chin, a voice like warm honey and the desperate courage to stand her ground and lie when a man his size, in a temper, tried to threaten her? Yes, that was the calibre of woman he wanted. Now he just had to find an eligible lady with the qualities possessed by a shabby, skinny milliner. Without the lying and the mystery.

'My lord?'

'Mmm?' Startled, Marcus sat bolt upright in the chair by the fire. He hadn't been dozing exactly, more brooding, he told himself.

Wellow was too well trained to appear surprised by anything the family might do. 'I beg your pardon, my lord, but we thought you had gone out.'

'Why? What is the time?'

'Ten, my lord. Would you like me to have a supper laid out in the Small Dining Room?'

'Good God.' Marcus considered his club, then Perdita's apartments, and found that, after all, the thought of a supper in his own dining room was more enticing. 'I lost track of the time, Wellow. The family has dined, I take it?'

'Yes, my lord, on the assumption you were at your club, my lord.'

'Quite. Supper, if you please.' He felt no enthusiasm for an evening of erotic negotiation with Mrs Jensen. Damn it, was he sickening for something?

What if he comes to the shop? Salterton, the dark man? What if he asks me what happened at Lord Narborough's house? Do I tell him? Or lie? Do I try and find out about him and then tell Lord Stanegate? But he *is a Carlow.*

There Nell's train of thought stuttered to a halt and she sat staring rather blankly into her cooling cup of black coffee. A night's restless, dream-disturbed sleep had done nothing to calm her.

She was afraid of Salterton, she realized, although she did not know why. Something about him made her think of knives. But she was afraid of Stanegate too. He had power and influence, and however unwittingly, she had been the cause of his father's collapse. Only he did not believe it was unwitting.

If only that were all. Lord Narborough was his father and he had been her own father's friend, she knew that much. Something had happened when she was very young and her father was taken away. And then Papa had died and Mama had never smiled again—and she spoke the name of Carlow like a curse.

Over the years, growing up, Nell had pieced together a little. Papa must have done something wrong, she had concluded. But she was a girl and a child and no one worried girl children with hard truths, even when not knowing seemed worse than whatever it was that had plunged them into disgrace and penury after her father had gone. Perhaps Nathan and Rosalind had known more; they were older than she. But it had never been spoken of, and the far-off days when there was a big house and her memories of rooms full of treasures and a park might only be a dream, not truth at all.

Something bad, very bad, had happened to Papa. So bad that it stained them all with its tarnish, so bad that he…died.

Nell should hate the Carlows, she knew that, because her mother had told her that George Carlow was responsible for everything that had befallen them. *Traitor,* she had called him. *False friend, treacherous.*

But there was something about his son, the viscount, that seemed to fill Nell's consciousness, to stop her thinking straight. And it was partly, she was honest enough to admit, a very basic attraction, something in his masculinity that called to the feminine in her. As though he was the man who haunted her dreams, her ideal, the man who would be her friend as well as her lover.

Fantasy. Marcus Carlow would haunt her in truth if he found her, there was no doubt about that. Nell shivered and put the cup down on the hearth. Her toast was getting cold. She nibbled it, telling herself that to huddle by the meagre fire, instead of sitting up at the table like a lady, was justified in this cold weather and had nothing to do with a primitive need for safety.

Yes, fantasy. Men were not like that god in her dreams, none of them, and viscounts would certainly have one use, and one use only, for unprotected milliners' assistants.

She got up and put the dirty earthenware in a pail to wash up with her supper plates, then shook out her pelisse and tied her bonnet strings. Reticule, gloves, handkerchief... Her thoughts skittered away, back to the aching worry. Was Lord Narborough better? What had she done? He had seemed kind when that flustered young footman had shown her in. Tired, but kind. But that had to be a mask. What secrets was he hiding?

If her father was still alive he would be the same age as the earl. She wished she could remember him, but all that came back from that distant time was the sound of weeping and her mother's curses.

Shivering with more than the cold, Nell locked her door and went down the stairs, narrow at first, then widening as she reached the lower floors. This had been a fine house once; traces of dignity still hung about the width of the doorframes, the bewebbed cornices, the curl of the banister under her hand as she reached the ground floor.

'Mornin', Miss Latham.' Old Mrs Drewe peered out of her half-open door, seeing all, noting all, even at half past five in the morning. Did she never sleep?

'Good morning, Mrs Drewe. More fog, I'm afraid.' As she closed the front door behind her, she heard the wail of the Hutchins' baby on the second floor. *Teething*, Nell thought absently as she turned onto Bishopsgate Street and began to walk briskly southwards.

She was lucky to have her room, she knew that, even if it was on the third floor of a Spitalfields lodging with nosy neighbours and crying babies. It was safe and secure, and the other tenants, poor as they were, were decent people, hard-working and frugal.

And she was lucky to have respectable work with an employer who did not regard running a millinery business as a subsidiary to keeping a brothel, as so many did. It seemed very important this morning, hurrying through the damp fog in the dawn gloom, to have some blessings to count. Even the fact that Mama was at peace with Papa now felt like a blessing and no longer a source of grief. Whatever this mystery was, at least Mama was spared the worry of it.

Past the Royal Exchange, looming out of the fog, gas flares hardly penetrating the murk, on down the street with the towering defensive walls of the Bank of England on her right and into Poultry. The crowds of early-morning workers were thicker now and she had to wait a moment at the stall selling pastries to buy one for her noon meal.

And then she had reached the back door of *Madame Elizabeth—millinery à la mode, plumes a speciality.* The clock struck the hour as she hung her pelisse and bonnet on her peg and put her pastry on the shelf in the kitchen.

It was warm and bright in the workroom as she tied on her apron and went to her place at the long table alongside the other girls. It was not out of any concern for her workers that Madame provided a fire and good lamps—warm fingers worked better and intricate designs needed good light—but they were a decided benefit of the job.

Nell smiled and nodded to the others as she lifted her hat block towards her, took off the white cloth and studied the bonnet she was working on. It was for Mrs Forrester, the wife of a wealthy alderman, a good customer and a fussy one. The grosgrain ribbon pleated round inside the brim was perfect, but the points where the ribbons joined the hat required some camouflage. Rosettes, perhaps. She began to pleat ribbon, her lips tight on an array of long pins.

'Your admirer coming back today, Nell?' Mary Wright's pert question had her almost swallowing the pins.

Nell stuck them safely in her pincushion and shook her head. 'He's no admirer of mine, if you mean Mr Salterton. I'm just the one who delivers the hats.'

'And does final fittings,' one of the girls muttered. It was a sore point that Nell had the opportunity to go out and about and to visit the fine houses the other milliners could only dream about entering. Her more refined speech and ladylike manners had not been lost on Madame.

'Well, he only wanted a parcel delivered,' she said, skewering the finished rosette with a pin and reaching for her needle.

'I'd deliver a parcel for him, any time,' Polly Lang chipped in. 'He's a fine man, he is.'

'How can you tell?' Nell's needle hung in mid-air as she stared at Polly's round, freckled countenance. 'I've never seen more than a glimpse of him.'

'He's got money; he can have a face like a bailiff, for all I care,' Polly retorted with a comical grin. 'You must have seen his clothes. Lovely coats he's got. And his boots. And he's dark. I like that in a man, mysterious. I reckon he's an Italian count or summat, *incogerneeto,* or whatever you call it.'

'Incognito,' Nell murmured, setting the first stitch. 'He's certainly that.'

The shop bell tinkled in the distance and Nell stabbed herself. Feminine voices. She relaxed, sucking the drop of blood from her finger. He wouldn't come back, she told herself; he had done whatever he had intended. Madame was not going to receive any more orders for extravagant hats fit only for high-flyers.

But how had a man with some grudge against the Carlows found *her,* of all people? Surely it could not be coincidence? The dark, controlled face of Lord Stanegate came back to her and she shivered again, a strange heat mingling with the anxiety. She had made an enemy there and somewhere out in the fog-bound city was another man, one whose face she could not quite picture, who might feel his unwitting tool was a danger to him.

The second rosette slipped wildly out of shape. She must be very, very careful, Nell resolved as she began to form it again, wishing she understood what she had become embroiled in.

Chapter Three

Marcus sat back against the carriage squabs and waited, patient as a cat at a mouse hole, his eyes on the back door of the smart little shop with its glossy dark green paint, gilt lettering and array of fancy hats in each window.

It had taken Hawkins just twenty-four hours to identify three milliners using the plait. It came from a small Buckinghamshire village and cost double the price of the more common patterns, he reported. Armed with Marcus's description of Miss Smith, one of the Hawkins daughters had penetrated the workrooms of each, pretending to be seeking employment, and had reported back that a young woman answering to that description was working for Madame Elizabeth's establishment in the City.

He had been there since four, the carriage drawn up off Poultry in St Mildred Court, as if waiting for someone to come out of the church. Ladies had gone in and out of the shop, deliveries had been made, a few girls had run out to the pie seller and scurried back, but there had been no sign of the thin girl with hazel-green eyes.

Now—he checked his watch as the bells of the City's churches began to chime—it was six and the fog was dark and dirty, full of smoke, swirling in the wake of the carriages, turning the torches and flares a sickly yellow.

Blinking to try to maintain focus, Marcus missed the door opening for a moment, then half a dozen young women spilled out onto the street, pulling shawls tight around their shoulders, chattering as they split up and began to make their way home.

'John!' The coachman leaned down from the box. 'The taller one heading up past the Mansion House. Don't let her see us.'

She looked tired, Marcus thought with a flash of compassion, wondering how early she had arrived at the shop and how it must be to sit bent over fine work all day. As the carriage pulled out into the traffic, he saw her pause on the corner of Charlotte Row to let a coal heaver's cart past. She put her hand to the small of her back and stretched, then set her shoulders as though bracing herself. After the cart passed, she darted across, zigzagging to avoid the worst of the waste and the puddles. With a glance at her drab skirts, the crossing boy turned away and began to sweep assiduously for a waiting lawyer, bands fluttering, wig box in hand, a likely prospect for a tip.

Yes, she was certainly a working woman. That much at least had been true. Marcus quenched the glimmer of sympathy with the memory of his father's face that morning, grey and strained, although he had protested he had slept well and had managed a smile for Lady Narborough.

But Marcus had not been able to rouse his father's

enthusiasm to give a personal message to Hal, and the earl had waved away an attempt to interest him in plans to plant new coppices at Stanegate Hall. He was sinking into one of his melancholy fits and, in the absence of the mysterious dark man, Marcus had only one person to blame for that.

She was hurrying up Threadneedle Street now, deeper into the City. John was doing well, keeping the horses to a slow walk, ignoring the jibes and shouts aimed at him for holding up the traffic. In the evening crush there seemed little chance she would notice them. Then she turned north into Bishopsgate Street, walking with her head down, hands clasped together in front of her, maintaining the steady pace of someone who is tired, but is pushing on to a destination despite that.

Just when Marcus was beginning to think she was going to walk all the way to Shoreditch, she turned right into a lane. It took John a moment or two to get across the traffic. Widegate Street, Marcus read as the carriage lurched over the kerb into the narrow entrance. Named by someone with a sense of humour. He dropped the window right down and leaned out. The street was almost deserted. Ahead, Miss Smith was still keeping the same pace, not looking back. Then one of the pair shied at a banging shutter, John swore, and she glanced back over her shoulder. Marcus caught a glimpse of the pale oval of her face below her dark hat brim. He saw her stiffen, then walk on.

'Steady, man,' he ordered softly as the coachman cursed again, under his breath this time. Ahead, the lane was narrowing into an alley, too tight for the carriage that was already glaringly out of place in the maze of back streets.

'Stop.' He got out as he spoke, pulling up his collar against the raw air. 'Can you turn? Wait for me here.'

'Aye, my lord.'

Marcus glanced up as he entered the narrow way. Smock Alley. He tried to get his bearings. They were heading for Spitalfields Church, he thought, his eyes fixed on the figure ahead, keeping in the shadows as much as possible as he padded in her wake.

His heel struck a bottle in the gutter and it spun away and shattered. She turned, stared back into the shadows, then took to her heels. Marcus abandoned stealth and ran too, his long legs gaining easily on the fleeing figure with its hampering skirts. Then his ankle twisted as he trod on a greasy cobble; he slid and came up hard against the wall, splitting the leather of his glove as he threw out a hand to save himself. When he reached the spot where he had last seen her, she was gone.

Marcus looked around. He could see the dark entrances to at least five streets and alleys from where he stood. Impossible to search them all. He walked slowly back to the carriage, cursing softly.

Nell flattened herself against the wall of the stinking privy in Dolphin Court, her ears straining as the sharp footsteps grew fainter. Finally, when the stench became too much, she crept out and studied what she could see beyond the narrow entrance. Nothing and no one. He had gone, for now.

Who had it been? Not Lord Stanegate; he at least could not know what she did or where she worked. Mr Salterton, wanting to know what had happened—or worse, intent upon silencing the messenger? Or was it as simple as some amorous rake bent on bothering a woman alone or perhaps a thief after her meagre purse?

Only, thieves did not drive in handsome, shiny carriages. Which left Salterton or a predatory rake. Shivering, Nell decided she would rather take her chances with the rake; she doubted that a well-directed knee would deter Mr Salterton.

When she reached Dorset Street she walked to the end, past her own door to the corner and watched for almost ten minutes, but no one at all suspicious came into sight.

It was an effort of will to force her legs up the three flights of stairs to the top of the house and even more of one not to simply fall onto the bed, pull the covers over her head and hide. Nell made herself build up the fire, fill the kettle from the tub of water the shared maid of all work had left on the landing and take off her pelisse and bonnet before collapsing into her chair.

A woman on her own was so defenceless, she thought, her fingers curling into claws at the thought of the men who preyed on those weaker than themselves in the crowded London streets. Or behind the anonymous walls in little rooms like this. Her vision blurred for a moment and her stomach swooped sickeningly. She would not think of that.

For the first time in her life she felt a treacherous yearning for a man to shelter her. Someone powerful and strong. Someone like Viscount Stanegate. She closed her eyes and indulged in a fantasy of standing behind his broad back while he skewered the dark man on the point of an expertly wielded rapier or shot him down like a dog for daring to threaten her.

In reality, that would probably be a horrible experience, she told herself, getting up to make some tea. The last thing she wanted was to witness violence, and the viscount was hardly going to act the knight errant for her in any case. But the vision of a handgun stayed with her. Somewhere, there was the little pistol that Mama had always carried in her reticule. Mama had never had to threaten anyone with it, and it probably wasn't even loaded, of course. But the sight of a weapon might give some randy buck pause.

Nell found the pistol after a prolonged search. She peered down the barrel, wondering how one told if it had shot in it. Eventually she opened a window, pointed it out over the rooftops and pulled the trigger, braced for a bang. Nothing happened; she could not even pull the trigger back properly. So it was at least safe to carry.

Despite that, her snug eyrie in the roof no longer felt quite so secure. Nell turned the key and wedged a chair under the door handle. Was it time to move again?

By the next day, Nell's unease had hardened into something like defiance. She was damned if some man, whoever he was, was going to frighten her out of her home. It wasn't much, but it was clean, it was dry and she was surrounded by good-natured, honest people. She had her pistol, she was forewarned. She would stand her ground.

That was easy enough to resolve in the brightly lit, warm surroundings of the workroom with half a dozen people around her and a large pair of sharp scissors to hand, she realized as she walked home.

Wary, she checked behind herself, yet again. There

were no carriages following at walking pace tonight, no suspicious pedestrians behind her. It must simply have been a lone buck taking a chance. With a sigh of relief she ducked through Smock Alley and turned left and then right into Dorset Street. Home.

The keys were slippery in her chilled hands and she fumbled getting them out of the reticule. They caught on the pistol and she heard a sharp click as she pulled them free. Then she saw the man: big, dark, menacing and striding towards her out of the gloom, just yards away. The breath left her lungs and she tugged the little pistol out of her reticule and held it in front of her.

'I am armed. Keep away!' Her hand was shaking, so she lifted the other to support her wrist.

'Miss Smith, put that thing away before you hurt yourself.' *Lord Stanegate?* He stopped, perhaps two feet from the end of the muzzle. The lighting was poor, his face was in shadow, but she would recognize that deep voice anywhere. He was apparently hanging on to his temper with an effort.

'It is you it is pointed at, my lord,' she observed. 'It is not I who will be hurt.' Her heart was thunderous, her stomach was churning and there was nowhere to run to, but she would not let him see her terror.

'Have you any idea how to use it?' He sounded more interested than alarmed. Nell wished she could see his face properly.

'Of course I have! I aim it at the brute who is threatening me and then I pull the trigger. I can hardly miss at this range.' If she could keep him standing there long enough someone might come out of the house. Or Bill

Watkins might come home. Bill was a bricklayer, at least the height of the viscount and built like an ox.

'I was not aware I was threatening you, Miss Smith,' he said in a voice of infuriating calm, standing his ground. 'I merely wish to speak to you.'

'As you did before, I collect? That involved me being locked up in your house and intimidated with threats of Bow Street. And yesterday—was it you who chased me? Hunted me through the streets?'

'Yes, I must apologise if I alarmed you. That was not my intention.' He shifted a little so that light fell feebly on her hands and on the dark muzzle pointing at his chest. She could see his face better now, or at least the profile. Long nose, uncompromising jaw, high cheekbones.

'Oh no, not at all, think nothing of it,' she retorted with honeyed politeness. 'Alarmed? I merely thought it was either some buck set on rape or Mr Salterton thinking to dispose of his messenger. It would have been foolish of me indeed to have been *alarmed*.'

'Hell.' He put up a hand, rubbed it across his mouth, the first crack in his composure she had so far detected. 'I intended merely to follow you home and to make myself known. To talk to you. When you ran—'

'I see. Like a hound you chase anything that runs away. How civilised.' For such a tiny thing, the pistol seemed to be made of lead. 'How is the earl?'

'Better, a little, no thanks to you, Miss Smith.' The apologetic note in his voice was gone again. 'He is resting more easily, I think. In poor spirits, it depresses him to be so weak.'

'I can imagine. My mother—' She bit back the

words. This man did not want to know about her mother, nor should she weaken enough to confide in him, perversely tempting though that was. It must be something about the solid strength of him, she thought, renewing her grip on the weapon.

'Please go away,' Nell said firmly. Movement at the end of the street caught her eye. A black carriage, its glossy sides catching the torchlight, pulled in against the kerb a few yards behind the viscount. 'I do not wish to speak to you.'

'But I want to speak to you.'

'And what you want, you always get, my lord?'

'Mostly.' His mouth twisted wryly as though at a private joke. 'It is warm in the carriage and comfortable. I only want to talk.'

'No.' Nell edged back, searched for the step with her foot, found it and realized she needed a free hand for the keys. But if she opened the door he could force his way in. 'Stay there.'

The muzzle of the gun waved more wildly than she intended as she scrabbled for the key. The viscount moved suddenly to the right, she swung the gun round, he feinted and caught her wrist, the weapon trapped between them.

'Let it go!'

'No!' Part of her realized he was not exerting his full strength and that even so, she was completely powerless. Nell opened her mouth to scream and a gloved hand covered it. She bit and got a mouthful of leather. She kicked and he moved sharply; their hands, joined around the pistol, jerked and the gun went off.

Reeling with shock and half deaf, Nell fell back

against the railings. *It had been loaded?* It was a miracle no one had been hurt. And then she saw that Lord Stanegate was clutching his left shoulder.

'Damn it,' he said as she stared, aghast. 'Do you want to kill us all?'

'No! It was an accident—it wasn't loaded! I tried it. *It wasn't loaded!'* The driver must have whipped up the carriage, for it was there beside them. Behind her, windows were flung open and people were shouting; in front of her, the big man she had thought so solid was swaying on his feet as the coachman jumped down from the box.

'My lord!'

'Get her into the carriage.'

'No! I—' Nell was picked up ruthlessly in arms that were more than capable of controlling a six-horse drag and thrown without ceremony into the carriage—to be followed by the viscount who slumped onto the seat.

The front door of the house opened; there were raised voices and someone shouted, 'Murder! Call the Watch!'

She reached for the far door handle and was jerked back against the viscount with enough force to make them both gasp. 'You shot me,' he said between gritted teeth. 'Now you can stop me bleeding to death.'

'I'll get you home, my lord, just you hang on there.' The coachman slammed the door and the vehicle lurched forward.

There was something hot and wet under her hand. Nell held it up in front of her face. Blood.

He was struggling with the buttons of his greatcoat. Nell pushed his hands away and tore it open herself, shoved it back over his shoulders, ignoring the grunt of pain. Stopping the bleeding was more important than worrying about hurting him. *He deserves it*, she thought fiercely, trying to ignore the panic churning inside her. *I have shot a man. Dear God, I have shot a man.*

The carriage lurched again and more light came in. They must have reached one of the major streets. Nell yanked at the greatcoat, then his open coat, then the buttons on his waistcoat. 'Sit still and let me undress you,' she snapped as he tried to help her—and was rewarded with an unexpected gasp of laughter, choked off as between them they pulled his arms free.

He was in his shirtsleeves now. His neckcloth would be useful as a bandage, she told herself, trying not to think about what would be revealed when she got the bloodstained shirt off him. Nell ripped down the buttons, careless of them flying loose, and dragged at the shirt. He was not helping now; she rather thought he was close to fainting.

She tipped him forward to rest against her while she pulled the shirt free, struggling with the weight of his body, her nostrils full of the metallic smell of blood.

Then she pushed him back to see what damage had been done. She mopped at his shoulder then peered at the wound in the poor light. It was not, she told herself firmly, as bad as it might have been. There was a raw, deep groove torn through his shoulder but the bullet was not buried in his body.

But it was bleeding like a spring, the blood already covering his chest. Nell bunched up the shirt and held it to the wound. He grunted, half conscious. It needed something finer to make a pad she could tie on with the neckcloth.

Nell reached under her skirts, took hold of her petticoat and tugged a ragged length of cotton free. That, at least, was easier to deal with. She made a pad, pressed it to the wound and began to bandage.

The viscount was coming round from his faint, his head restless against the squab.

'My lord, be still. I cannot get pressure on this if you move.'

'Hurts like hell.' He grumbled. 'Don't know why I'm so damned dizzy. Hal said getting shot didn't hurt. Bloody liar.'

'You are dizzy because you are bleeding. And if it hurts, that serves you right, my lord,' she retorted, finishing her binding. 'You really are the most difficult man.' They passed a row of grand houses, each with a flaring torch set outside. Light flooded in and she saw the naked torso under her hands clearly for a few seconds.

Not the pampered body of an indolent nobleman, she realized. But then, she hadn't expected it would be. His ribs were strapped with muscle, hard under her palms. There were scars over his ribs, bruises. She frowned, puzzled, then guessed that he boxed, although that did not account for the scars.

Nell shivered, her hands sliding over the muscles, lingering on the scars. Crisp, dark hair tickled her palms. *He is magnificent,* she thought, suddenly breathless. Then he shifted, the muscle bunching and flexing, and she snatched her hands away, remembering what male strength could do, remembering who this was.

'Just do as you are told for once and be still, my lord,' she ordered. Blood was seeping through the linen. Nell put both hands on the bandage and pressed, kneeling up on the seat beside him to apply more force.

'Marcus,' he muttered.

'Who?'

'Me. My name. You cannot call me *my lord* every sentence, not when you've torn half my clothes off.'

He was teasing her?

'*My lord*,' Nell said with emphasis, 'we are nearly at Albemarle Street. You will kindly have your coachman drive me home the instant you are safely inside.'

'Oh no, Miss Smith.' He smiled thinly. Whatever his mood a moment ago, now she could discern no humour whatsoever. 'You stay with me or John Coachman will take you straight round to Bow Street and lay charges of attempted murder by shooting.'

Chapter Four

'Stay with you? You mean go into the house with you? No! Why are you doing this? Why won't you believe me?'

Nell heard the viscount grit his teeth as they went over a bump in the road, but his voice was steady and intense as he said, 'You lied to me. You do not work for a dressmaker and your name is not Smith.'

'Oh, very well!' How he had found her, she had no idea, but he had and now she must deal with it. 'My name is Latham, Nell Latham. Of course I lied to you. You were angry, you were blaming me for something I know nothing about. You are powerful, my lord,' she added bitterly, trying to tighten the knots on the bandage. 'I am not. I need every advantage I can gain. Oh, sit still for goodness' sake, or you will make it bleed badly again!'

'How can I sit still with you digging your fingers in like that?' He showed, unfortunately, no sign of faintness again. The carriage was rattling over the cobbles at a speed that would make it lethally dangerous to jump out, which seemed the only possible means of escape.

Nell turned back from a speculative study of the door handles and glared at her patient. 'I am attempting to stop the bleeding,' she scolded. 'I have to press hard. Now, I am sure we are almost at Albemarle Street and when we get there I expect your man to drive me straight home again—with none of this nonsense about Bow Street.' Perhaps a voice of firm reason would work.

'You shot me.' The piercing eyes were dark with pain, but they had lost none of their force. 'Shooting a viscount is not nonsense. You could get hanged for less.'

'It was self-defence, as well you know,' she retorted. 'I am a respectable woman, walking home at night, and a large man pounces on me at my door. What am I supposed to do?'

'Scream?' he suggested. 'Hit me with your reticule? That would seem to be the normal reaction. Few respectable women walk the streets of London armed to the teeth.'

'They do if they are made the pawn in some stupid game between men who ought to know better,' she snapped back, anxiety making her forget the wisdom of control for a moment.

Under her hands he went very still. 'Game? This is no game, Nell.'

'Miss Latham, if you please, my lord. I have not made you free with my name.' They were turning into Piccadilly, slowing. Her heart raced as she slid off the seat. 'I have scissors in my reticule. I'll see if I can cut a better bandage.'

The door opened smoothly as she twisted the handle. The horses were just picking up their pace again—too late. No, she must get away, must jump *now*. Nell launched herself forward, but was grabbed from behind and dragged back; she landed part on the seat, part on top of the half-naked viscount. The door slammed shut, the carriage lurched as the driver whipped up the team, and Nell took hold of whatever she could to keep from falling to the floor.

What she had done, she realized a split second too late, was to wind one arm around the viscount's neck and bury her face against his naked chest. His free arm came round and held her to him, his breath rasping in his throat as she wriggled. She managed to pull herself up so they were face to face, so close she could feel his breath on her mouth, see, in the flashes of light as they passed lamps, that his eyes were intent on her face with a kind of focus that sent answering heat surging through her.

He wanted her. Aroused, she supposed, by the chase, by the violence, by his half-naked state and her quivering body clamped to his, Marcus Carlow quite patently wanted her. And for an insane moment, she wanted him too, wanted that strength and the certainty and the sheer animal physicality that lay hidden beneath the veneer of the civilised gentleman.

Desire must have shown in her eyes, or perhaps in the way her breath caught, and he saw it, recognized it. His mouth, when it took hers, was hot and hard. Not polite, not questioning. He had seen the need in her; it met his and so he acted on it.

For a moment it was what she wanted, what she had dreamt of, powerfully erotic, all-consuming, sweeping her away from reality. He made no allowance for inexperience, his tongue thrusting into her mouth with arrogant demand, his lips sealing over hers, his arm shifting her to lie across his legs so she could feel the shameless jut of his erection against her buttocks.

What broke the spell, she did not know. Some sound, the play of the shadows, a touch? She could not be sure, but the dark memories flooded back and with them the shame and the fear. She was no longer a willing partner in this embrace, this primal sharing of heat and breath and desire. She was afraid, hurting, overwhelmed and helpless. Blindly, Nell struck out, fighting, desperate against the man imprisoning her.

One moment his arms were full of supple, warm, yielding woman, the next a fury was struggling to be free, hands and heels flailing, her gasps of passion replaced by sobbed words. 'No, no, no…'

Dizzy with loss of blood, with desire and pain, Marcus opened his hands. 'Nell, don't. I won't—Nell, it is all right…' She recoiled from him, wrenching free the arm that had been around his neck, her clenched fist striking his wounded shoulder like a hammer blow. The pain was exquisite, the world went dark. With what remained of his strength, he pulled her back against his body. 'Nell…safe.'

'My lord!' Wellow's voice? The butler seemed to be shouting down a well. Had he fallen down one? That would explain why there was all this pain. Marcus decided he had broken his shoulder; that was logical. It explained why he was cold and hurting, but it did not explain why he was sitting on something that rocked, or what the light against his closed eyes was.

Reluctantly, Marcus dragged his lids open and

prepared to deal with this. Only he was not down a well and he appeared to be in his own carriage outside his own front door, half-naked and with Wellow and three footmen all peering anxiously at him from the pavement. 'What the hell?'

'Get him inside,' said a decisive and irritated female voice from behind him. 'And send for the doctor. He has been shot; the bullet is not in the wound but he has lost blood. Hurry up, if you please! He will catch his death from cold out here.'

'Managing female,' he muttered, amused despite himself. If he could only recall who she was and why—

'Well, someone has to be,' she snapped.

Oh yes, Miss something… 'Nell. You taste of cherries.'

'You will have to carry him,' she continued, ignoring this. 'It will take all of you, he is so big.'

'Not helpless…can walk.' Marcus got himself upright by hauling one-handed on the doorframe. Hands reached out as he stumbled down the step to the pavement, then a shoulder was thrust under each arm and the footmen began to walk him towards the door. 'Damn it, I'm not drunk!'

'No, my lord.' That was Richards' soothing murmur. 'Of course you're not. We'll just get you into the warm, my lord.'

The heat and light of the hall made him shudder, suddenly realizing just how cold he was. Marcus freed himself from his supporters and straightened up. He was damned if he was going to be half carried to his own bed, felled by some chit with a pocket pistol.

It was coming back now. And it had not been *some chit*, it had been Nell Latham and she might have wounded him, but she had kept her head and stopped the bleeding despite being thrown into a carriage on top of the man who had frightened her so much.

He turned slowly on his heel to find her facing him, chin up, her arms full of bloodied shirt and ruined coat. And then his memory presented himself with the damnably precise image of what had happened next. He'd kissed the woman, ravished her mouth like a wounded barbarian dragging home a prize from the hunt. Her eyes widened as he stared at her, the fear flaring again as though she expected him to seize her, there and then, and force her on the marble floor.

'Peters, take those clothes from Miss Latham and show her into the White Salon. Bring her warm water and a towel for her hands. Richards, send for the doctor; the man may as well take up residence here at this rate. Wellow, have Allsop come down to the library with a shirt and my dressing robe.' The doctor could see to him down there; no point in making a fuss and attracting the attention of the family. 'And, Wellow, there is no need to disturb Lord or Lady Narborough or my sis—'

'Marcus!'

'Honoria, quiet, please! Papa will hear.'

She ran across the hall to him, her eyes wide, her cheeks pale at the sight of the blood on his chest and the makeshift bandage. But being Honoria, there was excitement and vivid curiosity behind the concern. 'What happened? And who is this?'

'This is Miss Latham who came to my aid when I was shot,' he said smoothly. 'If you could just take her into the salon—'

'Marcus!'

'Mama.' Was he fated never to get a sentence finished? Marcus gritted his teeth and produced what he hoped was a reassuring smile. 'I have suffered a minor flesh wound, Mama. Thanks to Miss Latham it is under control, the bleeding has stopped. I have sent for the doctor. Could you all go into the White Salon so I can get changed and Miss Latham can sit down? She has had a somewhat trying evening.'

Lady Narborough gave a little gasp at the sight of his blood-smeared naked torso, but nodded, took Honoria's arm and smiled back at him. 'Of course. If Dr Rowlands is on his way, I am sure there is nothing to worry about. Come along, Honoria. Miss Latham, we are so grateful for your help.'

Miss Latham coloured up, he saw. As well she might, seeing that she had shot him in the first place. It was something that she could blush, he supposed. 'Lady Narborough, it was really the least I could do. Now, if you will excuse me, I must go home.'

'But, Miss Latham, remember what we discussed?' He moved to her side, smiling down at her. Her eyes widened as though he had snarled instead. Perhaps he had. 'I really do not feel it is safe for you to do anything but stay here at the moment.'

'Safe?' Marcus felt a twinge of admiration for the way she held his eyes with hers. Her chin came up. 'I see you are serious about the threat,' she murmured, her voice dropping as she glanced sideways at the other women.

'Not a threat. I never threaten, Miss Latham. It was a promise.'

'You promised to keep me safe just now,' she retorted. 'I think.'

'And so I will, *if* you stay here.' Safe at least from whatever she was frightened of outside. Inside, he was not going to promise to keep his hands off her throat if she was not completely frank with him and soon.

'Did you say *threat,* Marc?' Honoria, her hearing as sharp as her eyes, turned in the doorway.

'I was shot in the street, very close to Miss Latham's house. I fear she could be in danger if she returns there so soon,' Marcus said, urging the three women through the door of the salon.

'Lord Narborough is ringing.' They all turned towards the stairs as Miss Price came down. 'I heard movement inside his room. He may be intending to come down if no one answers.'

'He most certainly is,' Lord Narborough said as he appeared at the head of the stairs, clad in a green silk robe, his stick in his hand. 'I've been ringing for the past five minutes. What the devil is going on?' He paused, stared at his blood-smeared son and grabbed for the banister. 'My God, Marcus, what has happened to you?'

'A flesh wound, nothing more. It looks worse than it is.' Marcus reached his father before the earl's knees gave way, his own legs feeling like sponges as he ran up the stairs. 'Sir, come back to your room. The doctor is on his way.' He closed his fingers on his father's wrist unobtrusively as they walked slowly back. He did not like his colour. Behind him he heard the rustle of his mother's skirts. 'I'll tell you all about it.'

Nell sat down on an upright chair, spine straight, shoulders back, as though impeccable deportment could armour her against whatever might befall her in this house. She could only hope that none of them recognized her from that first, ill-fated visit. What had happened in the carriage she could not even begin to think about. It had been too shocking, too violent, too complex to contemplate now, despite her body's betraying shivers.

Lady Honoria sat down opposite her, eyes bright with curiosity. She was very pretty and beautifully gowned, Nell observed, and she had an air about her of barely suppressed energy. A handful, Nell had no doubt. The other woman, clad in elegant simplicity in dove-grey silk, was a few years older, Nell guessed, noticing that her gown was home-made, with taste and skill. The paid companion, perhaps?

She tugged the bell pull and came to sit beside Lady Honoria. 'I am Diana Price, companion to Lady Honoria and Lady Verity. Tea should not be long. You were not yourself wounded in the attack, Miss Latham?'

'No. Fortunately. It was somewhat alarming, however.'

'Was it footpads?' Lady Honoria asked.

'With a pistol?' Miss Price countered. 'That is not their usual weapon, I would have thought.' She frowned at Nell, puzzled. 'What exactly happened?'

'I was on my doorstep, about to take my keys from my reticule,' Nell began, picking her words with care. 'And Lord Stanegate was passing. And then there was the incident and the gun went off in the struggle and he was hit in the shoulder. Fortunately the coachman was able to get him into the carriage.'

'Extraordinary.' Nell's heart sank. Lady Honoria was bubbling with excitement, too caught up in the drama to notice the gaping holes in Nell's account. Miss Price, however, was regarding her with cool, intelligent eyes, speculation lurking in their depths.

The arrival of the butler with the tea tray was a welcome distraction. The ritual of pouring and passing reduced the encounter to a normal social occasion. Nell accepted a macaroon with real gratitude and let herself relax. It was a grave mistake.

'But I have seen you before, Miss Latham,' Lady Honoria said, her brow wrinkled in concentration. 'I know I have. Now, where could that have been?'

'I am all right, don't fuss, my dear.' The earl managed a smile for his wife as Marcus eased him back into his wing chair. 'You let us talk, hmm?'

Marcus turned, met his mother's eyes and nodded reassurance.

'Don't tire him,' was all she said as she went out, the demi-train of her gown swishing on the carpet.

'Who shot you?' his father demanded.

'Miss Latham, who is, of course, the young woman who delivered the parcel the other morning.' Marcus kept his voice scrupulously matter-of-fact. If he was in his father's shoes, nothing would make him more frustrated and unwell than getting half-truths and evasions. 'I tracked her down to her place of employment, followed her home and startled her, looming out of the fog. It appears she carries a pistol in her reticule.'

As if speaking of it touched a nerve, a wrenching pang shot through the wound. Marcus gritted his teeth, looked longingly at the brandy decanter and decided that, on top of blood loss, even one glass would seriously impair his analytical ability.

'She meant to kill you?' His father's knuckles whitened on the head of his cane.

'Probably not.' Marcus shook his head, wondering why he had any doubts. Nell had seen his face and she had still held the pistol to his chest. Could she really not have realized it was loaded when she did not deny it was hers? 'But she's lying to me, still. I mean to keep her here for a day or two, see if I cannot pry the truth out of her. She's deeper into this business with the rope than she says. I know it.'

Beside anything else, he could recall the feel of the gun in his hand. It was a well-made lady's weapon with an ivory handle, not some ancient, cheap pistol bought on impulse from a Spitalfields pawnshop. Her confederate must have given it to her; that was the most likely explanation.

'Who can be behind it?' Lord Narborough frowned. 'Now, I mean. In ninety-four any of us were targets, and when Hebden and Wardale died, then I could have understood an attack.' He swallowed and made a visible effort to regain his composure. 'Feelings ran high.'

That was an understatement, Marcus thought, for the furore surrounding a murder, the unmasking of a spy ring, and a crisis of conscience that had never left his father in peace. 'Almost twenty years,' he pondered. 'Enough time for the Wardale son to grow up.'

'Young Nathan? He'll be a man now. Last saw him when he was nine or ten. Blond child, big watchful eyes. Solemn little soul.' He frowned. 'I don't suppose—'

'Miss Latham is most definitely female.' That earned an old-fashioned look from his father. 'Blond, you say? Nathan Wardale's not Nell's dark man, then,' Marcus added before the earl could pursue the question of why he was so certain of Nell's gender.

'Unless she's trying to deceive you with a description that is the opposite of the truth,' his father said, sitting up straighter. 'Could she be his mistress, do you suppose?'

'No!' Marcus startled himself with the vehemence of his response, then tried to justify it. 'She lives in cheap lodgings near Spitalfields church. Decent enough, but not the sort of situation to keep one's mistress.'

'And you would know,' the older man said with an unexpected crack of laughter. 'Come to an arrangement with Mrs Jensen yet? You've got good taste, I'll give you that. Expensive ware, that one.'

'Not yet, no, sir,' Marcus responded, refusing to rise to the bait. How the devil his father knew about Perdita, let alone any details about her, escaped him. It never did to underestimate the earl.

'So, what are you going to do about her?'

'Mrs Jensen?' he asked, playing for time.

'No, this Miss Latham.' The earl turned his gaze on his son, wicked amusement lurking behind the intelligence. It was not often these days that Marcus was reminded where Honoria and Hal got their wildness from, but it was evident tonight. The strain might be bad for his father's heart, but the puzzle and the excitement were good for his spirits and his brain. 'Do you think she'll try and kill off any of the rest of us?'

'I doubt it. She is not that foolish,' he said dryly. 'She'll stay here—if whoever is behind this sees we have his agent in our hands, that might provoke a reaction.'

'And how do you intend to keep her here short of force? Your mother might have something to say about that.'

'I have threatened Miss Latham with Bow Street and a charge of assault by shooting,' Marcus explained, grinning back as his father's face was transformed by an appreciative smile.

'Very good. And what was her response?'

'She said it was *nonsense,* but as she was ripping up her petticoats to bandage my wound, she was unable to develop the argument.'

'Stopping you bleeding to death certainly weakens the case against her,' the earl observed. 'She could have fainted conveniently and left you to bleed.' There was a tap at the door.

'Dr Rowlands for Lord Stanegate, my lord.'

'I'll be with him directly.' Marcus got to his feet and rested one hand on his father's shoulder. 'Don't worry yourself about this, sir. We'll get to the bottom of it soon.'

'Aye, and what are we going to find there?' he heard the older man mutter as the door closed behind him.

Nell was beginning to feel as if she was involved in a fencing match against two opponents. Miss Price, impeccably polite, appeared to be analysing every word she said and finding it sadly wanting. Her half smile expressed more doubt than if she had been on her feet accusing Nell of shooting Lord Stanegate deliberately.

Beside her, Lady Honoria worried away at the certainty that she had seen Nell before.

'A delightful bonnet, if I may say so,' Miss Price observed.

'Bonnet?' Nell put up her hand, surprised to find it was still in place after the evening's events. Lord Stanegate had pushed it off her head when he was kissing her and she vaguely recalled jamming it back as she gathered up his clothing before getting out of the carriage.

'Yes. An interesting pattern of plait; I noticed it at once. Perhaps you are a milliner?'

'I am, as it happens.' Plait? So that was how he had located her. She was always finding small bits clinging to her skirts when she got home after work, however carefully she brushed. And from the smile that curved the companion's mouth, she assumed she knew all about how Marcus had found her.

'Oh, I remember!' Lady Honoria announced triumphantly. 'You are the person who delivered that parcel the other morning. The one that made Papa ill…' Her voice trailed away as she realized the import of what she was saying. 'And now Marc's been shot and you—'

'Miss Latham was merely the messenger. She is assisting me in finding out what is going on,' a deep voice said from the doorway, silencing the young woman.

Nell turned sideways to stare. Marcus Carlow was, thank Heavens, dressed again—or at least, decently covered. His open shirt collar was visible between the wide lapels of a silk robe that was distorted on the left shoulder where he was bandaged, his arm in a sling. She felt the tension ebb out of her, then stiffened. What was she thinking of, to feel relief that he was here? Did he really mean he believed her about the parcel? Nell intercepted a satirical glance and decided that no, he was not convinced. 'She will be staying here for a while,' he added.

'I do not think so, my lord. I have told you all I know.'

'But, Miss Latham,' he said, smiling as he came in and sat down in the wing chair at right angles to her, 'someone shot me. You may well be in danger as a result. As we have already discussed.'

He meant his threat to accuse her of deliberate assault. 'I think I will take my chances on that,' she said, making herself hold his eyes directly for the first time since that kiss. It was a mistake.

Heat seemed to fill her; she could feel the blush colouring her cheeks. That broad chest under her palms, the sleek planes of his pectoral muscles, the utter assurance of his kiss, the taste of him still on her lips... Nell got a grip on herself before she licked her lips. Did he even recall that embrace? Or had he been in some sort of near-unconscious state?

The dark eyes looked back, bland and polite, and she realised she could not tell. 'I found where you live with very little effort, Miss Latham,' the viscount said. 'Others could too.' He waited, giving her time to think that over, but he had no need. The shivery image of knives that the thought of the dark man always conjured up was enough.

'Perhaps a night or two, if Lady Narborough permits,' she agreed, wondering why she felt she had surrendered far more than a few days of her life.

Chapter Five

'My dear Carlow, Marcus!' Marcus stood up as Lord Keddinton strolled into the library, the picture of dry, slender elegance from his raised eyebrows to the slim hand holding his cane. 'What is this I hear about illness and injury?' His sweeping gesture encompassed the earl's footstool and stick and Marcus's sling, his pale eyes bright with interest.

'A practical joke gone awry and an encounter with a footpad,' Marcus said easily. 'This is a mere scratch.' A night's rest allowed him to carry off the painfully throbbing wound with tolerable ease this morning. 'You will take a glass of wine, sir?'

'Thank you. If you still have that admirable claret I may stay all morning. A footpad, you say? Really, the streets are hardly safe at night these days.' With a smile, Robert Veryan—Lord Keddinton—made himself comfortable, crossed one leg over the other and steepled his fingers, watching Marcus pour.

Five or six years younger than the earl, Keddinton had risen high in the circles of government power since the days when Lord Narborough had been an active spy catcher and he had been a mere confidential secretary on the outskirts of the charmed circle of secrets and danger. His precise role was never spoken of publicly, but he had a reputation for knowing everything, most especially things people wanted to keep hidden.

'You are well informed, sir.' Marcus handed him a glass and set one beside his father. 'As always.'

'Oh, nothing is said outside these walls of the matter, I am sure.' Keddinton inhaled the bouquet for a moment, then took a leisurely sip. 'No, I called with a little gift for my goddaughter and she told me.'

'And what has Verity done to deserve a gift?' enquired the earl.

'Nothing whatsoever—the best reason for giving a lady a present, I always think. Merely a set of enamelled buttons I saw this morning in Tessier's. A pretty trifle.'

'You spoil her.'

'My godchildren interest me.' Viscount Keddinton twirled the wine glass, admiring the colour against the light. 'I like to keep in touch.'

'That must take some effort, you have quite a few,' Marcus observed.

'I have been honoured by the confidence their parents place in me.' Keddinton turned to the earl. 'A practical joke, you say?'

'Some friend of Hal's, I have no doubt,' the earl said easily. 'Sent Marc a parcel which I opened—thought there was a snake inside! Gave me such a start my blasted heart was all over the place.'

'And it was not a snake?' Veryan set down his glass and fixed his full attention on the earl.

'No. Merely a cord of sorts. How are Felicity and the family, Veryan?'

The conversation passed to family matters. Marcus sat letting the two older men talk, his mind on the puzzle of the rope. He would speak to his father about confiding in Veryan; the man knew all about the scandal of ninety-four. They had discussed it only that Christmas when Keddinton had visited in company with his new confidential secretary who expressed an informed, if tactless, interest in the case. Keddinton had long been at the centre of the shadowy world of secrets that surrounded the heart of government. He could be an excellent source of information and would bring a powerful brain to bear on the mystery.

'Let me show you out, sir.' When his father's friend finally took his leave, Marcus strolled down the stairs beside him, restless with his own weakness from loss of blood and his inability to see clear to the heart of this strange threat.

'There was no message with the parcel?' Veryan asked abruptly.

'No. As I say, a prank misfiring, that is all.' He must speak to his father first before confiding in Veryan.

'Of course. Please give my compliments to your mother. I am sorry to have missed her.'

Marcus stood staring at the hallstand and its gleaming card tray for a long moment after Wellow had closed the door behind Lord Keddinton.

'Where is Miss Latham, Wellow?' He had been putting off that confrontation all morning. Sleep had not only rested his hurts, it had also ensured that he faced the morning feeling rather more clear-headed than he had the night before. And one picture that was very clear indeed was of Nell clawing her way out of his embrace—if that was not too polite a word for how he had taken her. The fact that there had been an answering flash of desire in her eyes, just for one moment, did not excuse falling on a virgin like a starving man on a loaf.

She had not come down to breakfast; no doubt she wished to avoid him, he concluded ruefully. It would be easier to mistrust her if the wrongdoing were all on her side, he told himself with a grimace at his own thought processes.

'Miss Latham is alone in the White Salon, my lord. Lady Verity having just gone shopping with Lady Narborough and Miss Price having accompanied Lady Honoria for a dress fitting; Miss Latham is reading, I believe.'

He should probably call his mother's dresser to sit in the corner for propriety, Marcus thought, opening the door. But if he did, he could hardly discuss last night.

'Miss Latham.'

She was sitting very upright at the table in the window, a book open in her hands, her bent head making a graceful curve of her neck above the simple leaf-brown bodice of her gown. As he spoke, she looked up and closed the book, keeping one finger inserted to mark her place.

'My lord.'

There was little of the weary, frightened milliner about the woman in front of him, just a dignified young lady in a plain gown interrupted by a man when she thought she was alone. Then the colour flooded her cheeks and she stood up with more haste than grace, dispelling the illusion. No, Nell had not forgotten that damned kiss.

* * *

'My lord.' Nell bobbed a curtsy, all too conscious that she had behaved as though she were an equal by remaining in her seat like a guest, not the milliner that she was. She had allowed Miss Price to take care of her last night, to lend her night things. She had been sent up supper to her room, and now she had forgotten her place in the sheer comfort and luxury of it all.

My place might be to curtsy and defer, but I will not let him take advantage of me, not after last night. Nell had lost a great deal of sleep, lying wide-eyed in the darkness, wondering what on earth had come over her to let the viscount so much as touch her, let alone to have responded for that fatal moment.

'Marcus,' he said, smiling his cool smile. 'I told you last night. You have no need to stand up for me, Nell. May I sit down?'

'Of course.' How polite they were being. 'I hope the fact that you are downstairs means that the wound is not troubling you too much this morning?' That had been another waking nightmare: that he contracted a fever, the wound became infected, he died—and she became a murderer.

'A trifle uncomfortable, that is all. There is no fever.'

She lowered herself to her seat cautiously, in time with him. 'My lord, I cannot call you by your given name; it is not suitable. It would give the impression of an intimacy…' She ran out of words.

'And after a certain incident last night, intimacy is the last thing you wish to encourage?' he asked, leaning back in his chair and studying her across the circumference of the table.

He was nothing if not direct! The colour left her face; she felt it as a chill on the skin. 'Indeed.'

'I apologise. I have no excuse for my loss of control. It will not happen again.'

Instinct told her not to believe him; men could not be trusted. But his eyes were wide and candid. Serious. Nell blew out a small, pent-up breath, her conscience pricking her. 'I…it was not entirely your fault. For a moment I just wanted to be held.'

'And then you changed your mind?' She had fought him like a fury, that was what he meant, she acknowledged. Wounded and dazed as he had been, a good push would have been more than adequate to repel him, she was sure. There had been no need to struggle like a wild thing.

'Er…yes,' she said. There was speculation on his face for a moment, then it was gone. 'My lord, I should go home.'

'No.' He said it flatly and for the first time she actually believed that he would keep her by force if necessary. 'You are not very obedient, Nell, and I know you have more to tell me than has yet come out. You will call me Marcus when we are alone. Is Nell Latham your real name?'

'Yes!' It was. Or at least, it was one that long use entitled her to.

Marcus Carlow studied her with openly sceptical eyes, but he did not comment, only seemed to reach a decision. 'This is how it will be. You will go this afternoon with Miss Price and me to your lodgings and we will collect whatever you need for a prolonged stay and make sure your valuables are secured—'

'I cannot stay here for days! I have employment that will vanish if I am away. Today is Saturday, thank goodness, but on Monday—'

'I will write to Madame Elizabeth informing her that the Countess of Narborough requires your presence,' he continued as if she had not spoken. 'It would take less than the very broad hint I will give her of future patronage, should she continue to employ you, for your post there to be secure.'

Lady Narborough and the Misses Carlow would not thank him for having their choice of milliner dictated! Or perhaps he would send his mistress there. Nell eyed him, her thoughts concealed behind a mask of composure, then could not resist a jab at his assumption of control.

'Madame does good business providing for the convenients of rich city merchants, as well as their wives,' she observed. 'But perhaps the mistress of a viscount expects a milliner of the top flight?'

Lord Stanegate—*Marcus*—gave a snort of laughter, surprising her. She had expected one of his quelling looks. 'You remind me of a small matter of business I must conclude. *Convenients* indeed, what a very mealy-mouthed euphemism, Nell.'

'Birds of paradise, lightskirts, Cyprians, demi-reps?' she countered. 'Is that free-spoken enough for you, my…Marcus?'

He smiled again. What a very attractive smile he had, especially when his eyes held that wicked twinkle. He was not, she guessed, thinking about her. Not with that look. She felt a fleeting twinge of envy for the woman he was contemplating and a sensual frisson of recollection.

'Where was I?' he continued. 'Ah, yes, we have dealt

with your employer. On what terms do you settle with your landlord?'

'Weekly, in advance. But—'

'We will pay him for, let us say, a month to keep your room.'

'A month! But that is ridiculous, I cannot—'

'You say *but* and *cannot* too often for me, Nell.'

'What am I to say, then? Yes, Marcus? Anything you say, Marcus? Whatever you say, Marcus, however ridiculous? You are too used to having your own way, my lord! I cannot, and will not, stay here a month, and that is that.'

'We are not staying here, we are going into the country, to Stanegate Court, our family seat in Hertfordshire. There we can consider this puzzle in tranquillity, my father can rest—the local doctor is excellent—and the girls can stop dragging their mother around every shop in London.'

'You do not need me for that. I know nothing more than I have told you.'

'I do not believe you. You are a liar, Nell,' he said, still smiling that smile she had thought so attractive just a moment before. 'You know it and I know it. You have secrets you are not telling me.'

But they are secrets I hardly know myself and do not understand, she wanted to say, closing her lips tight on the words. 'You cannot force me to leave London and to go into the country,' she said at last, realising as she spoke that her very lack of denial increased his suspicions.

'Of course I can. How are you going to stop me? Young women are kidnapped all the time, but rarely into comfort as a houseguest. Will you run to Bow Street and lay an information against Viscount Stanegate? Will you protest that I forced you into this house last night, that I forced you to converse and take tea with my sister and her companion?

'And after that brutality you took supper and allowed one of our maids to tuck you up in bed without a murmur of protest? They will be appalled at such a tale.'

'You chose to be sarcastic, my lord.' Nell glared at him, trying to see a way out. 'Well, now I realize how foolish I was to have stayed and will walk out of the front door. What will you do about that, pray?'

Marcus shrugged. 'If you chose to try and escape, I will have you bundled into a locked carriage, transported to Stanegate, locked up in one of the estate cottages and guarded, but you won't do anything that foolish, will you, Nell?' All the amusement had gone out of his eyes.

'It would certainly give you cause for complaint, if you found yourself in the presence of a magistrate eventually, but who would they believe, do you think? Or would you prefer to go home, unprotected, and see if your dark man has done with you, knowing that I am in the country, too far away to call upon?'

A tirade about the inequality of their positions was not going to help. 'You think that this is more than a practical joke, don't you?' Nell said at last when she had her seething temper under control. 'You believe Salterton means real harm in sending that rope—and it was not intended to scare Lord Narborough into thinking it was a snake, it has some other meaning. You suspect you know what lies behind this.'

It was Marcus's turn to fall silent. Nell wondered if he meant to answer her at all. Then he said sombrely, 'I may be wrong, but if I am correct it is an old story, a nightmare that should have been long forgotten. You know all about old nightmares, do you not? I can sense it.'

The shudder that ran through her must have been visible to him. He seemed suddenly focused, as though he would read her mind. The piercing grey eyes were hooded; he knew he had scored a hit. *An old nightmare. Yes, that is exactly what I feel stirring. But it is coincidence, surely, that has brought me here? If it is not, if Salterton knows who I am—then he knows my real name. He knows more than I do about my past.*

'You are afraid.' It was a statement.

'Yes,' she admitted. 'I dislike mysteries. I dislike insecurity. And that man makes me think of knives.' *And I am afraid of you and your family because Mama spoke your name with hate and yet you have all been kind to me, so now I do not know what to trust.* But the man in front of her had not been *kind.* He had been autocratic, bad tempered, sexually domineering—and yet… 'And I dislike not understanding you,' she snapped, provoking another of his disconcerting laughs. 'And I do not want to be kidnapped, you arrogant man.'

'All you need to understand about me, Nell, is that I will keep you safe.'

From the dark man perhaps. Salterton. But from *him?* Marcus Carlow wanted her safe entirely for his own purposes and she was certain he had not told her them all.

'Your definition of safe differs from mine, Marcus.' How easily she had slipped into using his name. But the image of a great house in the country was powerfully seductive. Big, safe, warm, with people all around and strangers immediately obvious.

Nell tried to tell herself that it was only for a few weeks and then she would be back in her old world. But that was not warm, not safe, and she would be all alone again. What harm could it do to escape for just a little while? It could hardly make things worse. Could it?

'Very well,' she conceded.

'Thank you. This afternoon, after Miss Price returns, we will go to your lodgings.' There were sounds of a bustle from the hall, a young lady's laughter. 'In fact, I think that may be her returning now.'

The journey to Dorset Street was enlivened at the beginning by Miss Price sinking into the carriage cushions only to start up with a cry and produce a small pistol from under her skirts. 'What on earth?'

'Ah.' Marcus reached across and took it, slipping it into his pocket. 'The footpad's weapon.'

'A thief with a nice taste in ivory-handled ladies' pistols,' Miss Price remarked, settling herself again.

'No doubt stolen from a previous victim,' Marcus said. He and the companion chatted easily, with the air of two people who had known each other for a long time and who, even if they had little in common in terms of station or interests, were comfortable together.

It was no doubt a relief to Marcus to know that with his mother so preoccupied with her husband's health, his sisters were in safe hands. Nell felt a twinge of envy, contemplating Miss Price's neat apparel and her position in the family.

It had not occurred to her to seek such a post herself as Rosalind had done. She felt a pang, recalling her sister, wondering, yet again, what had become of her.

Perhaps she could have followed in her footsteps, but at first her mother had needed her, especially in that nightmare time when they had found themselves utterly alone. Then, in Nell's grief after her mother's death, it had seemed so much easier to continue with the familiar and the secure, however humble.

Perhaps, when all this was over, she could talk to Miss Price, ask her advice about securing a similar position. But that assumed that this would all be resolved simply and happily with her reputation and her secrets intact.

'Here we are.' Marcus helped the two women out and Nell stood on the pavement looking at the tall, shabby house with new eyes, seeing it as her companions must, contrasting it with the crisp elegance of Albemarle Street.

'I am fortunate in my neighbours,' she said as the front door opened and they were greeted by a strong smell of stewing mutton and onions, a squall of crying from the Hutchins' baby and the powerful voice of Bill Watkins who appeared to have been imbibing rather freely with his Saturday noon meal and was now roaring out one of the latest ballads.

'Is that you, Miss Latham love?' Mrs Drewe put her head round her door, chattering on despite the presence of two strangers. 'Only Mr Westly was round for the rent.' Her gaze was avid.

'We called at his offices a few minutes ago,' Nell said. 'Thank you, Mrs Drewe. I shall be away for a few weeks, visiting friends. Mr Westly is keeping my room for me,' she added as she led the way to the stairs. 'So there's no need to worry.'

'They are all very honest,' she murmured, trying not to sound defensive as they toiled up the stairs.

'I am sure they are,' Miss Price said tactfully as they reached the top landing. She sat by the cold hearth while Marcus went to stand at the window. He had his hands clasped behind his back, and was pointedly not staring round at a room that seemed to Nell even smaller, darker and shabbier now his tall, elegant figure was in it. She set about packing.

Her few clothes, her hairbrush and toilet things went into two valises, her gold chain and simple pearl stud earrings she was wearing already, another bag was sufficient to hold her few books. Nell bit her lip in indecision: should she take the other things, the items that were so carefully hidden?

'My lord, would you be so kind as to move the bed to one side?' She had, thank goodness, placed the chamber pot in the bedside cupboard, so his lordship would not be edified by a view of that. His servants' rooms were doubtless infinitely more respectable than this. 'Thank you.' The narrow bed shifted easily on the well-waxed boards. She poked out the knothole in the middle of the floor, hooked her finger in and pulled.

'Cunning,' Marcus observed, then tactfully looked away while she lifted out the items inside. A bag containing the emergency reserve of money she kept in her room—the rest, her small savings, were in the bank—was tucked into one of the valises. The only other thing in her hidey-hole, a worn writing slope, held her parents' letters and her mother's diary.

'Read them,' her mother had urged in those last few days after the sudden fever had taken hold of her lungs. 'Read them and understand, you are old enough now.' But Nell had never felt strong enough to do so. She knelt on the hard floor, lifted the lid and looked inside, wondering if she would find the name *Carlow* in those yellowing pages, whether she wanted to know what they held. Finally she turned the key in the lock, hung it on its ribbon round her neck inside her bodice, replaced the floorboard and stood up, the box in her hands.

'I will take this; it contains my mother's letters,' she said, hoping that sentimental reason was sufficient explanation for wanting to take a battered old box with her.

'You are all alone?' Miss Price asked, enough sympathy in her voice to bring tears to Nell's eyes. She nodded, unable to speak for a moment and the other woman turned away under pretext of scolding Marcus for slipping his arm out of the sling.

'Miss Latham and I are quite capable of managing two valises and a writing slope between us, if you take the other bag,' she said with some asperity. 'Why is it, Miss Latham, that gentlemen insist on treating us as though we are weaklings?'

'Good manners, gallantry—' Marcus began.

'A desire to show off your superior muscles?' Miss Price murmured, shaking her head, and he gave in, thrust his arm back in the sling and picked up just the book bag on his way to the door.

Nell stood for a moment, wondering why she felt such a strong premonition that she would never come back here. Something must have shown on her face, for Miss Price tucked her free hand under her arm. 'Ready? You must call me Diana. I am sure you are going to be very happy staying at Stanegate Court.'

'Thank you. And you must call me Nell,' Nell responded, managing to find a smile from somewhere.

Mrs Drewe was lurking when they reached the front hall again. 'Did the other gentleman find you, Miss Latham?' she asked, her eyes darting over every detail of Marcus's tall figure. 'Forgot to ask when you came in.'

'Other gentleman?' she asked. 'Which other gentleman?' She could guess the answer.

'The dark one. Looked like a foreigner, if you ask me, duck. One of those Italians, I'll be bound. Nice clothes though, for all that.'

'No,' she said steadily, conscious of Marcus moving up closer behind her. 'Did he leave a message?'

'Oh no, duck. Just to say he'd catch up with you when he needed to.'

Chapter Six

Nell travelled to Stanegate Court in the carriage with Diana Price and the Carlow sisters. Lord and Lady Narborough took another carriage and a lumbering coach followed conveying valets, dressers and luggage.

Despite the cold, Marcus rode, giving Nell an excellent opportunity, should she feel so inclined, to admire his horsemanship, his well-bred mount, his glossy boots and the breadth of his shoulders under the caped riding coat. He appeared to have discarded his sling. After one glance, she turned her attention firmly to the interior of the carriage and told herself it was his business if he chose to aggravate the wound by vigorous exercise. She was not responsible for male pride.

'Marc prefers riding to driving,' Verity confided. The direction of her gaze had been noted. 'He rides very well.'

'So does Hal. He rides even better,' Honoria said, with the air of someone continuing a long-standing argument. 'Hal is our other brother and he is a cavalry officer, Miss Latham.'

'Marc drives better than Hal,' Verity retorted.

Diana rolled her eyes at Nell. 'Your brothers ride like centaurs,' she said. 'Both of them. They also ride neck or nothing, have been brought home on a hurdle many times and I hope I do not have to remind you, Honoria, not to try and emulate them.'

'Miss Latham—'

'Nell.'

'Oh, thank you, that is much cosier.' Verity, with her engaging smile, seemed little more than a girl, hardly ready for her first Season. Nell smiled back. 'It is very nice that you are able to join us. But I didn't know Marc knew you, so how—'

'Verity—' Diana began.

'Nell saved Marc from a footpad,' Honoria said, regarding Nell's flushed face a little quizzically. 'And she delivered that parcel for Papa, only—'

'It was such a shame that when your brother went to thank her he met someone with a pistol,' Diana said brightly.

'Oh, I see.' Verity subsided, obviously satisfied with the explanation. Honoria, it was equally obvious, was putting two and two together and coming up with at least six. A little smile tweaked at the corner of her very pretty mouth and there was a twinkle—not unlike Marcus's—in her eyes.

She thinks he and I are…involved, Nell thought with a sudden flash of insight, followed by a wave of embarrassment. But surely she would not think her brother would bring his mistress to his parents' house?

'Lord Stanegate is worried that the man might attack me, because I was a witness,' she said with what composure she could, telling herself that she was refining too much upon every change of tone or fleeting glance. 'He may well live near my home, you see.'

The remainder of the journey passed safely enough, aided by Miss Price's travelling chess set and Honoria's bag full of fashion journals, although not without both sisters bemoaning the necessity of their father's health requiring country air so close to the start of the Season.

Stanegate Court was a surprise. Nell had not known what to expect, but it had not been this low, rambling house of half timbering and mellow red brick, its roofs swooping in the comfortable sag of age, and woodlands of ancient beeches and oaks crowding close on the frosted hillside behind. If she had visualised Marcus anywhere it would have been in chilly Palladian splendour with ordered rooms and ranks of pillars.

'It is bigger than it looks,' Honoria commented as the carriage drew up in front of a vast timbered porch. 'There are wings at the back at all sorts of odd angles. Mama and I think the whole thing needs pulling down and rebuilding in the modern style, but Papa and Marc wouldn't countenance it.'

'But it is perfect,' Nell breathed as she alighted, stopping to admire it as the other women walked towards the door. 'Perfect.'

'You think so?' She turned to find Marcus behind her, reins in hand. He was white about the mouth and had thrust his right hand between the buttons of his coat to support the arm.

'You should not have ridden,' she said, frowning at him and ignoring the question. 'You have doubtless inflamed the wound.'

'Your concern would ring more truly if you had not

been the instigator of the damage,' he replied, his voice
as chilly as she was beginning to feel. He was tired and
in pain, she was certain. And of course, being male, was
not going to admit as much, let alone that it was his fault,
so his temper was raw.

'It would be most inconvenient for me if you were
to die,' she darted back at him. 'And besides, it was
entirely your fault!'

'That you were carrying a loaded pistol?'

'I did not know it was,' she protested.

'Oh, come now. I was not born yesterday.' Marcus
handed the reins to a waiting groom. 'Thank you,
Havers.' He stood frowning after the horse as it was led
away. 'No intelligent person carries a weapon when they
do not know if it is loaded or not. They most certainly do
not point it at someone.' He brought his attention back
from the horse to fix on her face. 'And, whatever else you
may or may not be, Nell, you are intelligent.'

'I pulled the trigger when I found it—pointed out of
the window, of course—and nothing happened. The
trigger must have been jammed and came unstuck when
I was trying to get my keys out.'

He looked unconvinced as they turned to walk into
the house.

'I suppose you've been sitting on that horse for
miles in the cold with your shoulder hurting more
and more, too pig-headed to give up and ride inside
and it has put you thoroughly out of temper,' she
observed. 'I can see you find my carrying a weapon
suspicious and think that I should have waited in a
ladylike manner to be attacked and then screamed in
the hope of some gallant rescuer rushing to my aid.

'Well, in my world, my lord, knights on white chargers are somewhat thin on the ground and defenceless females have to fend for themselves. Good afternoon,' she added punctiliously to a startled-looking butler who was standing just inside the door.

'Watson, the Blue Guest Suite for Miss Latham and find a girl to wait on her.'

'Certainly, my lord. Lord Narborough has retired to his rooms. Her ladyship has sent for the doctor. However,' he added as Marcus swore under his breath and turned towards the stairs, 'I collect it is more in the nature of a precaution, my lord. His lordship was in, er, good voice a few moments ago.'

'The country suits Lord Narborough?' Nell ventured, more concerned about the earl's welfare than prolonging her quarrel with his son.

'Mama is happier when he is in town because she sets much store in Dr Rowlands. My father is happier in the country. My sisters are unhappy to be torn, as they see it, from their preparations for the Season. Miss Price, no doubt, is less than delighted to have to deal with their moods.' He looked at her from under levelled brows. The butler, who appeared to sense atmosphere with considerable accuracy, melted away towards the rear of the vast beamed hall.

'And you?' Nell asked, smarting under the double lash of his bad temper and her own nagging conscience about the pistol. 'Are you unhappy, my lord?'

There was a long silence while his lordship appeared to be counting. 'I, Miss Latham? I have been forced to leave town at the start of what I was anticipating to be an enjoyable negotiation with my next—what was your delightful word? Ah yes, *convenient*. And do not attempt to look scandalized at my mentioning her. You raised the subject in the first place. I have a furrow through my shoulder that hurts like the very devil.' She opened her mouth and shut it with a snap as he added, 'And do not tell me again I should not have ridden today or we will fall out most grievously. I have sulking sisters, an anxious mother and a secretive, lying milliner on my hands. Yes, Nell. I could be described as less than happy.'

'Then I suggest you count your numerous blessings, my lord. I am endeavouring to find some to count myself,' she retorted. 'If I could be shown to my room; I have no doubt I will see you at dinner.'

'Or just as soon as you choose to tell me all the truth,' he flung back.

Watching Nell sweep off across the stone flags with as much outraged dignity as a duchess in a temper, Marcus bit back an oath and found himself admiring the delectable rear view of his reluctant houseguest. Her gown might be old and shabby, but her deportment was that of a lady and the sway of her hips, downright alluring.

He unclenched his teeth and snapped his fingers at a footman. 'Help me out of this coat.' Damn it, she was right, he should not have ridden, he thought, wincing as the man eased off the heavy garment. He was behaving in a way that he criticized in his own brother, recalling sending Hal frequent lectures about failing to allow wounds time to heal.

It was time to remind himself that he was, perforce, the sensible brother, the one with the responsibilities, the one who held the family together. He was not the brother who made love to young women in carriages, got himself shot—or lost his temper, come to that. That was Hal, who managed with Janus-like dexterity to be an exemplary officer on one hand and a hellion on the other.

'Send my valet to me,' he said curtly, making for the stairs. A bath, a fresh bandage, a change of linen and some reflection in tranquillity were called for. 'And Andrewes,' he added as a further thought struck him. 'We must look after Miss Latham while she is with us. Ask Wilkins and Trevor to ensure she does not get…lost. If she goes anywhere, they are to keep an eye on her. This is an easy house to lose one's way in,' he added blandly as the footman struggled to keep the speculation off his face.

He opened his chamber door to find his mother sitting beside the fire. 'Mama?'

'Your father is resting with a book.' She fiddled with the pleats of her skirt. 'The journey gave me time to think. Why, exactly, have you brought Miss Latham with us?'

'Because I have concerns for her welfare.' Marcus kept his voice even as he strolled to the fire and held out a hand to the warmth. His mother watched him, her face troubled. Oh, to hell with it! He was not beating around the bush. 'Are you concerned that I have installed my mistress under your roof?' he asked bluntly.

'I, well… Of course not, you would never do such a thing. Only it is more than a little odd, my dear. She appears to be a very well-mannered, well-spoken young woman, but she is, after all, a milliner.'

'Who may be in danger from a violent man in her locality. Mama, this is not a subject I would normally speak of to you, but as you allude to it, I am discussing terms with a certain Mrs Jensen.'

'Excellent.' The countess stood up, colour bright in her cheeks as she brushed her skirts into order with some emphasis. 'Forgive me, my dear. I should remember before speaking that you are my level-headed son!'

'Indeed, Mama.' Usually undemonstrative, he surprised both of them by leaning over and kissing her cheek. 'Be kind to Miss Latham for me. I would wish her to feel at ease. Perhaps the girls could lend her a gown or two?'

A relaxed Nell would be easier to break down, he thought as his valet slipped back into the room. He was aware that his grim expression had Allsop tiptoeing around, but was disinclined to put on a false front for the man. Let Nell relax, enjoy a little luxury. He would be, if not charming, at least civil, and in time her guard would slip. And then he would strike.

Nell perched on the edge of the big damask-hung bed and tried not to appear impossibly gauche as she stared round the room. Miriam, the maid who had been sent to her, was unpacking her meagre possessions and conferring with another woman who bobbed a curtsy and left. Doubtless to inform the rest of the servants' hall just how humble the new guest was, Nell thought with a sigh.

The rich draperies that hung at the windows set off a dusk-darkened view of sweeping parkland, gilded frames surrounded landscapes and portraits. The furniture was frivolous, French and entirely feminine, and Miriam's footsteps were swallowed up in the deep pile of the carpet.

There was a dressing room with its own closet and a tub and room for a hundred more gowns than she possessed and it all seemed achingly familiar. Once she had known a room like this, when she had been very, very small. Mama had been there, young and pretty and laughing with a man she knew must be Papa, and she and Nathan and Rosalind had come in to say goodnight and Nell knew, with a deep certainty, that it was always like that when Papa had been with them. Warmth and luxury and laughter.

The scent had been the same too. Potpourri, sandalwood drawer linings, the aroma of burning apple wood; familiar and long-lost, just as the library smell had been. Which meant that once they really had been wealthy. Not just comfortably off—she could remember *those* days clearly: the little house in Rye, the modest respectability that had proved so fragile—but wealthy like this. And looking back she realized that Mama's style of manner and her insistence on deportment reflected the needs of a life quite different from the one they had been living.

Miriam had set the battered old writing slope on a table with as much care as if it was a costly dressing case. The feel of the tiny key around her neck had Nell pulling it out, turning it between her fingers. Should she open the box, read the diary and the letters? Which was worse? Knowing the truth or imagining it?

The other maid came back, garments draped over her arms. 'Lady Honoria and Lady Verity thought you might wish to borrow some gowns, Miss Latham, seeing as how your luggage got lost. And there's some indoor shoes, miss, just come from the cobblers, that Lady Verity thought would fit.'

The key on its ribbon slid back under her bodice as Nell got up. So, her face was saved in front of the servants at least. She smiled and tried not to show her emotions at the thought of those pretty gowns, the light fabrics, the big Paisley shawl, the brand-new silk stockings that lay on top.

'Dinner will be in an hour and a half, miss. Would you like to take your bath and to change now?'

'Yes. Thank you.' Time to get used to her new clothes. Time to practise walking and smiling and chattering of polite nothings so she could survive the first formal meal in this fairy-tale world into which Marcus Carlow had propelled her.

But her resolution to think of nothing but ladylike behaviour did not survive long once she was dressed and alone in the jewel box of a room. The writing slope seemed to call to her, crouching like a toad in the middle of the polished table.

Her hands shook as she opened it. Diary or letters? Just one letter, the most recent, that was all she could cope with. The pink silk ribbon was faded with age as she untied the bow and lifted the topmost folded paper. The paper crackled, brittle and yellow, as she smoothed it out. It was clear to read, a strong male handwriting in spluttering brown ink with a pen that had seen better days.

Newgate.

Nell dropped the sheet in shock, then forced herself to pick it up again.

March 16, 1795
My darling, tomorrow is my last day on earth. I have stopped hoping now that George Carlow will relent, will make any effort to save me. He could, if he wished, I know it. He has the ear of

those high enough, if only he will tell the truth about what happened. Why he will not, I do not know. Is it because of that sin I committed that you, my love, have forgiven me for? Could his priggish disapproval of adultery be enough to see me hang when he knows me innocent of the greater crimes for which I am condemned? Or is there some other reason?

I can hardly believe that. Yet others believe it of me. If it is true, if George is behind this tangle of lies, you must beware. Trust no one, least of all him. He will try and tell you his conscience and his honour dictated his actions, his treachery to his oldest friend. Honour? I hope he has enough to keep away tomorrow. I do not want to go to my Maker with the sight of his face before me.

Your money they cannot touch. They have taken my title, my lands, my wealth, my name—my life is the least of it. Your dowry is safe. Even at my most profligate, I never touched that. You know where to go, where to hide to start your new life.

I beg you not to come tomorrow. I want to know you are with the children, that you, at least, are safe. Kiss them for me. Tell them their father loves them as I love their mother. I have not always shown that love as I should, but I give it now, with all my heart.
Your devoted husband, to death and beyond,
William.

Her father had hanged for something so awful that they had stripped him of his title. *Hanged.* That was what the silken rope was about. She remembered now, a nobleman was hanged with that, not with coarse hemp.

The letter fluttered to the embroidered bedcover and this time she did not pick it up. Papa had gone to his death believing that George Carlow—the Earl of Narborough, that nice man who was so ill—could have saved him, and suspecting that he had the worst of reasons for not doing so.

Her father had betrayed her mother with another woman and had been forgiven for it.

Nell stared blindly at the wall. So much made sense now: her mother's reticence; her aloofness from their neighbours; their quiet, retired life. The money from a fixed income ebbing away inexorably as three children grew up and prices rose. Her bitterness and sadness.

Had Nathan and Rosalind known the truth? Nathan should have inherited a title, lands. She scrabbled through the pile of letters until she found an earlier one with the address wrapper still intact. *The Countess of Leybourne*. That made sense now, the memory of someone talking about the Earl of Leybourne when she had been small and of being hushed.

An earl. Hanged. She had known there had been scandal and tragedy surrounding her father's death, but not this, never this. A dry sob rose in her throat, but there were no tears. Perhaps it was the shock, but her mind was clear and her hands, as she folded the letter away and turned the key, were steady.

Courage, she told herself. Somehow her own tragic history had resurfaced; it was too much of a coincidence that she had become accidentally entangled with the Carlows just when someone decided to attack them with the memories of that old scandal. Someone was pulling strings, and she had no idea who or why.

Now she had to go downstairs, make conversation, sit and break bread with the man who had stood by and let her father hang. If her father's suspicions were correct, Lord Narborough might even have been guilty of something far worse than abandoning his friend. She had to keep her knowledge secret. If Marcus Carlow found out who she was, he would believe she had every motive in the world for seeing his father dead, for wreaking vengeance on the entire Carlow family.

There would be a time to let her emotions sweep her away with grief for the past, for her parents. But not now, not while that man watched her, alert for the slightest weakness.

Chapter Seven

It was as though the good clothes wrought their own magic, Marcus thought, studying Nell as she pecked at her dinner. With her hair dressed by the maid and in one of Honoria's evening gowns—its amber silk making her eyes greener and her hair more richly honey-brown—she looked every bit as much the well-bred young lady as did his sisters. But then, he realized, he had paid little attention to her clear speech and obvious education. She might be a milliner now, but she had not always been one. Miss Latham had been born and brought up a lady. More secrets. More lies.

She was very pale and avoided looking at him, which was an achievement, considering that he sat opposite her. With five women and only two men, the table was, of necessity, unbalanced. He was flanked by Verity and Diana Price, with Nell and Honoria opposite. His father had felt well enough to take the head of the table; his mother, elegant as always, was at the foot.

But Nell, while she did not look at him, could not seem able to keep her eyes off his father, her expression serious, questioning, as it kept flickering towards the earl. Was she watching him for signs of weakness, anxious about the effect her delivery of the parcel had had on his health?

She caught the fullness of her underlip in her teeth and the unconscious gesture drew his attention to her mouth and sent a lance of heat straight to his loins. He must have made some movement, for her eyes finally met his, colour touching her cheeks at whatever she saw there. She looked away again and listened to Verity's chatter about the plans for her come-out ball, but Marcus sensed her wary attention was still on him.

She had hardly spoken a word all through the meal. That might simply be the shyness of a young woman propelled into a world far above her own. But it was obvious Nell Latham knew the rules of polite Society. Faced with a table laid for a formal dinner, she had not made a single wrong move and her behaviour with the servants showed the polite self-confidence of someone used to domestic staff. And yet she lived in that garret. Yes, gently bred indeed—and what had brought about her fall?

He watched her now as she thanked the footman for refilling her water glass, her smile vanishing as she darted another glance towards his father.

'Mrs Poulson tells me that Lady Wyveton has returned to the Hall,' his mother remarked. 'Her house-keeper told Mrs Poulson that she is very low in spirits, poor lady. I mention it,' she added with a glance at her daughters, 'because I do not believe in whispering behind her back. Better that what has happened is known and a kindly discretion observed rather than gossip and speculation.'

'Wyveton deserves to be horsewhipped,' the earl said darkly. 'Carrying on like that with a married woman, right under his own wife's nose. And her own cousin at that. Outrageous.'

Nell was making no bones about staring at his father now. She was looking at him directly, a frown between her rather strong brown brows, her expression, if it was not too fanciful to think so, one of scarce-controlled anger.

'Will there be a divorce, Papa?' Honoria asked, eyes wide with the horror of it.

'One hopes not. Let this be a warning to both of you to consider most carefully the company you keep. It was an imprudent marriage, come to ruin.'

'Is the man beyond forgiveness, then, my lord?' It was the first remark that Nell had made, other than requests to pass the butter or the salt, or murmured thanks. Everyone stared at her. 'Might there not be some extenuating circumstance, or perhaps he has repented?' she persisted.

'It is unforgivable, whatever the circumstances,' the earl said, colour high in his cheeks. 'It always leads to degradation and disaster. I knew a case once—' He broke off, shaking his head. 'You will call upon Lady Wyveton, my dear?'

The conversation moved into safer waters, but Marcus kept his eye on Nell. How bizarre, that she should defend the adulterer. Most women would champion the wife—except in cases such as Lady Caroline Lamb's—and castigate the husband. Had Nell once been involved with a married man?

Warned earlier by his mother that keeping his father sitting over the decanters after dinner would earn her severe displeasure, Marcus lured him into the salon after one moderate glass with promises of backgammon. As it happened, Verity begged for a chess lesson which the earl granted with an indulgent chuckle, leaving Marcus free to observe his target.

His mother, Diana Price and Honoria were deep in discussion over the all-important gowns for the Carlow ball. Nell was sitting beside them, her expression politely attentive, her eyes unfocused, looking inwards. Just what was going on in that neatly coiffed head?

'Miss Latham?'

She started. 'My lord?'

'Would you care to stroll through the Long Gallery?'

'I confess some exercise before retiring would be welcome after such a long time in the carriage.' She rose, then hesitated. *Oh, artistically done, Miss Latham, now the excuse…* 'But you should be resting, my lord. Your wound—'

He had thrust his hand between the buttons of his swallow-tailed coat, refusing to attempt his dinner encumbered by a sling, and now his shoulder was aching like the very devil. 'Hardly a twinge,' Marcus lied. Nell's mouth pursed in a moue of disbelief, but she laid her hand on his offered arm and allowed herself to be walked to the door.

'This is a fascinating house,' she observed with the air of one determined to make polite conversation. Marcus led her across the Great Hall and up the shallow stairs with their grotesque carvings on every newel post. 'Is it Tudor?'

'Mainly. It was built by my ancestor, the first viscount. The land and the title were a gift from Henry VIII in return, so the family legend goes, for marrying an inconvenient mistress of the monarch's at the time he was courting Jane Seymour. The story is, of course, that she was with child.'

Nell shot him an assessing glance as though measuring him up to fill the monstrous monarch's shoes. 'Poor woman. I hope she had some liking for your ancestor.'

Marcus remarked, half jesting, 'You have no sympathy for an adulterous king then?' Nell tripped on the top step and he caught her arm to steady her. Far too thin, he thought in an attempt to deny the frisson that touching her produced.

'I imagine what he wanted, he took,' she said with a shiver that transmitted itself to his hand, still curled lightly about her upper arm. 'He had all the power and they had none, those women he ordered to his bed.'

'And yet you defended an adulterer to my father?'

'Every case is different, every person is different. To condemn without understanding is harsh.' Her voice was urgent with an undertone of distress and there was colour in her cheeks.

'You speak from experience then?' Marcus asked with every intention of provoking her into lowering her guard.

'Of adultery? You are suggesting I have been some man's mistress?' Nell tugged her arm free of Marcus's hold, conscious that she had let his fingers linger there too long, just for the illusory comfort they gave, and despising herself for it. 'You think I am Salterton's whore? Is that what you are implying?' The thought of the dark man with his air of menace and his dancer's sinister grace touching her, made her shudder.

'You were not born to the life you are leading,' he countered, his intelligent face watchful as he probed.

'And that makes me what, exactly? Other than unfortunate?' she demanded. 'I deliver a parcel and now you feel free to question my morals, probe into my life?' Would she be this angry, or less, if she had not discovered the sinister link between their families? 'You are no better than Henry VIII—overbearing, arrogant and perfectly prepared to browbeat a woman.'

'I will do what I have to, to protect my family,' Marcus said flatly, but there was colour on his cheekbones and his eyes were angry. 'Sooner or later you will tell me what I want to know.'

'After you produce the thumbscrews?' she flashed, flinging open the nearest door and marching through it. 'Drag me down to the dungeons? No doubt this house has them—to go with the warders who appear every time I walk anywhere alone.'

'The footmen are there for your protection and I very much regret the house has no dungeons,' he said with what she could swear was real feeling.

'I am sure you do— Oh!' She had found the Long Gallery, yards of windows on her left, their panes black onto the winter night and, on her right, portrait after portrait, ranks of them filling the space between the waist-heigh panelling and the ornately plastered ceiling, interrupted only by candle sconces and the carved stone of the fireplace. Charmed into forgetting their quarrel, she stood and stared.

'Let us call a truce and look at the pictures,' Marcus suggested, coming to her side. He made no effort to take her arm, but began to walk slowly, glancing up at the wall as he went. 'That's the first earl. A dull man with a genius for toadying to Queen Anne. There's the wife of the Tudor viscount with her eldest son.'

'Who looks nothing like Henry VIII,' Nell pointed out.

'All babies look like Henry VIII,' Marcus said. 'These are the early-eighteenth-century portraits.' Nell dutifully studied a number of sombre gentlemen in magnificent waistcoats and even more splendid wigs, flanked by their ladies who displayed considerably more bosom than she felt was strictly necessary.

'My father,' Marcus said, stopping beneath a full-length portrait of a young man holding the bridle of a stallion against a background of rolling parkland. The house could be glimpsed in the distance.

Lord Narborough was extremely handsome in those days. 'You resemble him closely,' Nell observed, not adding that the man in the painting looked as though he had not a care in the world while the one standing next to her had two sharp lines between his brows when he frowned. And he frowned a lot, mostly at her it seemed.

'Thank you, but you flatter me. I do have his colouring,' Marcus conceded. 'And here, at the end, are all of us together.' The family group showed a young couple, a baby in the wife's arms—that must be Verity—a small boy and girl playing with a puppy—Honoria and the absent Hal—and a serious boy leaning against the arm of his mother's chair. So, Marcus was frowning even at the age of nine or ten.

'Delightful,' she said politely. Somewhere, long since lost, there had been a portrait of her own family. She could just recall having to sit very still on Mama's knee, bribed with sweetmeats. 'When was this painted?'

'Ninety-four. I was nine. It was shortly afterwards that my father become…unwell.'

The year before Papa was hanged. Was he unfaithful to Mama even as they posed for their own portrait? Was he the man Lord Narborough began to refer to at dinner? And had Lord Narborough been so judgemental about this sin that he refused to help Papa when he was in danger of his life? Or was there more to all this? She must read all of the letters and the diary, however painful it would be. She had opened Pandora's box; now she was incapable of keeping the truths and the hurt locked away. A stab of grief lanced through her, almost upsetting her careful poise.

'What is it, Nell?' Something must have shown on her face as she turned from that happy family group, sitting in their sunlit garden. Marcus put out his hand to catch hers.

'You know where you belong, don't you?' she demanded, her own misery and confusion spilling out. 'Where you come from, who you are.'

'Of course.' He was puzzled. Naturally. He had always known who he was, no inner uncertainty of identity or purpose ever rocked Marcus Carlow's world. 'And you do not?'

Somehow he had pulled her gently to stand in front of him, his hand on her shoulder. It seemed the most natural thing in the world to take the one step forward that brought her close enough to lay her palm against his chest, and then, she was not sure how, her forehead was against the cool blue silk of his waistcoat.

He was so solid, so capable, so male. She wanted to touch him, to soak up that strength and certainty. She wanted to be held, to have someone stronger, more powerful than herself say that it would all be well, that she need not fight any longer, that there would be enough money for food and the rent, that there were no mysteries. She wanted someone to tell her that the past was past and could not hurt her any more. To tell her sweet lies, give her comfort. She knew it was fantasy, that she could not rely on anyone but herself and yet...

'Nell?' His voice was muffled by her hair, gentler than she had heard it before. Something thrummed through her, bone-deep, like the vibration of a great bell, felt rather than heard.

'I just want to be held.' The words spilled out as his arms came round her.

'Shh.' He rocked her gently, one hand cupping the back of her head, the other circling her shoulders. 'Let go of it, Nell. You don't have to fight *all* the time.'

He understands. It's so hard alone, so lonely. So cold. She tipped up her face to look at him, to tell him that and found no need for words as his mouth came down and took hers in a kiss that soothed and stroked and lulled her into a dream of safety and certainty.

Marcus's lips were warm, oh so warm. They caressed her mouth with a gentle pressure until she opened to him with a sigh that was like coming home and she leaned into the strength and the heat and felt her body turn to silk and flame and still he simply held her and spoke, silently, with his lips and his tongue and his strength while she melted, surrendering. *At last, at last.*

Gradually his breathing quickened; she felt his body tense against hers, and the hand that had curved protectively around her shoulders moved, urgent, seeking, found the swell of her hip, the dip of her waist, up to the curve of her breast and he became just *man*, just another male wanting her body, wanting her secrets, wanting her surrender.

'No!' She pushed him away, as desperate as she had felt in the carriage, the panic clogging her lungs, the pulse wild in her throat. 'Stop! Stop now!'

Marcus threw up his hands, stepped back, his eyes dark, his lips parted. They looked swollen. Hers must be too. That kiss, that foolish kiss, had been no simple brush of the lips.

It was insanity to have relaxed, to have trusted, to have dreamt. She could rely on no one but herself. Ever. To believe anything else was a delusion. How could she have let herself become so weak? How could she have let herself trust?

'Nell?' He reached for her and she batted his hand away.

'No. No. I am tired. *Tired*. I did not mean… How can I trust you? Any of you?' She turned and ran and knew he stood there watching her go.

Marcus flung himself down onto one of the sofas flanking the fireplace and ran both hands through his hair. His shoulder muscles spasmed with pain, but he ignored it. What had just happened? That had been more than just a kiss and far more than a simple response to a woman who seemed unhappy and confused. Why had he done that? God, he had wanted her. Wanted to comfort her, wanted to protect her and then, compellingly, wanted to take her.

His body was racked with need. Deliberately he set

himself to master the reaction, focusing until his breathing levelled off, the ache in his groin subsided, the demand of his body released its hold. *Think,* he told his intellect. *That's what you are supposed to be good at.*

Nell had been moved by that family portrait. *You know where you come from, where you belong.* So she does not know, any more. Whatever former life had given her the educated speech, the polished manners, the education—that had gone and now she was adrift, fighting every battle alone and aching for comfort.

Comfort, but not the comfort that two bodies entwined together brought each other. He had known, the moment the kiss became more than the desire to soothe her, know her, that he had lost her. That had been outright rejection, not shyness nor the maidenly alarm of a virgin experiencing a man's passion for the first time.

And yet, he could not believe she was experienced. Those kisses, her reactions, had been instinctive, not tutored. The only explanation that made sense to him was that she was in love with her dark man and to find herself in another man's arms, responding sexually to him, was a betrayal.

Marcus stretched out his legs towards the fire, ran one hand through his hair and let his head lean onto the back rail of the sofa. Despite his efforts at self-control, he still had an erection that was uncomfortable, his shoulder hurt like hell and he could not decide what to do about Nell. Other than take her to bed. Which was impossible.

He wanted her. He trusted her not at all, but he wanted her. And part of her, a part that she rejected, wanted him. A small hum of satisfied male conceit made him smile mockingly at himself. The smile cooled on his lips, became a twist of wry acceptance. Whoever Nell Latham was, she was steeped in deceit and lies. While he was ignorant of her secrets, she remained a danger to his family—a danger he had brought into their heart, the better to watch. He had to be certain that was the right strategy to have taken.

Four days passed and Nell began to allow herself to relax. She even learned to ignore the footman who was always hovering outside her door, unobtrusively padding along behind her wherever she went.

Lady Narborough became less distant, more natural towards her, and Nell realized with a jolt that perhaps she had worried at first that her son had brought his paramour into the household. Honoria and Verity simply accepted her as another young female friend. When they remembered her circumstances, they were tactful about their allowances and the difference in their circumstances. When they forgot, they lent her gowns and trinkets with total ease, as though she was a guest of their own station whose luggage truly had gone astray.

Marcus avoided any direct contact if he could help it, but she was conscious, constantly, of his regard. He studied her all the time, watching for what, she knew not. When she walked in the garden—well wrapped, her hands thrust into one of Honoria's fashionably vast muffs—she would look up and see him brooding on the terrace. When she strummed a few notes on the piano, trying to recall far-away lessons, he was there barricaded behind his copy of *The Times*. And when, defiant, she stared back to let him see she was aware of his scrutiny, his dark eyes held a spark of the heat that haunted her dreams.

In her turn Nell, from a wary distance, watched Lord Narborough. She was reading a few letters a day—all that she felt able to cope with—working back from that last, shattering message. But there were no clues that she could find to what her father's supposed crime had been, to the identity of his lover or why Lord Narborough had abandoned him. He was in prison for months, it seemed, and the letters held, for the most part, only anxious enquiries about the family and brave attempts to make prison life sound bearable.

Lord Narborough, the man she saw in his own home almost twenty years after the crisis, was kind to his daughters, obviously still deeply in love with his wife and proud of his sons. His attitude to the staff of the big old house was firm, but just, and it was plain that he knew them all, not just by name, but the details of their families too. All qualities that weighed on the right side of the scales with, so far, only his outburst about adulterous husbands on the other side. But most people would echo those sentiments, if perhaps with less heat.

By casual conversation with the girls, Nell discovered that the estates were extensive and prosperous and always had been. Money could not have been a factor in any betrayal, she decided. She was not going to discover more at a distance. Steeling herself, Nell made conversation with the earl, was persuaded into a game of backgammon and found herself liking her host more and more. And he appeared to like her too.

'Miss Latham would give you a run for your money at backgammon,' he teased Marcus after a close game one evening. 'And she has more patience than you have—no heavy sighs while I make up my mind about my next move.'

'That is not impatience, my lord,' Nell observed with a slanting look at Marcus. 'That is strategy. Lord Stanegate wishes to unsettle you.'

'He can try! Here, take my place, my boy.'

'Ah, no.' Marcus shook his head. 'Miss Latham will employ her strategies upon me.'

'I have none,' she protested.

'All lies,' he said lightly, his mouth smiling, his eyes dark as they took in her instinctive flinching at the word. 'You would sit and regard me with those green eyes until I could not think which way up the board was.' And he had strolled off leaving his father tutting good-humouredly about incorrigible flirts and Nell thoroughly flustered.

And so the first week passed, and Nell became used to the routine of the house, became part of it: running errands for Lady Narborough, paying visits with the girls when the heavy frosts eased enough to allow the carriage to be taken out, enjoying reading with Miss Price or playing backgammon with the earl. And every morning, before she got up, she would take the key from its chain around her neck and open her mother's box, take out the next three letters and remind herself who these people were and why she should not trust them.

Marcus had stopped interrogating her, which was almost more unsettling than his questions. She was acutely aware of his presence. On the Saturday morning, brushing her hair, she found herself daydreaming about his arms around her, his mouth on hers, and finally let herself wonder what it would be like to be made love to by a man like that.

The preliminaries would be…pleasant. She smiled a little at herself for the euphemism. The act itself would not be, of course, but perhaps the pain and the urgent crudity would be compensated for by being held afterwards. She closed her eyes and recalled the feeling of being caught against his chest, of the strength of his arms around her and the gentleness, so much at odds with his size and his temper. Would he lie with her a little afterwards, holding her, stroking her hair, murmuring something affectionate?

These thoughts took her as far as the breakfast room. Lord Stanegate, far from the urgent lover of her fantasy, was demolishing a sirloin while engaged in vigorous political debate with his father, who was peering irritably at the newspaper. The reality was so remote from her sensual daydream that she was smiling, not blushing, as she took her place at the table.

'The post, my lord.' Watson directed a footman to place a laden salver beside the earl's place.

Lord Narborough put down the *Morning Chronicle* and began to sort through, replacing his wife and daughters' letters on the tray for the footman to take to the countess and passing Miss Price and Marcus their own mail. Nell addressed herself to her omelette while the others began to break seals and exchange items of news.

'Maria Hemmingford has contracted mumps,' Lady Narborough informed them. 'So improvident, just before the Season!'

'The draper is unable to match that striped silk,

Honoria.' Diana passed her some samples. 'He says, will these do?'

'Do you know anything about the bloodlines of Nutley's carriage horses?' Marcus asked his father. 'Only my agent says that— Father?'

The other women, engrossed in a discussion of the silk samples, had not noticed Marcus's tone change. But Nell had heard him speak like that before. The earl was staring at a paper unfolded in his hand. Something fell from it, a twig with green needle-like leaves. Then the scent reached her: the peppery fragrance of summer and heat.

'Rosemary,' Nell said, identifying it. 'For remembrance, is it not?'

Both men turned to look at her, their likeness suddenly vivid as two pairs of flint-grey eyes fixed on her face. 'What do *you* remember, Miss Latham?' Marcus asked, his voice hard, and she realized that this was another part of the mystery, another threat and, it seemed, she had said quite the wrong thing.

Chapter Eight

Lord Narborough sat quite still for a moment, the fragrant sprig in his hand. Then he dropped it back into its wrapper, gathered up his post and rose. He was pale, but steady, and Marcus, who had reached out a hand to take his elbow, dropped it away.

'Excuse me, my dear,' the earl said to his wife. 'Would you join me in the study, Marcus?'

'Of course.' Nell, after her bright remark, had fallen silent. If she knew anything about this, then she was a good actress. He frowned at her, angry with himself for wanting to trust her.

The threat to his family, now that the initial shock of the rope was over, had strengthened his father, made him resolute, Marcus realized, watching the older man's firm jaw. He set himself not to fuss.

'As Miss Latham says, rosemary for remembrance,' he remarked, closing the door. 'Does it mean anything to you, sir?'

'Oh yes.' The earl sat behind the oak desk and waved Marcus to the chair in front of it. 'That night, when Kit

Hebden died, I found him and Wardale together, locked in each other's arms just outside my study window. I told you.' Marcus nodded. 'There had been a great storm. A cloudburst. Everything was soaking wet, but the air was hot despite that and all the scents of the garden were intense. There was a big rosemary bush, under the wall just by the long window.'

'It is gone now.' Marcus struggled to recall the planting in the town house garden.

'I had it pulled out. They had crashed into it, the leaves were everywhere, we were all covered in them by the end. I could never smell it again afterwards without remembering.' He lifted the sprig and held it to his nose as if to defy its power. 'That and the scent of blood like hot metal.

'I was expecting them both to meet me in Albemarle Street to talk about the search for the spy—the traitor in our midst—who we were pursuing together. Then I got a note to go to the Alien Office. Some clerk had made a mistake over a message that could well have waited until the morning. Or perhaps it was a deliberate ploy to lure me away—I have wondered often about that.'

'You got back home, went through and found the long study window open.' Marcus nodded. His father had told the tale before Christmas when Veryan had brought his new assistant to visit and the young man had asked about the old mystery.

'Hebden died on the wet stone, in my arms. All he said was, *Verity…veritas*. It made no sense, he was rambling, Verity was a babe then. All Wardale could say for himself—standing there with the knife in his hands and the man's blood all over him—was that Kit had been stabbed when he arrived and he had pulled the knife out to try and help him. He wouldn't say where he had been earlier. I could guess. He had been with Amanda, Kit's wife.'

'The adulterer you spoke of at dinner was William Wardale, Lord Leybourne?' His father had not repeated that piece of incriminating gossip before.

'Yes. Hebden was no saint himself, of course. When he thought her barren, he had forced his wife to raise his own bastard son, which gives you some idea of his character. He was a clever devil, with a chip on his shoulder wide enough to make a refectory table. He was the one with the brains, but only a barony. We two earls, he was convinced, had the status but not the intellect to match his.'

His father shrugged. 'Mathematics and codes were never my strength. But arrogant though he might be, and neglectful and inconsiderate of his wife as he most certainly was, he was our colleague, our friend. Wardale had no call to seduce Amanda.'

'Perhaps she wanted comfort and he gave it to her,' Marcus mused aloud, thinking of another woman entirely. 'Was that enough motive for murder? One would have thought Hebden, the wronged man, would have struck the blow.'

'If Wardale was the traitor, it could have been a motive,' his father said slowly. 'We both knew Kit was getting very close to cracking the intercepted coded letters. At least, that was what he would have us believe. And when he had done that, the man's identity would be revealed.' He held out the rosemary to the candle flame and it caught with a dry crackle, burning into scented ash. The earl brushed his fingers fastidiously. 'We never found Kit's notes or the letters after his death. The trail went cold and the spy ceased his activities.'

'As you'd expect if he was in prison,' Marcus commented.

'Exactly. How could I defend Wardale? How could I not say what I had seen? He was my best friend—but he killed a man in front of me, he was apparently betraying his country. What should I have done?'

It was the old torment that had stolen his father's peace of mind, his health; and it had never left him.

'Nothing, in all honour,' Marcus said, as he had said when he had first heard the story. And he believed it. 'So. The silken rope a peer is hanged with, a sprig of rosemary from that last desperate fight. There is no doubt now that they refer to Hebden's death, the search for the traitor and Wardale's execution.'

'But who is sending them—and why now?' The earl ran his hands through his hair as though to force some answers into his head.

'We're back to Wardale's son again, aren't we? That's the only way I can make any sense out of the timing—a child grows into a man, a long-held resentment festers into an obsession with revenge.'

'And your Miss Latham is his accomplice? I find that hard to believe. She's a delightful young woman.'

'So was Lucrezia Borgia, by all accounts,' Marcus remarked darkly. It was important not to let his guard down, not with his body telling him to trust her and his mind half inclined to follow it. 'She's hiding something, more than one thing, if I'm any judge.'

'This wasn't franked.' The earl flipped over the folded sheet. 'No postal marks on it at all.'

'Hand delivered. It could have been her; we have rosemary growing all over the garden here. I'll ask Watson about it.'

'Marcus.' He stopped, halfway to the door. 'There is no need to let your mother know about this.'

'Of course not, sir. Are you…all right?'

'Yes, thank you. Better than I've felt for a long time, strangely.' His father shook his head, a rare smile on his lips. 'It's like the old days, having someone to confide in, think with. I'm glad you're here.'

Something twisted inside Marcus. 'I've always been here, Father.'

'I know, and I've leaned on you harder than I should have done. But this isn't estate business, this is a mystery, danger. And, damn it, it is painful remembering, but do you know—I'm enjoying it.'

'Good.' Marcus swallowed, suddenly fearful that the sensation behind his eyes was tears. 'Good,' he said again, gruffly, and left while he was still in command of himself.

Nell closed the door into the flower room quietly behind her. She had managed to shake off her persistent footman escort by dint of joining Lady Narborough in her sitting room and had just completed an errand for her to the gardener to ensure there were more evergreens included with the hothouse flowers.

Now, there was nothing to stop her thinking about the sprig of rosemary that had so shaken Lord Narborough. What on earth had that been about? It made no sense.

At least she understood the silken rope, for that was what a peer of the realm was hanged with. Although why someone was trying to terrorize the Carlows now with that reminder of her father's death was a total mystery.

And what had possessed her to quote that foolish old saying when it should have been apparent from the men's faces that something was very wrong? Something else that Marcus would blame her for, no doubt.

'Watson?'

There he was. Nell drew back into the cover provided by a massive suit of armour as Marcus stopped the butler in the middle of the Great Hall.

'My lord?'

'This letter that came for his lordship this morning. Delivered by hand, I assume?'

'Indeed, my lord. It was handed in at the kitchen door by young Francis, Potter's son.'

'The under gamekeeper? Find out who gave it to him, will you, Watson.'

'I have already ascertained that, my lord. I do not appreciate post for the family arriving in such a manner. According to Andrewes, who took it from the lad, it was handed to young Potter with a small coin by a man early this morning.'

'A stranger.'

'Just so, my lord. Do you wish me to make further enquiries?'

'If you would. A fuller description would be helpful.' Nell took a cautious step backwards and then froze as Marcus continued. 'Was Miss Latham about early on? Perhaps taking the air before breakfast?'

'You think she may have seen the transaction, my

lord?' Being well trained, Nell thought bitterly, Watson did not ask the obvious question: why did Marcus not speak directly to her? 'To the best of my knowledge Miss Latham did not leave her room between retiring last night and breakfast this morning, but I will enquire.'

She waited until the butler left, then, not giving herself time to think, stalked out from her hiding place. 'Marcus!'

He turned on his heel to face her, a frown on his face as she said the first thing that came into her head. 'Do you never stop scowling?'

To her surprise, he laughed, transforming himself from a handsome, hard figure of authority into a charming, and much younger, man. 'I have much to scowl about, Nell.'

'Is your father ill again? That rosemary was another threat, was it not?'

'It was. And, curiously, I believe he is invigorated by the puzzle.'

'My lord.' They turned as Watson advanced down the length of the hall. 'I have spoken to young Potter myself; he was loitering in the kitchen. The man was unknown to him, but he assumed from his dress, speech and general demeanour that he was a groom. A short, wiry individual with brown hair, so the lad says.'

'Thank you, Watson.' Marcus put one hand under Nell's elbow and steered her through the nearest door into a small panelled chamber. 'Not your dark man, then.'

'His agent perhaps?' Nell perched on the edge of a great oak chest, her feet dangling. Sinking into one of the deep chairs would make her feel trapped, she sensed, yet standing around stiffly felt awkward. 'My lord— Marcus. What have I to do to convince you that I know nothing more of this?'

But she did, of course. She knew of a dark and painful episode in the Carlows' family past. She knew that Lord Narborough had known her father, had been involved, in some way, with his death. It was certain her family tragedy was linked somehow to whatever lay behind this persecution. Had Lord Narborough gone through life making enemies? Surely it was too much of a coincidence that she had been the messenger. If she told Marcus who she was it would probably help him solve the mystery—and she would be handing him the most perfect motive for her involvement.

'I am just a milliner,' she said. 'I do not know who is doing this. If I could help you, I would.' As she said it, she almost believed it, crossing her fingers behind her back. *It all depends what the letters show,* she qualified to herself. Did Lord Narborough simply fail to help her father—or was his role more sinister?

'You have to let me go home.' Marcus was staring out of the window, hands thrust into his breeches' pockets, seemingly paying her no attention. 'I cannot stay here. I must earn my own living.'

'Go home to that garret?' he asked, swinging round. 'To scrape a living working long hours while your fingers are still nimble and your eyes sharp? And then what? Where will you be in ten years, Nell? Twenty?'

'I will manage. I must. Thousands of women have to.' Nell tried to keep the desperation out of her voice, not to listen to the little voice, the one that kept her awake at night, the one that murmured about insecurity and poverty and a slow slide into destitution. *You are all alone,* it would insist. *All alone.*

'There are alternatives,' Marcus said.

'Domestic service?'

'You are an attractive woman. If you were not so thin, not so anxious, you would be a beautiful one.' There was a note in his voice that reached inside her, a hint of husky desire that twisted a hot ache low in her belly.

'You suggest I should sell my body?' she demanded harshly.

'Find yourself a protector.'

Nell made herself meet his eyes, her chin up. 'Are you offering me a *carte blanche,* my lord?'

'Perhaps.' He moved closer, almost touching her knees. Nell gripped the edge of the chest and fought with herself.

Marcus Carlow was strong and powerful. He would protect her—for as long as she was his mistress. He would be generous, and if she was prudent, she could save. He was attractive. *Oh God, so attractive. And that is why you are giving even a second's thought to this insanity,* she argued with herself. *You are discussing selling your body, putting yourself in a man's power. Ruining yourself.*

But she was so tired of being alone, of fighting every day for food and respectability and some semblance of a decent life. 'Why?' she demanded. 'Why me? I thought you had a new mistress.'

'Not yet.' Marcus moved a little closer, his thighs pressing against her knees as she perched on the high chest. 'Why? I wish I knew. I tell myself I do not trust you and yet I read more fear than cunning in your eyes. You are too thin, you throw out no sophisticated lures to attract me—and yet, when I have kissed you, there has been a spark of such fire in you that I am in danger of burning up.'

As she stared back into the intent, dark gaze, her throat tight, her heart banging against her ribs, he nudged his leg between her knees, parting them. And then he was standing between her thighs, the heat of him soaking into her trembling limbs, the scent of his body filling her senses, the breadth of his torso filling her sight.

'There is a kind of purity about you, Nell,' he murmured as he lifted his hand to run the back of it down her cheek. She shivered, turning her face against his knuckles, trying to control her breathing as a primitive pulse began to beat where the heat of his body met the aching warmth of hers.

Purity. He thinks me a virgin. I can't... I want him. Is this so wrong if I want him? But I must tell him.

'Marcus.' His hand slid round to cup her chin, turn her face up to him. 'There is something... I am not a virgin.'

For a long moment he stood quite still, then he flung himself away from her, leaving her shivering with the sudden withdrawal of his heat. 'Then I was right. You are his mistress.' There was a curious kind of bitterness in his voice and, keyed up to tell him what had happened, she was thrown off balance.

'Whose mistress?' Then she saw what he was thinking. 'You believe I am his whore? Salterton's whore.'

'Don't use that word.' Marcus swung round, his face dark with anger. 'Don't ever use that word of yourself.'

'Why not?' Nell slid off the chest, jarring her heels as she landed on the bare boards. 'It is what you think, what you would make me, is it not? Or are you too much of a hypocrite to face it? You leap to conclusions, accuse me on no evidence, cannot wait one moment to let me explain—but of course, you are disappointed so you make wild accusations. You want a virgin, don't you? That's what men always want, after all.

'Well, I am not a virgin, so you can go back to your expensive, skilled mistress and make her an offer and enjoy her expertise and her practised tricks. Not as titillating as fear and screams and pain, but I am sure it has its satisfactions.'

'Nell, for God's sake!' Marcus reached for her as she stood there, panting with anger and the terrible relief of pouring it all out at long last. 'Nell, come here.'

'No.' She lashed out at him, hitting his face more by luck than intention. They stared at each other as the sound of the slap echoed against the carved panelling of the little room, his eyes so wide she could see her own tiny reflection in them. '*No.*'

Fear and screams and pain... The words buzzed in his head, more painful than the sting of Nell's fingers on his cheek or the ache of unsatisfied arousal in his groin. She had been forced? Had the ferocity with which she had fought him in the carriage, the rejection in the Long Gallery, had those been terror and not the sudden recollection that she was betraying another lover?

'Hell!' he said out loud into the empty room as the echoes of the slammed door died away. What had he done? But he knew. He had raked up a past that was agony to her. He had offered a sexual relationship when that was the last thing she needed. In his male arrogance he had crowded her with his body, his strength, blocking her escape, reminding her, inevitably, that he had the power to do with her what he wanted.

Marcus strode to the door and then stopped. Nell did

not need him pursuing her all over the house. She needed, he was certain, another woman to talk to and there was no one here but strangers she could not trust. As he had shown her she could not trust him.

Nell ran up the stairs, scrubbing at her face as if she could stop the tears by brute force. *Damn him!* Now he knew what had happened to her and he would despise her for it. It was always the woman's fault, of course, the woman who was ruined as a result.

By dint of sheer willpower, she stopped crying, got the hiccupping sobs under control and looked around. She was somewhere on the first floor, but in her distress she had missed the turn to the wing where her bedchamber was and now she was lost. The old house rambled like a living organism. Passages led off from corridors, doors might open onto chambers or stairs or more corridors. Small flights of steps appeared for no apparent reason.

At random she opened a door and found herself in a small library. There was a desk in the window, a fire in the grate and a pleasant smell of apple-wood smoke and leather. A book—that would help her compose herself. Nell walked across and began to examine the shelves, taking slow breaths as control returned.

It was a very masculine selection, she decided, opening a copy of the *Racing Calendar* for 1810 at random, then replacing it. Heavy bound editions of the Classics did not tempt her either. There was a glass-fronted bookcase on one wall. She tried the handle as she peered in. Locked. The books inside did not seem particularly valuable: a row of matching volumes, each with the date in gilt on the spine. Diaries, she supposed.

With a sigh Nell dragged her sodden handkerchief out and blew her nose again.

'If you want poetry and novels they are in the main library downstairs, Miss Latham,' said a deep voice behind her.

'Ah!' She jumped and spun round. 'Oh. Lord Narborough. I do apologise, I had no idea this room was occupied, I was just—'

'Looking for somewhere to hide?' He put down a book, rose from his deep winged chair and held out a large white handkerchief. 'Here, take this.'

Beyond trying to pretend nothing was wrong, Nell took it and applied it to what she was certain was her very red nose. 'Thank you, my lord.'

'Homesick?' She shook her head. 'Marcus?'

'Yes. He does not trust me and I am afraid we… argue. I have just slapped his face,' she admitted in a rush.

'Do him a world of good, I've no doubt. Pull the bell, would you be so kind? What we need is a cup of coffee. Now, you sit there, my dear.'

'But, Lord Narborough, you do not understand.' And what was she going to tell him, exactly? That his son had offered his protection and she had hesitated for long, betraying minutes before refusing him?

'Have you got anything to do with that rope or the rosemary at breakfast?' he asked her abruptly.

'No!' Nell bit her lip. 'I have things I wish to keep secret and Lord Stanegate can tell that. It makes him suspicious. But, I give you my word, my lord, I do not know any more about why you have been sent these mysterious objects than I have said.'

'Well then, we have no need to speak of it any more.

Ah, Andrewes. Coffee and biscuits if you please. And, Andrewes, should anyone—anyone at all—be enquiring for Miss Latham, you believe you have not seen her since breakfast.'

'Very good, my lord.'

'Now then.' He settled back in his chair, steepled his fingers and regarded her benignly. 'Tell me how to make a hat.'

'But you cannot want to know that, my lord.'

'I most certainly do. Have you any idea how much I pay for hats for three ladies in a year?'

'One hundred guineas?' Nell hazarded.

'Nearer three. Now, I want to know what is involved in making a hat. I would like to know where my money goes.'

By the time the gong sounded for luncheon, Nell had forgotten Marcus, her distress, even who the man she was so comfortable with was. They drank coffee, ate all the biscuits; he asked questions about hats, teased her, told her about the latest litter of hound puppies in the stable. She asked about the history of the house and found he was an authority on it.

'Really? A priest hole?' she gasped, wide-eyed.

'A hidden room, certainly, and it was used during the Civil War—we stood for the king, you understand.' George Carlow regarded her with a smile. 'You know, you remind me of someone. I wish I could remember who. There's something when you smile…'

'Oh.' *Mama.* She had always been told that she was the image of her mother, except for her colouring, which was her father's. If Lord Narborough had been so close to her father, she realized, the realities flooding back, he would have known her mother well also. 'Listen— wasn't that the gong for luncheon?'

The elusive memory escaping him, Lord Narborough got to his feet. 'So it is. Shall we go down?'

Nell stuck to his side on the way downstairs, then took refuge between Verity and Honoria at the table. But Marcus was absent. After half an hour, when she felt physically sick every time the door opened, Honoria put her out of her misery by remarking, 'It's too bad of Marcus, going off to Aylesbury like that without stopping to see if there's anything we want from the shops.'

'He's gone to the bank, darling,' her mother remarked. 'And then he's dining with the Wallaces. You cannot expect him to trail round haberdashery counters for you.'

'Well, if he was going to the Wallaces, he could have taken me,' Honoria persisted. 'It is an age since I spoke to Georgina.'

'I believe it was a last-minute decision to go. He is just dropping in on them to take pot luck,' Lady Narborough said. 'We will invite Georgina and Harriet over next week if the weather holds.'

So, Marcus had made an unplanned trip, just to avoid her. Nell shivered, anticipating the look she would see in his eyes next time they met. Pity? Or disgust?

Nell retired early that evening, the puzzle of her feelings for Lord Narborough driving her back to her mother's box. She liked the man, she trusted him instinctively. Could she be so wrong about him?

The diary lay at the bottom of the box. Nell stood, twisting her hands together for several minutes before she reached in and lifted it out. The red morocco cover was scuffed and dull and a brown pressed flower fell out and crumbled into brittle fragments as she opened it.

Resolutely Nell began to read, the earl's big handkerchief tight in one hand.

An hour later she laid the book down, dry eyed and drained. In 1795, her father, William Wardale, Earl of Leybourne, had been convicted of the murder by stabbing of Christopher Hebden, Baron Framlingham, in the garden of the Carlow's London house. He had been found, literally red-handed, by Lord Narborough. The woman he had been having an affair with had been Hebden's wife, Amanda. And almost worse than anything, her mother had written on the tear-blotched pages that he had been suspected of spying for the French, although that had never been made known publicly.

Somehow that, and the name of his lover, had been kept a secret. He was stripped of his title and his lands by Act of Attainder, meaning her brother, Nathan, could never inherit. And so he was hanged.

Stunned and shaking, now she could see it all laid out so clearly, Nell put the diary back in the box and locked it. No, it was impossible that her unwitting involvement in this was coincidence. Someone had deliberately implicated her in their plot against the Carlows. But why? If her father had been guilty, then he had paid the terrible price for his crimes. His family had all paid it with him. Why should anyone seek to involve her now?

If her father had been innocent, then why not come to her, tell her? It was as though someone wanted revenge on both families.

The clocks began to strike. Midnight. Lord Narborough was often late to bed; she had heard his wife nagging him about it. He might still be awake, and if he was, then she was going to confront him, tell him who she was, demand to know the truth about what had happened.

Before her courage failed, Nell tied her wrapper, put on her slippers, picked up a chamberstick and let herself out into the dark corridor.

There was no light under his door, no sound from within. Frustrated, Nell leaned against the panels feeling absurdly let down. It was foolish to have this sort of conversation at this time of night in any case, shocking to visit a man's bedchamber at any hour. Much better to speak to him in the morning, she told herself, shivering with cold and reaction.

As she straightened up, there was a sharp noise from the room, the sound of breaking glass. Then silence.

She stared at the door. Perhaps the earl had knocked over a water glass. Or perhaps he was ill, flailing out in the throes of a heart stroke. She could not simply ignore it. The doorknob turned silently under the pressure of her hand as she stepped inside. Nothing, just the sound of heavy breathing from the curtained bed. Then she felt the draft from the window, saw movement from the corner of her eye, spun round. Her candle blew out but there, silhouetted against the faint light, was a lithe figure. A figure she had seen before.

Nell grabbed for him, saw the flash of metal in the gloom and was thrown roughly to one side. She staggered, reached out, found nothing under her groping hands as she fell. She opened her mouth to scream as her head struck something hard and solid. The darkened room was spinning—or was it her? Everything went black.

Chapter Nine

'Good night, Andrewes.' Marcus left the night-duty footman to lock up behind him and go back to the hooded porter's chair by the front door. As he strode down the Great Hall to the staircase the clocks chimed midnight from every corner of the rambling house.

A convivial evening with Sir James Wallace and his family had done little to help him decide how to approach Nell in the morning. It certainly had done nothing to quieten his conscience. He was not normally so unperceptive, he told himself, his boot heels clicking on the broad wooden treads as he climbed.

The truth, he thought, refusing to let himself off the hook, was that he had been attracted to Nell from the start and that had clouded his judgement. He looked at her, he wanted her and he knew he should not. So, he concluded with a wry smile, he had convinced himself she was not to be trusted in order to boost his flagging willpower. Not a very comfortable admission to have to make. And quite how he was going to put it to her when he apologised, he had no idea.

In London the night would be young, his mother and sisters out at parties, himself at one of his clubs. This evening it seemed everyone had decided on an early night. The house was silent and no light showed under his mother's bedchamber door as he passed it. He walked softly on down the considerable stretch of corridor marked only by the doors into her sitting room and her dressing room, then round the corner.

Marcus stopped in his tracks. His father's door was ajar onto darkness and from within came a low moan. He ran, shouldering the door wide. There was no sign of his father. The curtains billowed in the cold January air, the flame in the lamp he held guttered wildly and, on the floor huddled against the dresser, was Nell. As he stared at her, she closed her eyes as though to block him out.

He wrenched back the bed curtains in a rattle of rings and saw his father, night cap in place, snoring gently against his piled pillows. As Marcus looked down at him he shifted slightly, then the reassuring rhythm of snores resumed. Beside the bed was one of the medicine bottles from the still room. He picked it up and sniffed: Mama's fennel infusion, the smell familiar from childhood fevers and toothaches.

Quietly he drew the curtains closed and walked back to Nell. Beside her hand was a snake-like coil. *Another silken rope.*

Something turned cold and hard inside him as he bent and dragged Nell to her feet. She came up limply, her arms lax as though passively resisting him.

'I told myself to trust you,' he snarled, shaking her. 'And I find you letting in your bloody accomplice. Where is he?'

Her eyes opened slowly, as though she too had taken a sleeping draught. In the soft light of lamp the greenish hazel irises seemed black. 'Why would I need to break the window?' she asked, her faint voice full of dull anger. 'Why upstairs?'

Marcus glanced at the casement, let her go, then went to pull the window closed. The small pane nearest the handle was broken. Glass crunched under his booted feet. It had been broken from the outside, he realized, leaning out. Below the window, the bare stems of the wisteria made a strong, twisted ladder, the topmost stem scarred with a fresh cut.

'You would not,' he began, sick with himself for his own suspicions. He turned back as Nell's legs gave way and she began to slide inelegantly down the glossy front of the dresser, one hand to her head. Then he saw the blood. Her fingers where she had touched her head were red.

'Oh God. Nell.' He caught her under the arms and held her against his body. 'Where are you hurt? Show me.'

'Head, here,' she murmured. He tipped her against his shoulder, his fingers searching in the mass of hair until they found the lump. She flinched against him as he touched it and his hand came away stained as hers was. But there was no ominous movement in her skull around the lump and she was still conscious.

Marcus scooped her up. He couldn't be certain it was superficial, he needed better light to see by. His room was nearest, Allsop dozing in the armchair as Marcus swept in. The valet came to his feet in an instant. 'My lord! Shall I send for the doctor?'

'Miss Latham has suffered a blow to the head; I am

not sure how serious it is. Bring the lamp and more candles over here, let me look at the wound.' Nell was passive in his arms, whether from shock, weakness or loss of consciousness he was unsure. There was blood matting her hair on the right side over her ear and, as he parted it gently, he could see the raw skin, crowning a lump the size of a bantam's egg.

'It's a graze, not a cut, so it needs no stitching. Get me warm water, cloths, the basilicum powder. Nell!' Nell opened her eyes and blinked at him as he settled her back against the pillows. 'Look into my eyes, let me see your pupils.' Obediently she stared back. Her eyes seemed normal. 'How many fingers am I holding up?'

'Three.' He laid her back against the pillows, but she kept her eyes on him. 'It was the dark man, Salterton… I recognised the way he moves. Lord Narborough…'

'He had taken a sleeping draught. He slept through it all, quite undisturbed,' Marcus said as the valet set down the water. 'Allsop, someone attempted to break into his lordship's bedchamber. Fortunately Miss Latham was passing, heard the window break and frightened him off, but not before he hit her and knocked her down. I imagine he has gone for the night, but just to be on the safe side, go and sleep on the truckle bed in his lordship's dressing room, will you? Take the pistol from the case in my closet.'

'My lord.' Imperturbable, the man bowed himself off, leaving Marcus regarding Nell, suddenly prey to doubts that he could manage this without hurting her.

'Would you like me to send for the doctor?'

'No—' she shook her head, eyes closed again '—fuss.' She lay still for a moment then admitted with a shaky smile, 'Don't like doctors.' Marcus grimaced in sympathy. She was brave and she was unexpectedly strong, but nothing and no one should hurt her. The thought of Nell's delicate skin being prodded, perhaps patches of hair shaved away, turned his stomach. He found he could not look at her face in case the sight of her distress affected him too strongly.

'I do not think you are scared of anything, Nell,' he said, attempting to sound bracing and unworried. 'Let me see if I can clean it and stop the bleeding, and we'll review how you are in the morning.' As he said it, the impropriety struck him. 'Would you like me to wake Miss Price, or Mama?'

'They'll worry about Lord Narborough,' she murmured, her eyes fluttering open. 'Things are so scary in the middle of the night. It doesn't matter. Trust you.'

That, if anything, made it worse. What cause had she to say that? 'You're cold.' He realized that she was beginning to shiver in her thin wrapper. 'Take this off and have my robe—Allsop's had it warming by the fire.'

He helped her with the wrapper, untying the belt, slipping it off her shoulders until he could remove it, noticing the plain fabric, worn thin in places, each small tear or hole painstakingly darned. He rubbed his finger over a line of tiny stitches, thinking of Nell in that drab, dark little room, darning a garment no one else would likely ever see until her eyes ached, rather than let her standards drop.

Damn it, how could he have thought for a moment that she was some man's paramour? Everything she owned spoke of a long, solitary battle against poverty. He did not care how improper it was, he was going to buy her something warm and luxurious and pretty just as soon as he could get to a Bond Street shop.

Nell lay back, too dizzy and queasy to worry about the fact that she was on Marcus's bed in his thick silk robe, alone in his room with him. The little blade he was using to cut the lint flashed in his hand. 'He had a knife…'

'I'm sure he did,' he retorted, gently parting her hair.

'Do you think he meant to murder Lord Narborough?'

'There was another silken rope, on the floor. I may be wrong, but I think his purpose is to frighten us, not to kill. But he would be armed in case of discovery. Hold still.' The warm water trickled over her ear as Marcus began to clean the wound. Nell bit her lip and tried to keep still. 'Am I hurting you?'

'It stings,' she admitted. He was so gentle, his big hands moving over her scalp as though he was handling a baby. Nell focused her eyes and watched him rinsing the cloth in the water, intent on his work. He had taken off his coat and rolled up his shirt sleeves, exposing strong forearms dusted with brown hair.

She felt a curious compulsion to raise her hand, stroke the dark pelt. She lifted it, then let it drop. *Mustn't touch him.* 'I didn't let him in, Marcus. I know it must seem suspicious, my being there.'

'Why were you?' She could not see his face, only his chest, so close as he leaned over to tend her head.

If she told him now, on top of this fresh attack, would he believe her innocent? His immediate thought on discovering that she was not a virgin had been that she was Salterton's lover. When he had found her just now he had accused her without hesitation. How could she convince

him of her good faith when he knew who her father was?
And yet it hurt so much to lie to him.

'I couldn't sleep, I was restless. Your father had been
telling me stories of the history of the house and it
seemed so romantic. So I decided to walk a little in the
Long Gallery. As I was going past Lord Narborough's
door, I heard the noise of breaking glass, just a sudden
sharp crack in the silence. I opened the door in case
something was wrong, another heart stroke perhaps,
and the man attacked me. It was dark,' she added. 'My
candle blew out but I recognised him. Salterton moves
beautifully.'

'He'll be crawling like a crippled cat when I get my
hands on him,' Marcus promised with a lack of
emphasis that was chilling in itself. He began to sprinkle
basilicum powder into her hair. 'I'll put a pad on that
and then bandage it. It is not as bad as all that blood
made it appear—a deep graze rather than a cut—but you
are going to have a most piratical appearance. You are
being very brave, Nell.'

Her head ached now, a deep throb that made her
think about Marcus's wound. He had shown no sign of
it since their arrival here, and yet it must have pained
him far more than her head. There was no sign of ban-
daging under the fine linen of his shirt. She found her
gaze lingering on his broad shoulders, on the open V of
his shirt, and steadied her voice.

'It aches,' she admitted. 'But it is nothing, I imagine,
compared to your shoulder.'

'Men are supposed to put up with these things,' he said
curtly, apparently focused on winding the bandage firmly
around her head. 'What sort of bastard hits a woman?'

Was he going to refer to the morning and his assumptions about her *lover?* Marcus was tidying away the bandages now; he could not pretend absorption in his medical activities for much longer.

He got up, cleared the water bowl away then came and sat down by the bed. 'I have to apologise to you, Nell.' He met her eyes at last.

'You do?' Perversely the tenderness she felt for him, here in the midnight intimacy of his room, did not incline her to make this easy for him.

'This morning I should not have made the suggestion that I did. And then I leapt to a conclusion that was utterly unwarranted. I insulted you and I failed to recognise that you had experienced something…terrible.'

'Yes.' She wanted to close her eyes, lie back, sleep. But Marcus was apologizing and she could not, for some reason, bring herself to snub him after all. 'I had— *have*—a brother and a sister. But Mama and I lost contact with them when I was seventeen. My brother vanished one day, Mama was ill, there was no money. Our landlord told me he would let us stay, for free if I would…if I would lie with him. I refused. You can imagine the rest.' She was not going to remember it any more than she could help.

'What was his name?' There was a pain in her hand. Nell looked down and saw Marcus's hand gripping her fingers. He followed her gaze and released her with a muttered curse.

'Why?'

'The man needs dealing with. I would ensure he was never able to do that to a defenceless woman again.'

'Harris,' she said. The name had been that of a bogeyman for so long. It was a liberation to find that speaking of it to this man began to disperse the terror. She could see her landlord now as an unpleasant, manipulative bully, not the ever-present monster he became in the endless dark nights.

'He will be long gone. Mama and I had to get away. We left, but then she became worse. It was a nightmare, and when it was all over, by the time she was better and I was sure I would not bear Harris's child, then we realized we had lost all contact with the others. It was not a very nice part of London we found ourselves in,' she added with considerable understatement.

'My sister, I hope and pray, is still in respectable employment. My brother may be dead, I do not know.'

Marcus had repossessed himself of her hand and she let him hold it. Warmth and strength seemed to flow into her and she felt her eyes closing again.

'Oh, Nell. The carriage and then the Long Gallery. I was not gentle. I can imagine you never want another man to touch you again.' His grip opened and she curled her fingers into his to hold him.

'So I thought,' she agreed, beginning to drift towards sleep now. 'I find it depends on the man.'

Marcus was halfway to his feet. At her words, he moved sharply, as though caught off-balance, and his free hand brushed the side of her breast. She opened her eyes as he snatched his hand back, his face stark. 'I am so sorry, Nell, that was an accident.'

They both seemed to have stopped breathing, still linked by her grasp on his left hand. Nell managed to find enough air for two words. 'I know.' He was standing there, tall and strong and worried for her, her blood on his shirt where he had held her in his arms, his big, elegant hands that had tended her wound stilled with the fear that his touch would terrify her.

Nell felt tears welling up at the back of her eyes and swallowed them away, making her voice light. 'You know, it is a very long time since anyone just held me. I think…I think that would be nice.'

'Nice.' The frown lines between his brows vanished. 'You would like me to hold you?'

'Mmm. In your arms. In bed.' Her eyes were growing heavy again and the room was drifting away, along with vague inhibitions. She shouldn't ask that of him, she knew, but somehow she couldn't quite recall why not. 'I think I would feel safe then. I think I could sleep.'

Nell was almost asleep already. What he should do, Marcus knew perfectly well, was to pick her up, carry her back to her own room, ring for her maid and leave her.

And if she woke in the night, alone, in pain, worried that her attacker might return? That should not matter. All that should matter was decorum and propriety.

'Well, be damned to that,' he muttered, tugging off his boots and throwing his waistcoat and neckcloth onto the chair. He would stay with her tonight, and he would show her that it was possible for a man to be gentle, to touch a woman without an ulterior motive.

She was asleep now, honey-brown hair loose on the pillows, the rakish bandage incongruous around her head, no colour in her cheeks. He turned back the covers on the far side of the bed then lifted her across, settling her snugly, before sliding in beside her, still in his breeches and shirt.

It took some arranging to get his arm around Nell without touching her breasts or jolting her head, but he managed it at last, ending up with her left cheek on his shoulder and one arm over his chest. He suspected that his own arm was going to be numb by morning, but it was worth it to experience the soft warmth against him, the silky slide of her hair touching his neck, the cold toes curling confidingly against his stockinged feet.

'Are you asleep?' he murmured.

'Yes,' she replied, making him smile as she burrowed a little closer. 'You are so warm, Marcus.'

'And your feet are so cold.' But then she was truly asleep, her breath whispering through the open neck of his shirt to tease the skin. He had never before lain with a woman like this, innocently. With innocent intent, he corrected himself. What he felt was not at all pure, and strangely, it was not the obvious things that were inciting the need to run his hands over her body, to kiss her, to rouse her to passion. It was those small, cold feet, the feel of her hip bone jutting against him, the dark shadows under the down-swept lashes that reminded him that she needed feeding up, resting. It was the things that reminded him that this was Nell.

He wanted to look after her, pamper her, indulge her. And make love to her until she forgot those damned men who haunted her and filled her life with ever-present fear, forgot everything but the feel of his body possessing her, the scent of his skin in her nostrils, the heat of his mouth on hers.

'Oh, well done,' he muttered into the darkness, contemplating the painfully insistent erection he had managed to conjure up. *Think about Salterton, think about Father, think what you are going to do in the morning.* He settled Nell firmly against his side and willed himself to sleep.

Nell woke to the four soft *tings* of the little French clock on the bedside table and lay blinking in the light of the lamp Marcus had left burning. He was asleep, his right arm holding her against his body where she must have lain for hours, warm and safe.

The colour burned warm in her cheeks as she remembered asking him to stay with her, sleep with her. Hold her. She must have been almost feverish to have dared do such a thing.

He was still dressed. Her bare leg brushed against the heavy cloth of his breeches, her side was pressed to his shirt. She had trusted him instinctively and he had been gentle and caring, the antithesis of Harris, the opposite of what she had come to fear any man would be like.

He was frowning in his sleep, she realised, smiling at those sharp lines between his brows. She was becoming rather fond of that expression. It no longer seemed forbidding, more the sign that he was worrying about his family, worrying about her. Caring.

Nell shifted a little and winced at the stiffness in her neck and the jolt of pain in her bandaged head. Would he let her see his own wound, judge for herself how well it was healing? She thought not. Being injured appeared to be a physical affront to him, she thought with a smile, remembering his indignation at the pain, his own weakness. A weakness he had overcome through sheer, bloody-minded determination instead of allowing his body time to rest and heal.

She risked letting the tips of her fingers stroke across his chest. 'Marcus,' she whispered, her eyelids drooping again. 'Love…'

Chapter Ten

The single chime of the clock beside him brought Marcus out of a dream of Nell, her hands drifting across his body, her lips warm on his skin, her hair flowing, murmured words of love on her lips…

He turned his head on the pillow. Quarter past four. It was important to wake up early, he knew that, but why?

Against his side, someone stirred, soft, warm, curling round his body. *You idiot, Carlow*. What the hell had he been thinking last night? Not thinking at all, he decided grimly, just going with his feelings and his instincts, which now, in the cold dark of dawn, were obviously wildly awry.

Nell was no dream; she was here, in his bed, where he had put her when she had been in no state to know what was right or wrong, when she was vulnerable. She was now, for all the utter innocence of their behaviour, completely compromised.

Or she would be, if she were a lady. But Nell was a milliner, a working girl. She was no less ruined for that, but his position was completely different. The son and heir to an earldom did not marry a milliner, not if he had any care for the family name, for his duties and responsibilities to his inheritance.

But she was his responsibility now, more than ever. He lay there trying to think through all the ramifications of this. Getting her back to her own bed was the priority. Then removing all traces of her from his, making sure Allsop kept his mouth shut, finding an excuse for her head injury to satisfy his mother and sisters, explaining it all to his father, putting an effective guard on the house...

Hell. Double hell and damnation. What if she clung to him, thought that after last night he should—what? She wasn't really ruined, not if no one knew. She was not a virgin after all. He mentally kicked himself for that thought. *Crass.* But a week ago he would have concluded, without a twinge of conscience, that a woman in her position should be grateful to be paid off. But this was not just any woman, this was Nell, and besides, a painfully stirring conscience was telling him that his previous attitudes were nothing to be proud of.

Against his side she moved, snuggling closer, disturbing the covers so the scent of warm, sleepy woman filled his nostrils like a drugging incense. It sent his body into a state of instant arousal that did nothing for his already guilty conscience. With a muttered curse Marcus slid out of bed, found her wrapper and threw back the covers.

'Nell.'

'Mmm?'

'Wake up, you've got to go back to your own room.' Slippers, had she had slippers? He found them, averting his eyes from the sight of Nell cuddled in his robe, while she sat up rubbing her eyes.

'Ouch,' she complained, then seemed to realize where she was. 'Oh.' Her face was a picture. If things had not been so serious, he would have smiled at the combination of feminine embarrassment and the dissipated appearance of the lop-sided bandage. 'Oh, dear.'

Marcus schooled his face into studious neutrality; she did not need him appearing to laugh at her. 'Oh, dear, indeed.'

'I should not be here.'

'*Quite,*' he said, with some emphasis, controlling a quite inappropriate urge to grin. She coloured up. 'Do you think you can walk or shall I carry you?'

'I am certain I can walk, thank you,' she said, her voice suddenly cool. 'I had better put my own robe on.'

He handed it to her, turning away while she got out of bed. There was a soft sound as his own robe landed on the covers. Marcus turned round to find her pulling on her slippers. 'Ready?'

'I can go by myself, thank you.'

'But your head—'

'Aches. Probably as much as yours does.'

'Mine?'

'I assume you were drinking last night or I would not have ended up in your bed, my lord,' she said crisply.

'You asked to stay, Miss Latham.'

'I had just been hit over the head,' she retorted. 'I think I was hardly responsible for my own actions at that point. You, on the other hand, had *not* been hit on the head. Who are you going to tell about this?'

'That you spent the night in my bed?' This was not

how he imagined the conversation this morning would go. This was certainly not the clinging, fragile young woman he had been braced to deal with.

'No.' The look she sent him was scornful. 'About the intruder.'

'No one except my father. Allsop is highly discreet.'

'Excellent. I shall tell Miriam that I slipped last night and hit my head on the dresser.'

'And bandaged it yourself without calling her?' This degree of independent thought was beginning to rile him. Marcus reminded himself that he did not want a fluttering female throwing herself embarrassingly upon his chest and expecting goodness knows what from him. But for some reason cool rationality was decidedly galling. She had spent the night in his arms, for Heaven's sake! Women usually expressed some appreciation after that experience.

Nell unwound the bandage and lifted the pad cautiously, wincing as it pulled on her hair. 'I will sponge my head with one of my handkerchiefs; that will be quite gory enough to satisfy her that I doctored myself. And as for managing by myself—why, my lord, I am unused to living in such style and hesitated to disturb the maid at a late hour.'

'You will rest in bed today.' Marcus reined in his rising temper and the urge to throw Nell over one shoulder and take her back to her own room before she came out with any more cool, calm, sensible remarks.

'That sounds more like an order than a suggestion, my lord.' Nell smiled, obviously fully intending to set his teeth on edge. 'I have no intention of causing Lady Narborough any concern. I will see you at breakfast.'

She paused at the door. And this time the smile held no touch of acid. 'Thank you, Marcus, for looking after me last night. You were very gentle.'

And then she was gone, leaving him feeling as if he'd been slapped and then had the weal tenderly kissed better. He looked at the clock. Half past four. The youngest scullery maid would be creeping about soon, riddling the grate in the kitchen range and laying the table for the staff breakfasts. He would go down and have her make him a pot of coffee; somehow he did not think he would get any more sleep this morning.

Lord Narborough looked quite revoltingly alert to his heavy-eyed son when he followed Felling and the laden breakfast tray into his lordship's room.

'That will be all, thank you, Felling.' The earl waited until the valet was out of the room before raising one eyebrow at Marcus. 'And why have I woken up to find my window broken and your valet in my dressing room?' He peered more closely. 'And why are you looking as though you've been up most of the night?'

Marcus walked over to the dresser and picked up the length of silken rope. Nell's nightcap, as plain an object as a Quaker maiden might wear, was lying in the corner. He retrieved it and pushed it into his pocket.

'You had a visitor last night by way of the wisteria.' He tossed the rope onto the bed.

'And there I was, sound asleep after one of your mother's famous soporific cordials and missing the excitement. I could sleep through a thunderstorm after a dose of that.' Lord Narborough peered across the room at the small pane of glass. 'That wouldn't have made much noise. I might well have slept through it in any case. Who raised the alarm?'

'Miss Latham happened to be passing, on her way for a midnight ramble in the Long Gallery. Apparently your tales of the house made her restless to explore.'

His father put down his coffee cup with a rattle. 'Miss Latham confronted the rogue?'

'In the dark. He knocked her across the room, fortunately just as I was passing on way to my bed. She has a sore head, but nothing more serious, thank God—she is telling Mama that she fell and hit herself. Near enough to the truth, and we don't want to worry the others.' Marcus shot his father an assessing glance. He was taking these revelations very well. 'He had a knife, she thinks.'

'Had he indeed? For my ribs, do you suppose?' The earl sounded quite cheerful about the idea.

'I doubt it. He seemed easily routed for a man on a lethal mission. No, I think his intention was to alarm us, to leave the rope.' Marcus got up to look out of the window. Through the ancient panes, the garden seemed strangely distorted, just like his thoughts. 'I thought by moving out of London we would wrong-foot him, but he seems as at home here as on the streets.'

'If it were just us, we could make it easy for him, lure him in.' The earl put his tray aside and got out of bed, walking barefoot in his nightshirt to join Marcus at the casement. He studied the broken window. 'But not with a houseful of women.'

'I agree. Defence it is then. I'll speak to the keepers and the gardeners, arrange patrols around the grounds at night.'

'Doesn't solve the problem of who and why though.' His father pulled thoughtfully at his ear lobe.

'True. We are certain it is connected with the Wardale matter,' Marcus thought out loud as he went to sit in the armchair, leaving his father to get back into bed with his cup of coffee. 'We need to think who it might possibly be.'

'A relative of Wardale is the most obvious,' the earl said, spooning sugar into the cup. 'The son, of course. The other two children were girls—I suppose they could have married. The Hebden's baby son died soon after the murder. His wife, Amanda, married again, some country gentleman. There are stepsons I fancy—but why would any of that family bear a grudge in any case?'

'I suppose,' Marcus ventured cautiously, 'that there is no possibility that Wardale was working with someone else?'

'No sign of it at the time.' Lord Narborough frowned. 'There will have been a file, of course. We were reporting directly to John Reeves, who was heading the Alien Office at that time, and John King, who was under secretary at the Home Office. Veryan was King's junior confidential secretary in those days; he'll know how to lay hands on things.'

'I'll write to him.' Marcus got to his feet, restless, glad of something positive to do. He wanted action. If truth be told, he wanted violence. 'And I will speak to the keepers.'

'Leave the letter to me,' his father said as he tugged at the bell pull.

'Then I'll take it to the receiving office.' A ride was what he needed. A flat-out gallop. Something physical. His shoulder gave a protesting twinge as he closed the door. He ignored it.

* * *

Nell sat in the deep window seat in Honoria's bedchamber, her eyes on the park sweeping away towards the river, less than half her attention on the Carlow sisters and Diana Price. Her headache had settled to a dull background thud and she had managed to persuade Lady Narborough that the lump did not require dressing.

Verity was bent over the desk, sucking the end of her pen, writing, so she informed her sister, to Rhys Morgan. 'I haven't heard from him for at least two months,' she complained. 'I hope he is all right.'

Honoria turned from her excavations in the clothes press. 'Are you still in love with him, Verity? He won't do, you know.'

'No, I am not,' Verity responded with dignity, somewhat spoiled by her indignant blush. 'I grew out of that *years* ago. He's another of Lord Keddinton's godchildren,' she explained to Nell. 'I used to think I'd like to marry him—when I was little—because I thought he looked so handsome in his uniform, but now we're just friends. I write to him.'

'Verity writes to everyone,' Honoria teased, emerging from the folds of a riding habit she had pulled over her head. She made a futile attempt to button it. 'I simply cannot get into this habit any more. My bosom has grown.'

'We could have it taken out,' Diana remarked, turning back the bodice to study the seams.

'I never liked the amber colour much.' Honoria wriggled out of it and went in her petticoats to Nell's side. 'It would suit Nell though. Do you ride, Nell?'

'Yes,' she said, then realized that riding was hardly

a common accomplishment for a milliner. 'But not for more than ten years.'

'Oh, one never forgets,' Honoria said airily. 'Do try this on and if it fits we can go riding later.'

It seemed easiest to do as she was asked. At least no one could expect her to make conversation while struggling into voluminous skirts and complicated bodices. 'You need a habit shirt underneath,' Diana said, extracting one from the pile.

What would Marcus say, seeing her masquerading as a lady on horseback? He would be less than happy, Nell decided sadly, if his cool demeanour that morning was anything to go by. She had woken to the lovely warm glow of being cared for, the tingle of excitement of his closeness, only to have that dashed by the wariness in his eyes, the chill in his voice. *Indeed. Quite.* The clipped syllables were like tiny slaps as she recalled them.

No doubt, in the cold light of day, he regretted the kindly impulse to take her in his arms and help her through the night. He probably expected her to make demands, have expectations. Or perhaps his suspicions had come back in the night; her explanation of what she was doing at Lord Narborough's door must seem highly circumspect.

'…if they fit you.' Honoria was holding up a pair of boots. 'I've just remembered them. I've had them years and I am sure your feet are smaller than mine are now.'

'I'm sorry. I was wool-gathering.' Nell pulled on the boots and stood there trying to smile at the image in the mirror. Even in the days when they were living in a modest rented villa, Mama had encouraged her children to ride, although the hired mounts became more and more elderly and sluggish as the money diminished. Now, seeing a Nell who had vanished more than ten years ago, she half expected Mama to appear and tweak her skirts into order, tut-tut over a split in her glove, warn her against jumping fences. 'Thank you.'

She bent to pull the boots off again, when Miss Price remarked from the window, 'It looks as though Lord Narborough and Lord Stanegate are riding. See, the groom is leading Corinth out.'

'Wonderful, we can all go. I've finished my letters.' Verity scrambled out of her chair and joined the companion to peer down at the drive below. She tugged the bell pull.

'Lady Verity?' The footman averted his gaze from the heap of feminine underthings on the bed.

'Send to the stables and have Firefly and Sapphire and one of the hacks saddled up please, Trevor. We will be riding with Lord Narborough.'

'His lordship is not riding, Lady Verity. I believe Lord Stanegate is going to the receiving office.'

'Verity,' Diana Price reminded her, 'you and Honoria promised to help Lady Narborough with her sick-visiting in half an hour.'

'Oh.' Verity's face fell. 'So we did. Never mind, Nell, you can still go. You have Firefly, my mare. She's very sweet. Tell the stables please, Trevor.'

'I—' Nell bit back her instinctive protest. A ride to the receiving office sounded mild enough. She could manage that, surely? And it would give her an opportunity to put Marcus right about any misconceptions he might be harbouring, even if it took a plain and embarrassing declaration that she might have been foolish enough to ask him to spend the night with her, but that did not mean she expected anything further as a consequence.

There had been that lovely glow last night when he had looked at her, treated her with such tenderness. She dreaded his response destroying that memory if he was hurtful today.

'Hat!' Honoria pursued her to the door, a rakish low-crowned hat in one hand, hat pin in the other. 'And gloves and a whip.'

Nell made her way down to the stables, wondering if this was such a good idea. What if she could not remember how to ride after all? What if Marcus snubbed her completely?

'Here we are, Miss Latham.' It was Marcus's groom, Havers, holding the head of a pretty bay mare. 'His lordship left before Lady Verity's message arrived, but he's still in sight.' And sure enough, walking sedately away down the long carriageway was Marcus on the raking grey hunter with a dark tail so long it brushed its fetlocks.

The groom made a cup with his hands for her foot and tossed her up into the saddle. 'She's got nice manners, miss, never you fear.' Somehow Nell's limbs seemed to remember what to do, her balance came back instinctively. 'Just you trot along and you'll soon catch him up,' the man said, giving the mare a slap on the rump. 'She's a bit fresh,' he called after her as Firefly trotted out of the stable yard under the clock tower arch. 'But you won't mind that.'

A bit fresh? She was certainly that. The mare had seen the gelding ahead of her and broke into a canter. Nell gripped the pommel firmly, resisted the temptation to hold onto the mane and told herself that a smooth canter was much more comfortable than a bouncy trot. *I can do this, we've almost caught him...*

Then the horse ahead of her reached the gates and instead of turning and trotting off down the lane, Marcus put him straight at a low hurdle in a gap in the hedge on the other side. The big grey sailed over and she caught a glimpse of the crown of Marcus's hat vanishing beyond the hedge line.

The hurdle was perhaps three feet high. *I can't do this!* Nell told herself, taking a firm grip on the reins and pulling. Nothing happened. Firefly, nice manners or no, had obviously decided that her rider did not know what she was about and was taking over. Her ears pricked up, she adjusted her stride. Nell had a sidelong glimpse of a startled gatekeeper and then they were in the air.

'Ough!' The landing was neat on the mare's part, totally inelegant on Nell's. She grabbed the pommel, lurched violently, her hat slid down to her nose and for several stomach-lurching seconds she was convinced she was going to fall off.

It was a surprise to find she was still in place when she shoved her hat painfully back on her head and collected the reins together in some sort of order. Firefly was cantering steadily, and ahead the elegant figure of Marcus was still visible, although receding down the meadow towards what Nell had a horrid suspicion was a river. There was no sign of the decorous trot now, the hunter was galloping flat out.

Firefly lengthened her pace while Nell considered her options. Hauling on the reins was not working, falling off was highly dangerous. That left staying in the saddle and enjoying herself. Ahead, the hunter rose in a long, low jump over what must be water, his rider apparently welded to his back, and took the slight rise on the other side in ground-eating strides.

'You are *not* going to jump that!' Nell ordered, reining in as hard as she could. The mare's ears flicked back, she fought the bit and did not slow, but at least she could not jump either. They went through the wide, shallow stream at the gallop, muddy ice-slush, water and watercress flying everywhere.

'Now, go and catch him up.' Nell dropped her hands, tightened her grip and gave the mare her head. She would never match the big hunter, seventeen hands if he was an inch, to her fourteen, but the little mare threw her heart into it with Nell, thrilled and terrified in equal measure, staying put by a miracle of balance, luck and desperation.

They swung out of a gap in the hedge and on to what Nell recognised as a well-made-up toll road. Far ahead, Marcus had the grey galloping along the wide grass verge, and the mare had no objection to following Nell's tug on the rein—or maybe, she decided, risking one hand to pull back the hat from over her ear, Firefly preferred the grass anyway.

And then she saw buildings and the hunter was slowing, turning under a swinging inn sign, and she realized this must be the receiving office and the nearest stop for the mail coach.

Firefly seemed to know where she was, or perhaps without the horse ahead to chase she was prepared to slow down. Whichever it was, she dropped to a trot as they turned into the yard and allowed Nell to rein her in at last.

Nell slumped in the saddle, breathless, and shoved the wretched hat back on her head. Her hair was coming down. The occupants of the yard turned and regarded her in silence as she got her skirts into some kind of order. An ostler paused in mid-stride, bucket in hand, mouth open, the straw he had been chewing dangling. A pair of small boys stopped chasing the chickens and gawped. Marcus turned in the saddle to see what was entertaining them, took a long, hard look and closed his eyes as though in pain.

'I came for a ride,' Nell said, a strange, unfamiliar feeling building painfully in her chest, threatening to bubble up, overcome her. Then she realized, as the hat finally won over the hat pin and slid off, bouncing from her mud-spattered skirts to the cobbles, what it was. Laughter.

She wanted to laugh. How long had it been since she had felt like doing that? Giving way to unrestrained, joyous laughter? Not a polite smile, not a social gesture, but real laughter?

Too long, Nell thought, her lips twitching as she watched Marcus open his eyes. He sat there on the raking hunter, immaculate, elegant even in country buckskins and plain coat, and there she was, panting, dishevelled, muddy and unrepentant—and the masterful Lord Stanegate had not a clue what to do with her.

She doubled up over the pommel, gasping, her eyes blurring with tears of sheer amusement and laughed until her stomach ached.

Chapter Eleven

'Nell?'

'Yes?' she managed.

His lordship had dismounted and was standing by her side, hand on the reins, lips compressed. 'Why are you having hysterics on that horse?'

'Because it is funny?' she ventured, hiccupping faintly. 'You looking so—' She waved a hand about, searching for the right word and failed, so wiped her eyes with it instead. 'And me so—'

'Quite. I certainly cannot find the *mot juste* for your appearance,' he remarked severely. And then she saw the sparkle in his eyes and the smile tugging at the corner of his lips, despite his struggle to repress it. 'I am afraid Verity's mare has got away from you. I had no idea it was such a spirited animal.'

'Or I such a poor rider,' she said ruefully, lifting her leg over the pommel and allowing herself to be helped to the ground. Marcus seemed to find her no weight at all, which either meant he was as strong as he appeared or that she was thinner than she should be.

Somehow, he acquired a private parlour and got her into it before they both gave way to their mirth. 'Oh, Nell.' Marcus sank down in the nearest chair, buried his face in his hands and choked with laughter. 'You look as though you have been through a hedge backwards. And that ridiculous hat!'

'That is Honoria's,' Nell said in alarm, looking round for it.

'Beyond help, I fear.' Marcus looked up at her and she could not help smiling back. 'I will buy her another, don't worry. But what on earth possessed you to think you could ride? And how did you get that horse out of the stables?'

'I can ride,' Nell said with dignity. 'Only I haven't for a very long time. And Verity and Honoria thought I should ride with you. It has certainly cleared my headache,' she discovered in surprise, pressing the sore lump above her ear with caution.

Marcus came and hitched one hip onto the table beside her. 'And how does a milliner learn to ride?'

'It was a long time ago, when we had a little money. We all rode, dreadful job horses, of course.' She hesitated. 'I did not always have to work for my living, Mama had a few savings.'

'I have not asked you about your father.' Marcus's voice was gentle, still husky from the laughter.

'Oh, he died some time ago.' Her stomach swooped down sickeningly. 'Before…before things got so bad.' There was no reason to suppose he would question it; such stories were commonplace. 'He managed land,' she added, grasping for something near the truth.

Sometimes she thought she could recall the broad

parkland, the groves of trees, the fallow deer. Sometimes she was certain the scent of roses on a hot June day was a memory and not a dream of a paradise lost.

'I am sorry, Nell.'

She looked up, wondering how those hard grey eyes could look so kind, how that strong, sensual mouth be so gentle. 'I—' Somehow she was holding out her hand to him, somehow he had pulled her into his arms, to stand between his thighs.

'Sweet Nell.' And the huskiness in his voice was no longer from the laughter as he bent his head and found her lips. Slow, oh so slow, the caress of his mouth on hers. And so fast the shock of sensual longing that made her limbs heavy, her blood race, sent that strange hot pulse beating deep and low inside her.

She quivered, would have moved closer, but his hands cupped her shoulders, held her still, and he made no move to touch any other part of her, only her mouth, his own asking questions that she only half understood.

When he lifted his head, she was as breathless as she had been after her ride. 'I wanted to talk to you,' she managed, before she lost what nerve she had left. 'I wanted to say about last night. I am sorry, I know I placed you in a difficult position. I need you to know that I would never presume upon that…I do not want you to think that I expect anything. Anything at all.' Only he had just kissed her. What did *that* mean?

'No,' Marcus said, standing up, lifting the weight of her loosened hair in his hands for a moment before letting it drop. 'I know that. I recognise innocence when I see it.'

'I am not innocent,' she began. Harris had taken that from her.

'Innocence,' he repeated. 'Other people's actions do not count, Nell.'

'You believe me, then?'

'I acquit you of throwing out lures, of being any man's mistress. I believe you did not let Salterton in last night.' He smiled at her a little ruefully and ran his finger down her cheek. 'But I know you still have secrets.'

'Oh.' The impulse to confide in Lord Narborough had not survived the night and she felt none to confess now. 'I am sure you have too. Everyone has secrets.' She had to ask. 'Marcus, why did you kiss me just now?'

'I don't know,' he said, getting up abruptly. 'Insanity, probably. I suppose you have lost all your hair pins?'

The abrupt turn of topic back to the banal braced her. 'All of them. I will tie it into a tail with my pocket hand-kerchief.' There was a spotted mirror over the fireplace. Nell turned to it, feeling the physical separation as she moved away from Marcus. She raked her fingers through the tangled mass, trying not to meet his eyes in the glass.

At least he was honest with her; he knew she was hiding something. And he kissed her and did not know why? She would not have thought that Marcus Carlow had any impulses he could not account for. Perhaps it was simply lust and he did not want to frighten her with the truth. But whatever the reality, that morning's coolness had gone and with it the weight of unhappiness that had balled into her stomach.

'How is your head? I should have asked sooner, but the sight of you on that mare quite drove it out of my mind.' He made no move to approach her.

'Sore when I touch it, that is all. There, that will have to do.' She looked a raggle-taggle Gypsy.

'Are you tired of riding?' Marcus asked.

'I suspect I am going to be very stiff tomorrow,' Nell acknowledged ruefully. 'But no, I am not tired.'

'We can go the long way home,' he offered. 'Through the woods and up over Beacon Hill at a nice sedate pace. You will like the view.'

She led Firefly to the mounting block herself before he could help her, gathering up her mired skirts and settling into the saddle. The mare, now she was in company, was behaving as though an out-of-control gallop through the meadows would never occur to her.

'We are very respectable now,' she observed as they walked out of the yard onto the road.

'I am,' Marcus retorted. 'I am also far too much of a gentleman to describe what you look like, Miss Latham.'

She was beginning to be able to read the humour behind his more flattening remarks and to see beyond the frown when it was turned in her direction. 'You already mentioned hedges,' she pointed out meekly, earning a flash of amusement before his face was straight again.

He turned off within sight of the turnpike gate, taking a track up through the fields towards the edge of the beech woods that climbed the steep scarp. Even in January the golden-brown dead foliage clung to its twigs and the horses' hooves brushed through the great drifts of last year's leaves as they climbed, following the track as it zigzagged back and forth.

A jay flew, screeching, as they passed. In the distance the laughing cry of the green woodpecker mocked them and, faintly, Nell could hear the thud of axe on timber.

'Cutting firewood,' Marcus said, following the direction of her gaze. 'Or bodgers. Wood turners and hurdle makers working in the woods,' he explained. 'This way.' He put Corinth to the bank and urged him up, then turned to watch as Firefly, agile as a cat, scrambled up beside them, buried to the hocks in the thick, rustling leaf carpet as Nell clung to the pommel.

Now they were deep in the woods, the tall, straight grey trunks of the beeches looming above and around them like pillars in a cathedral. The air smelled fresh and spicy, full of the aromas of dead leaves and bruised stems as they passed along the narrow path.

And then they were out into the open on close-cropped grass dotted with gorse, the yellow flowers still blooming despite the cold. 'Like climbing up a bald man's head,' Nell said as they reached the gently rounded summit.

'Don't be so disrespectful of our Beacon Hill,' Marcus chided, smiling. 'An Armada fire was lit here. Look, you can see for miles over the Vale of Aylesbury.' He sat, one hand nonchalantly on his hip, utterly at home and relaxed, she realized. Corinth, knowing a familiar stopping place, cocked one hoof up and slouched rather less elegantly than his rider.

'Mmm. Sunshine.' Nell turned up her face to the sun. There was no warmth in it, but the sight of a clear sky was a luxury after London's smog.

'It will snow later if that reaches us.' Marcus pointed far to the west to the bank of dark, big-bellied cloud. 'It is going to get much colder.'

They were on the edge of the scarp. It was like standing on a cliff with the Vale below instead of the sea. The chalk hillside that rolled away to either side of them was deeply indented with dry valleys, beyond each another bald crown, all a little lower than the one they stood on.

'Someone has lit fires.' Nell pointed to the trickles of smoke rising straight up into the still air. 'Is that the bodgers?'

'Possibly. Or Gypsies. They pass through all the time. Some of the tribes we know, others not.' He shifted his stance to watch a buzzard soaring overhead. Then something moved on the edge of the wood on the opposite headland and a figure walked out into the open. Dark haired, lithe, in loose trousers and dark coat, the man strode across the open hilltop then stopped, wary as a deer, and turned. He seemed to stare into her eyes.

Nell gasped, her hands tightening on the reins and Firefly backed, tossing her head. Marcus reached for the bridle. When she looked back, the hill was empty.

'What is it?'

'I…nothing. I was not paying attention and jabbed her mouth, I'm afraid.' Why lie? But the man had gone, and Marcus would think she was hallucinating or making it up. And perhaps she was. Three deer walked out of the wood, just where he had been— surely they would not do that if a human was close? Was it the blow to her head? Only, she could have sworn that had been Salterton in those strange clothes.

The dark man. Marcus was convinced he had now seen him for himself. He schooled his features so Nell could not read his knowledge that she lied. Why had she? He almost asked her, straight out, then bit back the question. Perhaps he would find out more by pretending he had seen nothing. Was Salterton, if that was his name, following them, or had it been coincidence? But nothing, his instincts told him, were coincidental where that man was concerned.

He had been dressed like one of the Rom. A good disguise for anyone with the colouring to pass. The local people, half afraid of the wandering bands, could not single one individual out from another.

'Time to get back,' he said, and brought Corinth's head round, away from the gathering clouds, pregnant with snow. Nell was drooping in the saddle a little now. Marcus watched her covertly from the corner of his eye, as she straightened her shoulders and sat up. She shouldn't have been riding, not after that blow to the head, and he suspected she would suffer for it tomorrow, but he was glad he had not missed that moment of shared laughter. How long was it since he had given in to unrestrained mirth like that? Too long. Not since Hal had been at home.

Nell had gained weight and curves and some colour in her cheeks since the day he had first seen her, he decided. Her figure was recovering the shape it was meant to have and the sharpness had gone from her cheekbones and wrists. She was a lovely woman, perhaps not in the conventional manner of the young ladies gracing Almack's—she was lacking their trained poise and perfect grooming—but her naturalness was far more appealing to him.

Corinth took advantage of the slack rein to turn his head and nuzzle Firefly, who tossed her head and took a few tittupping steps.

'Stop flirting, you old rake,' Marcus admonished,

getting a grip on both the reins and his wandering thoughts. Beside him Nell gave a little snort of laughter and he felt his own lips quirk in response.

Damn it, but she was seducing him somehow. She had no obvious wiles, no tricks. Every time he thought he had been mistaken in his doubts about her, something happened to make him suspicious all over again, and yet he could not stop thinking about her in ways that were utterly unwise. And acting that way as well. Why had he kissed her in the inn? He wished he knew, because every time his mouth touched hers he was left with yet another memory to torment him at night and no answers to his questions.

Nell would not admit it out loud, but the sight of the house was very welcome. Her thighs ached, her bottom ached—she did not remember having bones just there but they seemed to be sticking into the saddle—and her shoulders ached. She lifted her chin a notch as they went through the stable yard arch and made herself smile at the groom who came to take Firefly's reins.

As Havers went to Corinth's head, Marcus swung down, and came across to hold up his hands to help her. It felt so intimate as his fingers closed around her waist that her breath caught, even as she chided herself for such an unsophisticated response to the familiarity. He had lifted her down at the posting house. Ladies allowed grooms or gentlemen they hardly knew to assist them in this way without thinking anything of it. It certainly meant nothing to him, she assured herself, kicking her foot out of the stirrup and lifting her leg from the pommel. Then, as she began her controlled slide down to the ground, her eyes met his and she stopped breathing altogether.

Who would have thought those dark grey eyes could smoulder like that? With infinite slowness Marcus eased her down, her breasts brushing against his coat, the habit rucking up with the friction from his breeches. She felt her lips part, her lids felt heavy, and yet she could not break eye contact. And then the heat was replaced with doubt, with questions, and her breath came back with a force that made her dizzy, and she was standing on her own feet wondering if she had imagined it all.

'Marcus?'

'It is nothing. I have tired my shoulder, I should have let Havers help you down.'

And that was a lie, Nell thought, puzzled. If she had learned one thing about Marcus Carlow it was that he did not willingly admit to physical weakness. Had he glimpsed that enigmatic figure on the crown of the hill? In which case, why not say so? *Because he is determined not to trust you, of course,* she told herself. *You are not a lady so you are an obvious suspect. And if his father was innocent of wrongdoing when Papa died, he was most certainly guilty of a suspicious mind and lack of faith in his friend. Like father, like son.* At least Marcus had not renewed his offer of a *carte blanche*.

But when she came down before dinner, bathed, changed and rested, his mood had switched again. In fact, the entire family seemed cheerful and harmonious, and it did not take Nell long to realize that it was a significant improvement in Lord Narborough's mood that had lifted all their spirits.

'Papa is so much better,' Verity whispered, linking

her arm through Nell's and steering her towards the sofa. 'I heard him say to Marc that a little danger is always invigorating, which I do not understand. What danger? Unless he means Marc being shot, and one would hardly call that invigorating.'

'Absolutely not,' Nell agreed with feeling. 'But who knows with men? They may be talking about a dangerous wager on a cock fight.'

'Oh, yes,' Verity agreed, with her touching ability to think the best about everyone and everything. 'Did you enjoy your ride?'

Dinner was animated enough for Nell to retreat unnoticed into her thoughts. Slowly she was becoming accustomed to the reality of what had happened to her father. She had known something had been very wrong all the time she was growing up, she could see that now. She had not even been truly surprised about the manner of his death. At some point in her childhood, perhaps when she was far too young to understand, something had been said, something that as she had grown came to make sense—a sense that she simply had not wanted to confront.

So, what do you do, faced with a best friend who is accused of being a murderer and perhaps a spy? she wondered, watching Lord Narborough's expression as he talked to Honoria.

You help him escape, surely? But what if the victim is also a friend and you honestly believe the first friend to be a traitor? Would honour forbid you to help? Male honour was a touchy thing, she knew, beginning to have a glimmering of the dilemma that confronted Lord Narborough.

After the meal the men left their port early, coming

into the salon in time to applaud a spirited country dance Honoria was performing on the piano. Verity joined her for a duet, a sweetly sentimental ballad that had Lady Narborough dabbing at her eyes. Lord Narborough closed the backgammon board and settled back to listen.

The countess was persuaded to the piano to perform a short Mozart piece, but all his sisters' teasing would not get Marcus to sing.

'And what about Miss Latham?' the earl enquired, peering into her shadowy corner. 'Will you not play for us?'

'I am afraid I cannot, my lord.' She could just recall the presence of a piano in the parlour, but it had been sold early on.

'But you can sing?' he asked.

'Yes,' she admitted warily. 'But my voice is quite untrained and I have hardly sung for so long—' Not since before Mama's illness when she had sat with Mama and Rosalind, their voices mingling, all their worries forgotten in the music. Mama had a beautiful voice, Rosalind one almost as good. Her own performance she found hard to judge.

'Try now,' Lady Narborough urged.

Nell came to her feet. It seemed churlish not to join in the harmless entertainment. 'Very well, but I do not answer for the results; I may set the hounds howling.'

There was a pile of song sheets on the piano. Verity spread them out for her as Nell bit her lip, scanning them for something simple and familiar. 'This one.' She handed the music to Honoria, who propped it on the stand and played the introductory bars. Nell took a deep breath, fixed her eyes on a still life on the far wall, and began to sing.

Early one morning, just as the sun was rising,
I heard a maiden sing in the valley below.
Oh never leave me
Do not deceive me
How could you use
A poor maiden so?
Remember the vows that you made to your Mary?
Remember the bower where you vowed to be true?
Oh never leave me…

And this time Honoria and Verity joined in the chorus, falling silent again as Nell picked up the maiden's lament. When the last chorus was sung and the last note died away, Lady Narborough applauded, exclaiming in delight.

But as Nell looked round the room, she saw the earl was staring at her, as though he was not seeing her at all, but something else very far away. Marcus glanced sharply from his father to her.

'Father?'

'Charming, Miss Latham, charming,' the earl said at last, seeming to emerge from a trance. 'You remind me of…times long ago.' He got to his feet and turned to his wife. 'You'll excuse me, my dear. I think I will retire.'

Nell endured Marcus's speculative stare for another ten minutes before confessing, 'I am quite exhausted from my ride. I hope you will excuse me?'

Times long ago, Nell thought, climbing the stairs. It had been one of her mother's favourite tunes. Was her voice like enough to Mama's for it to stir a memory in Lord Narborough's mind, or was she simply refining too much upon the actions of a tired man who was not in good health?

But Marcus was not tired or ill. Why could he not believe her innocent of harm or bad intentions? Somehow his suspicions were becoming more than worrying; they were hurtful. She wanted him to like her, to trust her, she realized. And some foolish, unrealistic part of her that still clung to fantasy and to optimism wanted more from him, wanted…love.

The candle in her hand shook so hard that the flame guttered and went out. Nell stood on the darkened landing and forced herself to confront that word. It seemed she was in danger of losing her heart to Marcus Carlow, and one did not get more foolish than that.

I am the penniless daughter of an executed, disgraced man. I might as well long for the man in the moon. Only the man in the moon was infinitely far away, not so close that she could touch him, not so near that he could kiss her with casual arrogance and dissolve every iota of sense and self-restraint she possessed. The man in the moon had not shared her bed so that she knew what he looked like fresh from sleep, the shadow of his morning beard on his lean cheeks.

She could not tell them who she was, she realized. Not because she feared their anger or their retribution, but because she could not bear to see Marcus's face when he found out that she was deceiving him, could not face that final rejection.

Chapter Twelve

January 17

Twelve days since her world had turned on its head, less than a fortnight since she had first seen Marcus Carlow and lost her heart. Nell smiled at Trevor, who was adjusting the perpetual calendar on the hall table as she came out of the breakfast parlour, wondering at her own composure.

Why was her inner turmoil not showing on her face? Somehow it was possible to function without everyone pointing a finger at her, exclaiming that she was a presumptuous, foolish, infatuated woman who had no business even dreaming of such a man as the Viscount Stanegate returning her feelings.

'Good morning, Miss Latham. The frost's heavier this morning,' the footman observed, straightening the calendar and the silver salver. 'Very cold if you were thinking of a walk this—' The sound of horses outside sent him hurrying to the door. 'Excuse me, Miss Latham.'

'Who is it?' Honoria, her inevitable fashion journal in hand, emerged from the parlour behind Nell, effectively cutting off the retreat she was contemplating. The Carlows might disregard the fact that they were entertaining a milliner, but they would hardly wish to introduce her to their acquaintances.

'I don't know,' she began as Trevor opened the door for a bundled figure that, as it shed its voluminous carriage coat, was revealed as a slim, elegant man in his late forties.

'Lord Keddinton,' Honoria said with a smile, but no noticeable enthusiasm. 'What a very cold day to be visiting. Papa is in his study, I believe.'

'Godpapa!' There was no restraint in Verity's greeting. 'Where have you come from, not from Wargrave, surely?'

'My dears.' The man kissed Verity's cheek and smiled at Honoria, his gaze lingering as it fell on Nell. 'I came up from town yesterday afternoon, stayed with my friend Brownlow in Berkhamsted overnight. I have a trifle of business with your father before I turn south for Warrenford Park.'

'If the snow holds off, otherwise you will have to stay, which will be delightful,' Verity said. 'Oh, I am sorry, I am quite forgetting myself! Nell, this is my godfather, Robert Veryan, Viscount Keddinton. Godpapa, Miss Latham is staying with us.'

Nell managed a presentable curtsy. 'Good morning, my lord.'

'Good morning, Miss Latham. You have chosen a cold month for your country stay.' He smiled, nodded and followed the footman through the hall towards the study.

'What a lovely surprise,' Verity said. 'But I don't

expect he will be able to stay long, the roads must be so difficult with all this frost.' She settled herself by the fire with her embroidery frame and began to sort silks. 'You do curtsy nicely, Nell. I didn't think milliners would learn how to do that.' She went pink, suddenly realising that she had been less than tactful.

'There is no call for it,' Nell admitted, not wanting her to be embarrassed. 'But I learned how to curtsy properly when... We were not always very hard up, you see,' she finished lamely.

Honoria put down *La Belle Assemblée*. As usual, she was seeking out the most outrageous styles, guaranteeing another heated confrontation with her mother when they next visited the *modiste*. 'We wondered, because of your manners and the way you speak, only Mama said not to ask because it was tactless.'

'So it is,' Verity said, still pink.

'I grew up in moderate comfort,' Nell said. 'But then Mama was ill and then—well, the money ran out, so I had to work for a living.'

'What a pity you don't have a title,' Honoria observed, oblivious to Verity's frowns. 'Because then you could have opened your own millinery shop. Lots of aristocratic French ladies have; it gives a real *cachet*.'

But I do have a title, Nell thought, startling herself. *Or I did before they took it away. Lady Helena Wardale.* She could not recall it ever being used. That was another person, a long time ago.

'Well, even if I had, I do not have any money,' she said making her voice bright. 'It takes quite an investment to set up a business. I would have to rent a shop, buy materials and equipment, hire girls, advertise.'

'I suppose it must be expensive,' Verity said, threading her needle and beginning to add the leaves to a spray of roses. 'Oh well, perhaps Marcus will send his new mistress to the shop that you work at and your employer will be so pleased she will increase your wages.'

Honoria laughed. 'Really, Verity! I never thought I would hear you talking about such things.'

'He has got a new one, I'm sure,' her sister retorted. 'And mistresses are very expensive, aren't they, Nell?'

'I wouldn't know,' Nell said repressively, reducing Verity to bushing silence again. Her own cheeks were burning as she bent over Verity's work basket and began untangling a skein of pale blue silk. There had been that insane moment when she had been tempted by the thought of becoming Marcus's mistress, tempted to throw away her principles and her upbringing and risk plunging into the life of the *demi-monde*. For money. Or had it been for money? Had she been falling in love with him even then and not realized it?

'Damn it!' Marcus half rose from his chair as his father slammed his fist down on the desk, making the inkwell rock dangerously. 'Are you saying that Wardale was innocent? That I helped send an innocent man to his death?'

'No, no, my dear Carlow, of course not,' Veryan soothed. 'I was just asking if you'd thought of anything else, anything that could explain this persecution. I was simply speculating. You must remember, when I visited you in London you said nothing of this—the rope was a practical joke, Stanegate's wound the result of an encounter with a footpad, that was all.

'When I got your letter, I have to confess my mind was a total blank, and it isn't much clearer now. Of course the man was guilty, but just because that's a fact doesn't mean someone may believe otherwise. We discussed this before Christmas, you recall, and you did not feel so heated then.'

'Well, it sounds as though you were hoping he was innocent,' the earl said, subsiding back into his seat. His hands were not quite steady as they gripped the carved arms of the big chair and Marcus got up, splashed brandy into a glass and set it on the desk beside him. 'Part of me wishes it were so. Will Wardale was my best friend, for God's sake. But if he was blameless then there's injustice added to murder and treachery.'

'The roads must be bad,' Marcus remarked into the silence that greeted that observation. 'This frost seems to be hardening.' Veryan cast a sharp glance at him and Marcus tipped his head infinitesimally towards the door.

'Indeed, yes. Well, I had best be on my way.' One thing, Marcus reflected, Veryan was so damn sharp you never had to give him more than a hint.

'A pity.' Marcus steered him firmly towards the threshold. 'It would have been delightful if you could have stayed for luncheon, but Mama will understand.'

'Another time, perhaps.' Veryan looked back at his old friend. 'I've set Gregson, my confidential secretary, to dig out the old files while I'm away. He's a bright young man, we'll see what he can find. Good day, Carlow.'

The viscount stopped a safe distance from the closed study door. 'Well, this is doing your father no good at all, is it? A good thing, perhaps, that outburst was not heard by anyone but us or it might have been misconstrued as coming from a guilty conscience.'

'Damn it, Veryan!'

'I said misconstrued,' the older man said calmly. 'Is there anything else you want to tell me about it?'

'Possibly.' Still feeling defensive, Marcus opened the library door and motioned Veryan inside. 'I had hopes he was finding this more stimulating than upsetting, but the reminder that there might be some doubt about Wardale's guilt—that hit him hard.'

'So, what else is there?' Veryan strolled over to the globe and set it spinning, one long finger tracing across the continents like an emperor seeking new lands to conquer. 'Anything to do with that charming young lady I met in the hall on my arrival by any chance?'

'Miss Latham? She delivered the parcel that set this whole nightmare going.'

'And is she the owner of a pistol, one wonders?'

'Of course not.' He trusted Veryan, but the identity of whoever had shot him—a capital crime at worst— was not something he intended to reveal to anyone outside the family.

'No. Quite.' Apparently intent on the borders of Russia, Veryan did not lift his head. 'A young lady of mystery, then?'

'A milliner, that is genuine enough. She says the man who sent the parcel used her employer to secure its delivery.'

'Possible.'

'But she is hiding something,' Marcus said, half to himself. 'I want to believe she is telling me the truth and yet, somehow, I cannot.'

'Then trust your instincts,' Veryan said, looking up suddenly, his pale eyes intent. 'With a male suspect there are obvious methods of getting to the truth, regrettably coarse though some of those methods may be. With women, perhaps one needs to be slightly more… subtle.' His smile did not quite reach his eyes.

With an unpleasant taste in his mouth, Marcus watched Veryan's carriage disappear down the drive. Veryan's veiled suggestion that he seduce the truth out of Nell chimed all too closely with his own desires to be comfortable. It felt as though he had somehow let Nell down by talking about her to the other man and that he had revealed too much of his own thoughts to the experienced spymaster.

He gave himself a brisk mental shake and went back to the study, determined to take both his, and his father's, mind off the mystery by discussing coppicing and the troublesome flooding in the West Meadow.

Nell sat in the window seat, arms tight around her knees, staring out into the bright sunlight. The frosted world was radiant, untouched except for the marks of Lord Keddinton's carriage cutting through the whiteness on the drive and the birds' tiny footprints on the lawns. This place was so peaceful, so lovely, so apparently secure. Once, she had had a home like this, and that security had been built on sand.

'Beautiful, isn't it?' The deep voice behind her made her jump. *Marcus.*

'Yes, in London, snow or frost soon turns into filthy sludge,' she agreed without turning.

'Would you like to drive out with me?'

That brought her round, catching at her skirts to keep her ankles modestly covered. As she did so, Nell smiled at the impulse. She had been in bed in her nightgown with this man, for goodness' sake! It was past time for worrying about her ankles.

'You like the idea?' He had caught the smile, although he must be wondering about the accompanying blush.

'The ground is too hard for the horses, surely?' What was this? Another olive branch or an opportunity for interrogation?

'Not if we stay at a walk. There is a stand of timber my father and I disagree about. He wants it clear felled, I favour coppicing. A second look would be useful and the fresh air welcome.' When she did not respond, uncertain what she wanted, he added, 'And your company, of course.'

'Thank you, it would be pleasant, if you do not mind waiting while I find my coat and boots.'

'Borrow a muff,' he called after her as she whisked up the stairs, her mood lifting from mild melancholy to sudden happiness. Even if this house was less of a safe fortress than it seemed and the people within it not everything they purported to be, it was still a waking dream to cling to while it lasted. And she would be alone with Marcus again, that heart-stopping, frightening pleasure.

'You are very quiet,' he observed, glancing down at her as the curricle proceeded sedately along the drive. 'Or are you unable to speak under all that?'

Nell was wrapped up in her coat, a rug around her legs, a scarf about her neck, and Honoria's vastly fashionable muff covering her knees like a large shaggy dog. The matching fur hat came down almost to her nose, so she had to tip up her head to look at him.

'There is too much to look at,' she explained. 'This is like a fairy-tale scene at Astley's Amphitheatre.'

'You've been there?'

Nell made herself relax and tried not to feel defensive. Even milliners might save up to go to Astley's now and again. 'Oh, yes. Not often, of course.' When they had come back to London, selling the little villa in Rye and moving into rented rooms, there had been enough for occasional treats for a while. She remembered the lights and the spangles, the white horses and the acrobats, and she smiled.

'Is your head better?' Marcus asked abruptly when she did not elaborate.

'Yes, thank you. You are a good physician.'

'Not at all. But I am glad it is all right. My conscience was pricking me for not insisting on the doctor after all.'

'I expect I have a hard head,' she said lightly, watching her breath puff into the frigid air.

'You were lucky not to have been killed,' Marcus said, a snap of anger in his voice. 'How could he have hit a woman?'

'Perhaps he did not know I was one?' Nell suggested. 'My candle blew out almost immediately. But to believe that, you would have to accept I am not in league with him.'

'I do accept it.' The pair broke into a trot and were ruthlessly reined back in.

'But you still do not trust me.'

'Give me your word that you are hiding nothing from me, Nell, and I will take it.' The silence stretched on while she wrestled with her conscience. They were out of the parkland and into the woods before Marcus said, 'I thought as much. You mistrust me as much as I do you.'

'I might not tell you my secrets, but I do not lie to you,' she said bitterly. 'Admit that, at least.' She wanted him, wanted his trust and his belief and, impossibly, his love. She wanted to believe his father innocent of any wrong, to believe that he had only followed his conscience and his honour. She wanted her father to have been innocent and faithful. She wanted, she knew, the moon.

Nell twisted on the seat, clumsy under the thick rug, her knee bumping against his. 'Marcus—' she began, not knowing what she meant to say. The words died in her throat as she saw his face, unguarded. There was pain there, conflict. Need. This was not any easier for him, so fiercely protective of his family, than it was for her, she realized.

'Marcus,' she repeated, and he pulled up the pair, turned and looked down into her face. Neither of them spoke. But the vapour in the air betrayed the sharp breath he had taken and the look in his eyes stopped her heart for one dizzying moment.

They were at a fork in the road. Without speaking, he turned uphill, the pair working hard in the traces to manage the slope of the rutted track. After a few minutes they emerged into a clearing with a view down through the trees to the vale below. With its back to the woods stood a strange tower built of split flints, its battlements crumbling, its one window and door facing west.

'The folly,' Marcus said, driving the team into an open-fronted shack by its side. 'We picnic here, almost all the year round.'

Without explanation, he helped her down from her

seat, threw rugs over the horses and reached up to take a key from on top of a beam. Heart pounding, Nell followed him through the fake medieval door into a charming but chilly room in the Gothic taste with a stone floor, arched ceiling and a fireplace. Tin trunks and rustic tables and chairs made up all the furnishing.

Nell went to the window and rubbed at the small panes. 'It is very clean and tidy.' She had to say something, anything.

'As I said, we use it a lot.' Marcus was on his knees on the hearth, stacking kindling and wood shavings from the pile standing ready. The fire flamed into life as he added more wood. She stood watching him as he worked—his kneeling figure, his bent head, the vulnerable skin between his hair line and his collar that she wanted to touch so much—and felt the room grow warmer, far warmer than the blaze he was kindling justified.

When he stood, turned to face her, she found there were no words, not even a question. She knew why she wanted to be there, why Marcus had brought her there, and she knew, if she turned and walked away, he would let her go.

Nell laid the muff and hat on the table and unwrapped the scarf from round her neck. Her hands, as she peeled off her gloves, were suddenly quite steady. She loved him. She wanted him, and she was so tired, so very, very tired, of being alone. This would not be for long, she knew that; he would not want her again, once he had taken her. She had no arts, no experience of lovemaking to hold a sophisticated man of the world. What had happened to her would make her stiff and awkward in his arms however hard she tried to relax. But she would know, just once, what it meant to lie with a man in mutual desire and passion, and that memory would last for a lifetime of loneliness.

Marcus lifted the lid of one of the trunks and brought out blankets and cushions which he spread and heaped before the hearth into a makeshift bed and then slowly, his eyes on her face, he began to unbutton his greatcoat.

She followed his actions, her coat joining his on a chair, her fingers fumbling with the laces on her stout shoes as he sat and pulled off his glossy brown boots. He had more garments than she, but his were easier to remove—coat, waistcoat and neckcloth discarded while she was still undoing the buttons on her spencer.

And then he did move, stepping round the bed to draw her to the fire, holding her close, stilling her fingers on the fastenings of her plain wool gown.

There was cold air at her back and heat from the fire in front. She did not know whether she was hot or chilled until she felt the warmth of his body and slid her arms round him, holding him close, suddenly too shy to look up into his face.

'Nell.' Marcus knelt, bringing her with him, pulling a blanket up around her shoulders. 'Don't be frightened.'

She shook her head in denial that she could fear him. Her hands found his shirt, pushed it open, the buttons slipping free easily, and then she was inside the linen, her palms skimming the hot, smooth skin over his ribs, and he caught his breath with a sound that was almost a sob.

Impatient, she pushed the shirt back to reveal the muscled torso she had glimpsed on that nightmare carriage ride after she had shot him. There was a light dressing still on his shoulder; the bruises had faded, but the scars over his ribs still gleamed white.

'What happened?' Wanting to understand his body, she touched them lightly with her fingertips.

'A riding accident when I was eighteen. I took a header into a freshly cut and laid hedge. I was lucky nothing went straight in—there were enough spikes and sharp stakes.'

'Oh.' She pressed her palms to the marks as though she could sooth the long-ago pain. She brushed her fingers over the dark hair, shying round his nipples. She traced the line of his collarbone, the hint of a cleft in his chin, lifting her hand to stroke between his brows. 'You are not frowning now.'

'No.' Marcus smiled at her with his eyes, unmoving as she explored, daring to touch, too uncertain to caress. It was as though he understood that she needed to reassure herself that it was him, not that other man from her nightmares.

'May I?' He touched the buttons of her gown and she nodded sharply, feeling her body jerky with nerves and desire. 'Oh, Nell.' He seemed to find the sight of her bare shoulders, the curve of her breasts, in some way remarkable, for his hand remained where it was, a fraction above her skin, his gaze intent.

Nell tugged at the plain, worn chemise, suddenly conscious that he would be used to smoothing the fragility of silk and lawn from the pampered skin of his mistress, not much-washed cotton that was regrettably now less than snow-white.

'Nell,' Marcus murmured, catching her nervous hand in his. 'You could be dressed in sackcloth and you would still be lovely.'

'Oh.' She could feel herself blushing, but it was with pleasure now, her confidence building. Nell took hold of the ends of the tape that gathered the neckline together and pulled. 'I don't know what to do.'

'I do,' he said, smiling as he pushed the loosened straps from her shoulders. 'Trust me, Nell.'

With my body? 'Yes,' she murmured to the top of his dark head as he bent and kissed along the line where her corset ended. 'Oh!' His tongue slid between skin and boning, grazing the top of her nipple. 'Oh, *yes.*'

Chapter Thirteen

It seemed Marcus required no encouragement, which was fortunate, for Nell had no clear idea what she wanted, or what to do, only that she needed what Marcus was doing to her, and more of it, and for ever.

She found herself lying back on the heaped cushions, her skin tingling from the radiant heat of the fire, the chill of the draughts, the touch of his skin and the unpredictable caress of his fingers.

His weight came down over her and she fought the momentary panic. Then, as his mouth sought hers, she gave herself usp with a little shiver of relief. It was all right; this was Marcus. She was learning his mouth now, the taste of him, the teasing nips of his teeth, the arrogant thrust of his tongue. She became bold, nipping at his lower lip in her turn, letting her tongue roam into the hot, intimate secrets of his mouth.

He had raised himself on one elbow. As she emerged, slightly dazed from his kiss, she found his free hand sliding up, bunching her petticoat skirts until he could glide his palm over her naked thigh, up, nudging gently into the intimate heat between her legs.

Nell gasped. 'Marcus?'

'You want me to stop?' His hand stilled, fingers still laced into the moist curls.

'No! Only I—you— *Oh!*' The finger slid deeper, parted the folds, slipped inside her and she felt her hips lift in involuntary supplication, pressing the aching mound against his palm as her head fell back, helpless.

Instinctively her hand sought him, frustrated by his closed breeches, spreading impatiently over the hard swell. *'Nell.'* It was a groan as he shifted to sit up, one hand still on her while the other tore at the fastenings to free himself.

And then she could circle the heat and length of his erection. She was tentative, afraid to grip until he closed his hand over hers and showed her what he needed with almost desperate strokes, and she opened to him, arching and aching until he slid between her thighs. Her petticoat skirts ripped, unheeded, in the tangle of limbs and half-shed clothing and then she felt him nudge at her entrance. She drew in a shuddering breath of anticipation. And he stopped.

'Marcus?' She opened her eyes. He was looking down at her, his face intent, his eyes dark, his lips parted. He was rigidly still. Nell watched his Adam's apple move convulsively as he swallowed, a trickle of sweat running down the tendons of his throat.

'No,' he gritted out between clenched teeth. 'No.' He rolled off her, sitting up, knees bent, his forehead on his crossed arms. 'Damn it, I can't do this, not with you.'

Somehow Nell managed to sit up. Marcus shifted

sharply away as she laid a hand on his forearm. 'What is wrong? Did I—'

'You did nothing. Nothing. I want you and I would have taken you and that is wrong. You are a lady, Nell, and I would have made you a courtesan.'

'Once, if things had been different, I would have been a lady. But now I am a milliner and I am already ruined,' she said, managing to keep her voice from shaking as she hauled a blanket around her shoulders and tried to tell herself it was the cold that was making her shiver.

'Ruined?' He looked up at that, his smile twisted. 'No, you aren't ruined, Nell. You were assaulted, forced. What *I* was about to do would have ruined you. I would have made you my mistress. There is no way back from that.'

So, he had not been jesting when he had said he might take her as his paramour. He desired her that much—and he cared enough about her not to give in to the passion that was riding him so hard. If he felt like that—

'What do you feel for me, then?' she whispered.

Marcus met her eyes, his own dark, stormy and filled, it seemed to her, with a kind of frustrated anger. 'Feel? I want you, desire you. Are you in any doubt of that?'

'No,' Nell murmured, her spirits sinking. What had she expected him to say? That he was about to propose to her instead? That he loved her? As far as Marcus Carlow, Viscount Stanegate, was concerned, she was a fallen—in all senses—lady. Of course he could offer her nothing more than his protection for a while.

And what if he discovered who she was, that her birth, at least, was the equal of his? What would happen then? Nothing would change except that he would realize what a lucky escape he had had from a scandalous connection with the daughter of a man convicted of treachery and murder. And he would know the extent of the secret she had been keeping from him.

'I'm sorry.' Marcus got to his feet, stuffing his shirt back into his breeches. 'I should never have let this get so far. You are in no state to gainsay me, I know that.'

Nell looked down at her disordered clothing, the cold beginning to vanquish both the heat in her blood and from the fire. And with the chill came anger, a good deal of it directed at herself and none of it that she could explain out loud.

As Marcus turned away to pick up his boots, she scrambled to her feet, shaking out her skirts, pulling up her gown, forcing buttons into buttonholes with vehement jabs.

'I suppose you expect me to be grateful?' she enquired, making him turn sharply, one boot in hand.

'Grateful? No. I suppose one of us needed to be thinking straight and it should be me,' he said harshly.

'What if I would have enjoyed being your mistress?' Nell demanded, fighting with the recalcitrant sleeves of her spencer which had turned themselves inside out. Marcus, looking grim, did not answer her, but sat down and began to pull on his boots. 'Of course,' she continued, 'the genteel thing for someone of gentle birth fallen on hard times to do would be to simply dwindle to death without any form of occupation. That would be the respectable fate.'

'Damn it!' Marcus grounded his right foot with a slam onto the flagged floor. 'Are you saying that you really would have become my mistress? If I had asked you in cold blood as a business proposition instead of the pair of us getting carried away just now?'

'Perhaps I would.' Nell buttoned the spencer up to her chin. 'You appear to make love very nicely, which must be a benefit—not that I have much basis for comparison, of course, so I am really not a good judge.'

'Thank you.' Marcus ran his neckcloth through his hand with a snap. 'I rarely get any complaints.'

'How gratifying for you. Practice makes perfect, no doubt.' Where were her shoes? Nell spotted them under the table, sat down with more force than elegance and began to lace them up. 'I am sure that earning my living by submitting to your embraces would be considerably more pleasurable than getting eye strain and backache for pennies making hats.'

'I do not require my mistresses to submit! Damn this thing!' Marcus tied the neckcloth into a rough knot and thrust the ends into his waistcoat. 'And I might remind you that mistresses come to bad ends when their looks fade.'

'Not if they are prudent,' she retorted. 'It appears to be like any other form of business. One takes care of one's assets, charges a good price for them and invests the proceeds wisely.' Suddenly, shockingly, it seemed a not unattractive way of life. Provided one never let oneself fall in love, of course.

'Stop talking such damned nonsense.' Marcus lost his precarious hold on his temper, threw down his coat and grabbed her by both arms. 'You will do no such thing.' They glared at each other 'You have no idea what you are talking about or what the dangers are.'

'Balderdash.'

'Very well then. I will set you up in your own business. Millinery, a dress shop. Haberdashery or some such. That, at least, will be safe.'

'Why should you?' Nell demanded. 'You do not owe me anything, and that would simply make me your pensioner. At least, as a mistress, I would give something in return. I have my pride, believe it or not.'

'You have damn little else,' he ground out.

They were both furious now and Nell had very little recollection of quite why, except that her body thrummed and ached with unsatisfied desire and the man she had fallen in love with was lecturing her. He was probably right, which did nothing to soothe her hurt feelings.

'I am going back to London and then I will set about finding a protector. It will require a small outlay in clothes, I suppose, but I have my savings.'

'If you expect to find yourself a wealthy protector you will need more than a sewing girl's savings,' Marcus said, his lip curling in a way that had her longing to hit him. 'Clothes, shoes, fans, perfume. A coiffeuse, a maid…you must be seen in the right places, drive in the parks.'

'You know so much about it, you are just the person to advise me,' Nell said sweetly. 'Perhaps you would like to invest in me?'

Marcus let go of her arms as if he had been bitten. 'That, my dear, would make me your pimp,' he said, his voice icy. 'And, given that you need some lessons in lovemaking before you will be a worthwhile investment, I think I will not risk my social standing by a descent into trade just yet.'

'You—' Nell swept up her coat, crammed her hat painfully on her head and, fumbling with gloves, muff and scarf, stormed out of the door.

'Nell, come back here!'

'No! I am going to walk,' she threw over her shoulder, making for a narrow path through the trees that led in the direction of the house and ignoring the colourful language that followed her.

For a moment she thought he would pursue her, but after a few minutes she heard the sound of hooves on the hard ground and caught a glimpse through the trees of the curricle being driven away at a speed that could only be described as reckless in the icy conditions.

There was something hot on her cheeks. Nell dumped the muff and scarf on a tree stump, found her handkerchief and blew her nose. Anyone's eyes would stream in this cold, she told herself, pulling on her gloves, winding the scarf around her neck and beating the frost and twigs off the muff. Anyone's.

By the time she got back to the house, she could feel her face was red with exertion and the cold air, her feet were like ice and her hair was escaping from the fur hat she had bundled it into, but she was at least feeling calmer. It seemed that brisk exercise was a remedy for both sexual frustration and bad temper. But what she was going to say to Marcus when she saw him again, she had no idea.

'Thank you, Andrewes.' There seemed to be a new arrival. The footman ushered her into the hall which was encumbered with a trunk and a number of valises. A greatcoat was thrown over a chair and she could hear Verity's voice raised in excited speech.

'A new guest?' she hazarded.

'It's Lieutenant Carlow,' the footman said with a grin.

'Master Hal. Sent home on leave from the Peninsula now his wound's healing.' There was a feminine shriek of laughter from the drawing room and his smile widened. 'Their ladyships are very pleased to see him, as you might imagine, miss.'

'I'll go up and change,' Nell said with a glance through the window. No sign of a curricle. 'The family will want some time to talk together. Could you have some tea sent up please, Andrewes?'

Less than a fortnight ago, I was filling my kettle from a bucket on the landing and now I am airily requesting a tea tray from a liveried footman, she thought, trudging up the stairs. Had she really contemplated becoming a fallen woman in order to continue in such luxury? It seemed she had, which was a lowering thought. But somehow she could not regret the impulse, not if the man in question was Marcus.

Luxury seemed even more tempting when a tap on the door brought not just the maid with the tea tray, but footmen with hot-water pails. 'Andrewes thought you looked a bit chilled, miss,' Miriam said, shaking out Nell's coat while the sound of water being emptied into the tub came from the dressing room. 'Shall we wash your hair? Lady Verity's given me a bottle of her camomile hair lotion for you.'

'Oh yes, why not?' Nell drank her tea and contemplated the soft towels, the rose-scented soap, the fire in the dressing room. Sinless indulgencies for a guest. But, when she went home, the only way she could enjoy them was by committing the gravest sin for a lady: the sacrifice of her already tarnished honour.

Nell put down her cup and stood up, wondering if to

choose the life of a courtesan would be to take power or to lose it utterly.

Sliding into the warm embrace of the tub did nothing to banish the memories of how pleasurable some of the duties of a mistress might be. Idly Nell soaped her arms, squeezed the big sponge so that water flowed over her breasts, felt again Marcus's lips on her heated skin.

But she had fallen in love with him, maddening, suspicious man that he was. Was that why his love-making stirred her so? Could she give herself to another man, feeling like this? No, of course she couldn't. She would be disgusted at herself. It was Marcus's caresses she wanted and only his. She should be grateful that his scruples stopped him before they had done anything irrevocable. Which meant returning to a life of respectable, humble drudgery and the sooner she resigned herself to it, the better.

The gloom that these thoughts provoked half-tempted Nell into taking her drab gown from the clothes press and bundling her hair into a net. Stubborn self-respect made her submit to Miriam's best efforts with her hair, to the pot of flower-scented hand cream and the suggestion that she wear the prettiest of the afternoon gowns Honoria had lent her.

The effect, as she caught a glimpse of herself in the long glass in the hallway, was a shock. Her eyes were wide, intense. Her hair gleamed, there was colour in her cheeks, her skin was creamy above the elegantly modest neckline and her lips—her lips were curved into a provocative pout. Startled, Nell tightened them, to no avail. It must have been Marcus's kisses, she thought, wondering if she appeared to others quite as comprehensively abandoned as she felt.

The hall had been cleared of Lieutenant Carlow's baggage, but voices and laughter were still coming from the drawing room. Nell opened the door and hesitated, uncertain whether she should be intruding. But it was well past the usual hour for luncheon.

'Nell!' Verity, of course, was the first on her feet, bubbling with excitement. 'Come and meet Hal. Hal, this is Miss Latham.'

The man who rose from amidst the group beside the fire was unmistakeably a Carlow, favouring Honoria rather than Verity in his looks. As tall as Marcus, but of a lighter, rangier build, his hair was more of a golden brown, his eyes blue-grey, his tanned face devoid of any hint of his older brother's familiar frown.

'Miss Latham.' He came towards her, hand held out, a smile on his lips that made her feel that there was no one else in the room. 'I understand I am to thank you for rescuing Marcus.'

'Lord Stanegate was in no need of rescue, I assure you, Lieutenant Carlow,' Nell protested, taking the long-fingered hand that seemed reluctant to let hers go. 'He dealt with the situation most masterfully.'

'That I can believe.' The way his smile warmed his eyes sent a tingle right down to Nell's toes. *My goodness, he must have to beat the ladies off with sticks!* she thought, startled by her own reaction. *If I wasn't in love with his brother I would be a puddle at his feet.*

'Come and sit by the fire, Miss Latham.'

'I think it is time we all went in to luncheon,' Lady Narborough said, getting to her feet and smiling at her son. 'Miss Latham, you must be wondering if we were ever going to eat. I should have had the gong sounded half a hour since, but we were all so delighted to see Hal,' she explained, leading the way to the door. 'He has been giving us considerable anxiety.'

'You have been wounded, I believe?' Now that she had recovered from the impact of those smiling eyes, she could see that he was carrying little surplus weight and the skin under his eyes was shadowed as though by sleeplessness or pain.

'A ridiculous scratch from a sabre that provoked a fever I couldn't shake off. My commanding officer took exception to the fact that I kept falling flat on my face and ordered me to bed, then, once I got to my feet again he packed me off home. My regiment is here. I expect I will join it again in a week or two.'

'You must be very happy to have him with you, Lady Narborough,' Nell observed.

'I am delighted to have both my sons at home,' the countess said, taking her seat and gesturing Hal to sit beside her. 'I have to confess that I wish they were both not in such a battered condition.'

'They are both on the mend, my dear,' the earl observed from the other end of the table.

'Hmm.' Lady Narborough looked doubtful. 'They *say* they are.'

There certainly appeared to be nothing wrong with Lieutenant Carlow's appetite nor his ability to hold his own in conversation. He soothed his mother, passed on all the military gossip to his father, teased his sisters affectionately and still managed to give Nell the flattering impression that he could hardly keep his eyes off her.

It was all flummery, of course. She was under no mis-apprehension about him. She was the only female at the table to whom he was not related and Hal Carlow was a rake who flirted as easily as he breathed.

Nell had never been flirted with before. It was, she concluded, a most stimulating experience, even when one had a bruised heart. Or perhaps especially because of those bruises. A glance in the mirror reassured her. Yes, she was still looking remarkably fine. Experimentally she lowered her lashes and shot Mr Carlow a sideways glance. His lips curved appreciatively.

'We must invite some people over, Mama,' he observed. 'Get up a party. Dance a little. I am sure Miss Latham would like to dance, would you not?'

'I do not dance, Lieutenant Carlow.'

'On principle? Never tell me you are a secret Quakeress.' His gaze seemed to linger on her mouth.

'Because of lack of ability, sir. I am sure Lady Narborough has explained, I am not in Society.'

'But I could teach you.' The polite offer held suggestions of many things that Hal Carlow would like to instruct her in.

'Thank you, Mr Carlow, but I think it better not,' she said demurely, realising a moment later that he had simply taken that as a challenge. The blue-grey eyes laughed at her as she felt her cheeks warm.

He was still amusing himself by making her blush, and laugh, when they returned to the drawing room. 'You make those prodigiously pretty bonnets my sisters wear?' he asked.

'I make similar bonnets, sir.'

'These fingers are that nimble?' He lifted her hand

as though to examine it and she pulled it away, folding her hands together in her lap.

'It is a matter of practice and some natural aptitude. Lady Verity is just as skilled with a needle and has a far more artistic imagination than I,' Nell said, turning his attention back to his family and taking the opportunity while Verity fetched her latest embroidery to move to sit next to Lady Narborough.

'How proud you must be of your sons,' she murmured.

'Indeed.' The countess watched Hal intently. 'How I wish they would settle, though.' She sighed, then smiled. 'Now, Miss Latham, you have an excellent eye for colour. What do you think I should do about the curtains in here? This green has faded sadly and I am not convinced it was the right choice in the first place.'

Almost an hour later, when the tea tray had been brought in, sounds from the hall heralded Marcus's return home. Nell was helping her hostess, carrying a cup of tea to Lieutenant Carlow, when the door opened.

Mr Carlow's hand was over hers on the saucer, his smile warm as he thanked her, as Marcus came in.

'Hal!' His smile as he greeted his brother was broad. His eyes as they rested on Nell, were like fresh-split flint.

Chapter Fourteen

'Hal!' He had never been happier to see his hellion of a brother, and never been so close to wanting to strangle him. Hal had been in the house, what, a few hours? And there he was, smiling at Nell with *that look* in his eyes, his fingers all over hers.

And was she retreating in blushing confusion from a man she must know, with one glance, was a rake? Was she shaken and trembling after what had happened in the folly with him?

Oh, no. Miss Latham was smiling at his brother. Miss Latham was glowing. Miss Latham had never, he was damned sure, looked better in her life than she did at this moment, her hair gleaming in the candlelight, her skin soft and creamy, her figure admirably displayed by a gown that brought out the green in her eyes. And her mouth, soft and full with that delicious hint of a pout curving in appreciation of whatever outrageous flummery Hal had just spouted. The mouth that had opened under his that morning, the mouth that had trailed fire along his jawline.

Marcus smiled. Damn it, he knew he was smiling as he strode into the room, hand out to Hal; he could feel the muscles in his cheeks ache. But she had seen something in his face. Nell put the teacup down on a side table and retreated in a whirl of skirts to a seat on the far side of his mother, her eyes cast down, her hands in her lap, the picture of modesty.

'Hal,' Marcus said again, his fingers closing round the brown hand held out to him as his brother got to his feet. They embraced, hard, no need for words. Hal was back, alive, unmaimed. Under his hands, his brother's body felt slighter than he remembered, the lines of his face when he pulled back to look at him properly were fine-drawn with fever. He read the message in his eyes: *Don't fuss, don't ask.* He would, of course, but not until they were in private and the others could not hear.

'You look well,' he said instead, slapping him on his shoulder and taking the seat next to him. 'All that lying about in bed, I suppose.'

'Of course. Dreadful bore, but I caught up on my reading,' Hal drawled.

Marcus was not deceived. If Hal had been ordered to his bed—and stayed there—then he had been ill indeed and being kept from active service would have fretted his nerves raw. But there would have been diversions, he had no doubt. And pretty girls to play at mopping his fevered brow, and bottles of wine smuggled in against doctor's orders.

'Strategy and the Classics?' he suggested.

'But of course. French novels,' Hal added in an undertone. With a grin he turned back to the rest of the family. He knew his duty as the returning son: it was to suffer himself being fussed over for at least a day while they satisfied themselves that he really was safe and well. He picked up his teacup and proceeded to regale his mother and sisters with tales of Lisbon's shops and amusements and tease all three of them with hints about presents he had brought back.

Marcus caught his father's eye and nodded reassuringly, seeing the older man's shoulders relax. Lord Narborough had never had the easiest of relationships with his younger son, who could not recall his father fit and vigorous as Marcus could. The two found it hard to talk to each other and the earl's disapproval of Hal's wilder excesses resulted in a certain coolness.

Honoria and their mother were drawing Nell into the conversation about Portugal now. Didn't it occur to Mama that exposing Nell to Hal was not a good idea? Their guest was ignoring Marcus now, smiling and asking Hal questions, her apparent embarrassment when he had come into the room quite gone.

Marcus collected a cup and went to sit down, listening, studying his brother's face until his anxiety began to give way to a certainty that Hal really was on the mend.

With that reassurance, and not the slightest interest in the Lisbon pastry shops which seemed to so intrigue Verity, he let himself think about Nell. He had come back after an uncomfortable morning of soul-searching to apologise, to make her an offer of a partnership in a shop, a respectable business. Her talent and work, his money—a fair exchange with no obligations on either side beyond those that were strictly businesslike.

He would find something that would keep her safe and comfortable and not in any danger of being tempted to fall into the clutches of some man. A man like his brother. Like himself. Marcus shifted uncomfortably in his chair. His conscience was giving him hell. What had he been thinking of to equate Nell with the likes of Mrs Jensen and the rest of the muslin company? She would make a very good courtesan, he had no doubt, crossing his legs as the memory of her untutored passion came back with inconvenient force.

She was intelligent, thoughtful—oh yes, with time she would be magnificent, not because she was naturally wanton, but because she was the sort of woman that a man would be comfortable with and she would try to do her best whether she was trimming hats or learning sophisticated bedroom tricks.

Hal's rich, slightly wicked and utterly infectious laugh had them all smiling. And of course, Marcus thought, his own smile congealing on his lips, she has to storm back into the house after his crisis of conscience, straight into the company of a man who could most certainly teach her any bedroom trick she could possibly want to learn.

And why was she looking so damned lovely? He had come back braced for a furious, tear-drenched woman yet she appeared to have emerged from an experience that had shaken him severely looking not just untroubled, but blooming.

Marcus drained his cold tea and studied the tea leaves in the bottom of the cup as though to read his future there. He thought he could make out a gallows, which felt about right. What had happened up there in the woods? *I do not lie to you,* she had said, a thread of bitterness running through her voice. And he had looked at her and seen truth and pain and need in her eyes. Need for him that had called up an answering ache in his chest, the impulse to hold her, love her, claim her.

And the madness had seized him, swept way everything that might have held him back until that moment, almost too late, when he had found himself at the very point of surging into her body. It had been her eyes again—filled with trust—that had stopped him. *Trust.* And he was betraying it, whatever she thought she wanted or needed at that moment.

Damn it, why should she give him a second glance now? Hal was here: handsome, laughing—Hal never frowned—fun. *Good.* Excellent in fact, provided Hal did not seduce her. He would have a word with him about that, explain her circumstances, tell Hal all about the mysterious attacks.

Marcus looked across, satisfied he had now solved the puzzle of what to do about Nell Latham. All he had to do was warn his brother to behave, let her enjoy whatever parties or amusements that Hal's fertile brain conjured up, and then when this was all over, establish her in a neat little shop in a fashionable district. She could communicate with his man of business; there would be no need to see her again. That had to be good.

He caught Hal's eye and jerked his head slightly towards the door.

'I'll go up and er…rest before I change for dinner,' Hal announced, getting to his feet. 'Keep me company, Marc?'

'Of course.' He followed his brother out and they climbed the stairs together in silence until they were out of earshot of the footmen in the hall.

'What's afoot?' Hal asked. 'Mysterious ladies dis-

guised as milliners—or is it the other way round?—
gamekeepers all over the place, Mama putting a brave
face on something, you all here with only weeks to go
to the start of the Season. This is a damn sight more
interesting than I expected my convalescence to be.'

They walked into Hal's room to find his batman
laying out his evening clothes. 'Thank you, Langham.
Lord Stanegate will assist me.'

'It's a mystery,' Marcus said as the door closed and
he went to help Hal out of his well-fitting coat. 'And
a dangerous one, I suspect. I'd best start at the beginning. What do you know about the scandal of
ninety-four?'

'Nothing.' Hal began to unbutton his waistcoat. 'I
was five, remember? No one has enlightened me since,
and on the one occasion I asked, I had my head bitten
off for my pains. Life's too short to worry about
ancient history.'

'Not so ancient,' Marcus said, going down on one knee
to pull at his brother's boot. 'It's come back to haunt us.'

'Bloody hell.' After half an hour of concise explanation,
Hal had given up undressing and was still in his shirt
sleeves and stockinged feet. Military life had certainly
given him an ability to absorb facts, Marcus noted. The
questions had been few and pertinent, but Hal's eyebrows
still had to descend to their normal level.

'No wonder you've abandoned the field and surrendered the delicious Mrs Jensen to Armside,' he added,
when the tale was finally told.

'What? Damn it, I was on the point of settling with her.'

'I know. The clubs are full of it and Armside is smug

beyond bearing. Mind you, having seen the delicious Miss Latham—' He broke off as Marcus's fist clenched involuntarily. 'No?'

'No,' Marcus said with emphasis. 'Miss Latham is gently born but has fallen on hard times since the loss of her family and is now employed as a milliner. She is mixed up in this because, as I told you, our mystery man used her as a messenger.'

'That's not all, is it?' Hal began to strip off the rest of his clothing.

'No. She knows more than she's saying, but I can't believe— Hell's teeth, that looks sore!' A raw scar cut a jagged path down Hal's ribs. In the centre, there was still a dressing and the skin looked heated and slightly swollen.

'You might say so.' Hal squinted down at himself. 'The cut wasn't deep—more of a slice—but it took all sorts of rubbish in under the skin and by the time I got some medical attention it was a proper mess. Healing now, though.'

'I'm glad to hear it.' Marcus splashed warm water into the washbasin for him and propped his shoulder against the bedpost while Hal took the rest of his clothes off and began to wash. 'Another dashing scar to fascinate the ladies?'

'Well, not exactly *ladies*.' Hal grinned, comfortable in his nakedness. 'You were saying about Miss Latham?'

'That she might be hiding something and she might be a milliner now, but she has enough on her plate without you setting out to break her heart.'

'Me?' Hal managed a look of utterly unconvincing innocence as he pulled on his evening breeches. 'What you mean is, you were enjoying a pleasant flirtation when along I come, with my superior charm and elegant profile, and now you're getting all protective.'

'As yet the French have not managed to flatten your *elegant profile,* little brother, but believe me, if you compromise Miss Latham I will do it for them.' He managed to smile as though the threat was a joke.

'Compromise her? Certainly not.' Hal tucked in his shirt. 'Pass me a clean neckcloth, will you? But I'll enjoy cutting you out.'

Marcus contemplated retorting that his brother could try, then saw the trap. The worst thing would be to offer Hal a challenge, it was the equivalent of releasing a mouse in front of a cat. He shrugged negligently. 'Stop mangling that neckcloth. I need to change too.'

'I'm ready.' Hal tugged at his cuffs and followed Marcus out. 'So what, exactly, are we doing to solve this mystery, or does the family skulk out here for ever?'

'We can't do that,' Marcus said when they were alone in his room. 'The girls and Mama don't know what is going on. They expect to be back in London for the Season. If it were you and me and Father we could lure him in, but I daren't send the women away either, not without me.'

He tossed his shirt on the bed as Hal came and turned him by the shoulders into the light. 'So this is the famous gunshot wound from the footpad?' He lifted the edge of the dressing and drew a sharp breath. 'Nasty. But small calibre. One might almost say a *lady's* pistol.'

'One might, if one did not care about the consequences to the lady.'

'Ah.' Hal nodded appreciatively. 'What was she aiming at? Your head? Or your manhood?'

'Nothing at all, apparently. According to this hypothetical lady, she had no idea it was loaded.'

Hal adjusted the dressing again. 'Made a tidy mess of your shoulder. Hurt like hell, I should imagine.'

'It stung a trifle,' Marcus admitted with what he felt was commendable understatement. 'I was bleeding like a stuck pig. Miss Latham was remarkably effective in dealing with that.'

'Perhaps I can help her improve her aim,' Hal remarked as Marcus washed. 'It would be amusing to take her down to the Long Barn, assist her with getting a grip on a pistol.'

Marcus grabbed the soap so hard it shot from his hand into the basin. For a moment, the room vanished behind a red haze.

'Miss Latham is…fragile as far as men are concerned,' he said when he could master his voice. 'She has had much to fear from them and a very recent encounter with one who was not—' he searched for the word '—wise.'

Whether his brother guessed he was in the same room as the unwise man in question, he neither knew nor particularly cared. Hal could rag him all he liked, provided he left Nell's feelings unruffled and her heart intact.

Dinner passed uneventfully, with everyone focused on Hal. Nell retired into her shell, while the family bombarded Hal with questions and nagged him into eating more. With his own worries over his brother's health at rest, Marcus was left to watch Nell covertly and to wonder just why he was feeling so strangely unsettled. After all, he had a plan for dealing with her.

Lady Narborough refused to allow her menfolk to linger over their port, insisting that they had plenty of time to swap bloodcurdling tales of the battlefield later. So Hal was ensconced in the place of honour by the fire and fussed over, while Nell went quietly back to ponder the chess game she and his father were playing very slowly over several evenings. The earl, who seemed to enjoy teaching her, did not press her for a move, but sat back in his chair watching his younger son with an occasional smiling glance at Nell.

Marcus got up and sat beside her. 'That pawn?' he suggested, pointing. He had no idea whether it was a good move or not; his attention had been entirely on her face, not the board.

'Really?' She looked up at him, puzzled. It was obviously a foolish suggestion. 'But I am playing the red pieces.'

A very foolish suggestion. 'Of course, I was not thinking. You are not chilled after our drive this morning?'

'And my walk?' Nell met his eye with tolerable composure. 'Yes, I deserve to catch a cold with such foolishness, do I not?'

'It was my fault entirely,' he said. 'I am sorry.'

'You did not force me to get down from the carriage,' she pointed out, her voice low. 'What followed was just as much my responsibility.'

'I was tactless,' Marcus persisted, determined to apologise comprehensively while he was at it. 'Afterwards.'

'True.' Nell turned back to her contemplation of the board. 'And I was provoking.' She sent him a slanting glance from under her lashes, an utterly feminine trick to gauge his mood. Marcus felt his lips twitch, just a fraction.

'*Very* true,' he agreed, and she smiled, a small, secret smile that did the strangest things to his breathing. What the devil was the matter with him?

Her fingers poised over the chessboard, she hesitated, then moved a bishop. Across the table, Lord Narborough chuckled.

'Oh dear, have I walked right into a trap?'

'Most certainly. You see, I will now do this.' The earl leaned forward. 'And what will you do now?'

'I haven't the slightest idea,' Nell said, half laughing, half plaintive.

'Let me see.' Hal strolled over and studied the board, then leaned down and whispered in Nell's ear.

She went pink, laughed, bit her lip and sent Hal a roguish look that had Marcus's blood seething. 'Thank you, Lieutenant Carlow,' she said demurely, leaning forward and making a move that had Lord Narborough sitting up and frowning.

'Miss Latham will learn faster if you do not tell her what to do,' Marcus observed as Hal took up position leaning on the back of Nell's chair.

'But it is such fun to teach, don't you think so?' His brother's expression was bland and innocent, his suggestive words went straight to the most tender part of Marcus's conscience.

Teach Nell. Oh yes, that is what I want to do. Teach her to make love, teach her to love me. Love. His heart gave a sudden thump. Marcus stared at his own clasped hands, keeping his eyes down in case Hal read the truth in them.

He had fallen in love with Nell Latham. That was why he was so defensive, so possessive when Hal was close to her. That was why he could not make love to her like that, why the thought of her with any other man filled him with hot anger. That was why, whatever her secrets, he wanted her. Wanted to marry her.

Marcus got up abruptly, walked away across the room to the window and jerked back the curtain. His own face stared back, reflected in the glass. Wanted her for ever, as his wife. God. What was happening to him? He stared blindly at the dark world outside. It was like discovering something totally new about himself. He supposed it *was* something new, this feeling. It was certainly overwhelming.

He watched the scene behind him reflected as though in a mirror. His father frowning at the problem Hal's move had set him. Hal using his hands to describe something to his sisters that was making them laugh. His mother's smile. And Nell, quiet, contained, full of unexpected depths and passion. Nell, who had turned to liquid fire under his hands in that cold folly, whose skin smelled of roses and whose mouth tasted of cherries.

What did it matter that she had fallen on hard times, that she was having to earn her own living, that she had no family around her? He was Viscount Stanegate, heir to an earldom. He could do what he wanted. Just for once, he could do *absolutely* what he wanted. There would be gossip; he would have to deal with that, as much for her sake as for the family.

She must be from a gentry family, at the very least, he supposed. He would have his people look into it. There would be some respectable relative, however distant, who would be glad to oblige the Carlows by lending her countenance.

Now all he had to do was to find the right moment,

the right words. The seriousness of what he was contemplating was beginning to sink in. He was in love, and his world was no longer on its right axis, and perhaps never would be again. He was no longer in control of his emotions or his destiny.

That slim figure across the room was going to change everything. Everything he believed about himself, he realized, would be challenged and transformed. And yet, he had never felt more right in himself, more certain of who he was and what was important.

Marcus looked around the candlelit room that held everyone who mattered to him, a room set in the heart of the house and the estate that was rooted in his very being. If he had not stopped, up there in the folly tower, Nell could now be carrying the next generation to love this place, beneath her heart.

How long had he felt like this about her and not realized? How was he going to keep her safe?

Chapter Fifteen

'Checkmate.' Lord Narborough sat back and Nell laughed.

'Oh dear, I fear I am never going to get the hang of this game, even with Mr Carlow's assistance. Congratulations, my lord.'

'He's never beaten me yet,' the earl said smugly. 'So you learn from me, Miss Latham, not Hal.'

Still chuckling at Hal's snort of affronted pride, Nell glanced round for Marcus. He was watching her, unsmiling, almost grim. That frown was back and his eyes were darker than she had ever seen them. Darker than when he had accused her of trying to frighten his father to death. Darker even than they had been as he had lain over her, their breath mingling in the cold air, and he rejected her.

The bitter argument was still unresolved. He still desired her, still wished to make her his mistress, even though he knew he should not. And she, wanton that she was, still wanted him. If he had offered a *carte blanche* again, then she would have accepted it, Nell admitted to herself. It was the only way to have a part of him for her own, his body if not his heart.

But that hard, hot stare seemed to brand her as she sat there. What had she done so very wrong that he should look at her like that? Laughed and found pleasure in his father's company? Flirted a very little with his charming brother?

Dog in the manger, Nell thought. *You do not want me, but no one else can even be my friend.*

'Nell, will you come and talk about the party Hal wants us to hold?' Verity called.

'I—I am a little tired, Verity. Would you mind very much if we spoke of it tomorrow?' Verity's face fell and Nell had a strong suspicion that she would do what she often did and come round in her nightgown and wrapper to curl up at the foot of the bed for what she called a chat, but was usually a lengthy interrogation about the life of a milliner, which appeared to fascinate her.

Nell gathered up her things, made her goodnights and finally turned to face Marcus. He was still standing by the window, still watching her with what she could only interpret as dislike.

Two could play at that game. Nell lifted her chin and returned a stare of freezing disdain as she swept out of the door. Outside, she leaned back against it, shaken. He had seemed so gentle, almost teasing her over the chess game—until Hal had come over to join them. Perhaps he did not want her corrupting his brother.

'Miss Latham?'

'Oh. Watson. A moment's abstraction.' She smiled at the butler and went swiftly up the stairs. With Miriam dismissed, she turned the key in the lock; she really did not feel she could cope with Verity tonight.

Nell folded away the last of her father's letters and tied the ribbon. There was nothing more there to add to what she already knew, nothing in her mother's diary either, just despair and the death of hope.

She locked the writing slope and set it back on the table. The clock on the mantle showed five minutes to midnight. Time to sleep, if she could.

The tap on the door stopped her as she began to climb into bed. 'Verity, I'm sorry, but I am too sleepy to talk,' she called.

The tap came again, the handle turned. Nell sighed and went to the door. 'Verity—'

'It is Marcus. I need to talk to you.'

'At this hour? In my room? I very much doubt talking is what you have in mind,' she said, snatching her hand back from the door handle. 'Go away.'

'Nell, for Heaven's sake, stop sulking and let me in.'

'Sulking! I am doing nothing of the sort.' Nell heard her voice rise and got a grip on her temper. 'You are a complete hypocrite, Marcus Carlow, glowering at me for talking to your brother then accusing me of sulking,' she hissed at the crack in the door. 'I don't like you, I don't want you—'

There was a loud thump on the door panels that sent her jumping back in alarm. 'Nell!'

'Will you stop shouting! Do you want the entire household here? Do you want to shame me in front of your sisters? Go away!'

Silence. Then, 'You really are the most infuriating

woman I have ever met,' Marcus Carlow said. It must have been the muffling effect of the door, but she could have sworn he was smiling as he spoke. 'Good night, Nell.'

'Infuriating? Me?' But there was only silence. Nell turned the key in the lock and flung open the door, spoiling for a fight. The passage was empty save for half a suit of armour on a pillar. 'Oh!' The temptation to slam the door was almost overwhelming. Nell closed it with care, locked it and stalked back to bed.

What do you do, she wondered an hour later as she punched her pillow in an effort to find a position where she might finally sleep, *when you fall in love with a man whom you want to shake in exasperation almost as much as you want to kiss him?*

'The lake is frozen, so Potter tells me,' Marcus remarked as he tackled a large and bloody beefsteak.

Nell averted her eyes from both the man and his idea of a reasonable breakfast and addressed herself to her toast and preserves. She was finding it very difficult to ignore Marcus while at the same time not give the appearance of doing so.

'We could skate,' he continued. 'Potter says the ice is bearing—he and two of the other under-gamekeepers were on it last night.'

'Oh, yes!' Honoria was predictably enthusiastic. 'We can all go and take a picnic and have a brazier, just like we used to do.'

'I didn't know there was a lake,' Nell remarked.

'It is more of a long, large pond,' Lord Narborough explained. 'It was made by damming the river to create a head of water for the mill lower down. Most of the streams around here are shallow, but they feed the Woodbourne and it has a reasonable depth.'

'We crossed one of the tributary streams when Nell and I were riding,' Marcus said.

She saw Hal looked up at the use of her first name. 'So we did, my lord,' she said with a little emphasis on the title. Hal's lips twitched.

Unaware of the byplay, Lord Narborough tossed down his napkin and beamed. 'A good idea. The sun is out, the frost is hard. Watson, tell the kitchen that we require a luncheon hamper and have the footmen take the brazier and so forth down to the lake.'

'George,' Lady Narborough began, then looked round the table at her enthusiastic family and smiled. 'Oh, very well. The exercise will do us all good, I daresay. You have some stout boots, Miss Latham?'

'I will just watch,' Nell demurred. 'I have never skated.'

'You will love it. Please try, Nell,' Verity cajoled, despite Nell's firm refusals.

She was still saying *no* when they reached the lake-side an hour later. This was obviously a well-rehearsed excursion, with muffled-up footmen in galoshes throwing oilskin rugs over fallen trees for seats, a brazier and kitchen staff clustered around it making ready for hot drinks and luncheon. The staff seemed to be enjoying it as much as the family and it was hard, in the middle of so much laughter, to keep refusing to join in.

Nell stood by the edge, well wrapped up, watching while Lord Narborough executed intricate reverse steps with his wife, Hal whirled a shrieking Honoria in circles and Marcus fastened Verity's skates.

Diana strapped on her own skates with a practised air

just as Lord Narborough delivered his breathless wife back to the edge. 'Miss Price?'

They stuck out for the centre, collecting Verity as they went. Nell tried not to feel envious. It looked such fun, so effortless. Marcus came up, as sure on his skates as he was on firm land. 'Nell?' She fought the urge to turn away and take refuge by the brazier.

'I do not skate, my lord,' she said politely, conscious of Lady Narborough not so very far away.

'Nell, I want to make up.' Marcus was smiling ruefully at her when she finally made herself meet his eyes.

'Really?' She began to walk along the edge while he skated slowly beside her. 'After glowering at me last night and then hammering on my door for an argument? Do you assume I am going to corrupt your brother?'

'Hal? Good God, no! Quite the reverse, I am sure. Hal is the most appalling flirt; I would not want your heart wounded, Nell.'

Would you not? she thought, wondering what he would say if she told him that she feared he had already broken it. 'And that makes you scowl?'

'Was I so fierce? I am sorry, Nell. My thoughts last night were not easy. I had some hard thinking to do.'

'You seem more cheerful this morning,' she ventured. 'Have you made up your mind what you will do about your problems?'

'One of them, yes.' He came to a halt on the ice. 'I am looking for the right moment to do something about that. How to tackle our dark antagonist is still eluding me.'

'These woods are too big to hunt him in,' she said, looking up at the forested slopes. 'Could you set a trap?

Take away the patrolling gamekeepers, be a little careless with a window left ajar?'

'If it were only Hal, my father and I, that is exactly what we would do. With a houseful of women, no. But I refuse to allow him to spoil our fun. Come and put skates on, Nell. I will teach you.'

'I'll fall down,' she protested, allowing herself to be led back.

'Where's your spirit?' Marcus demanded, grinning at her. 'You ride a horse; this is much closer to the ground, even if you do fall.'

'Even? Oh, all right,' Nell capitulated. It seemed she had misjudged his mood last night and the dark, brooding gaze was not the outer sign of his feelings about her.

She sat on a tree stump and let him strap the skates over her boots, one hand steadying her foot while the other secured the lashings. Through the sturdy boots his touch could be nothing but chaste, yet there was still the memory of those same fingers trailing wicked delight up her legs, up her inner thighs, up to the most...

'Did you say something?' Marcus looked up and Nell shook her head. She must have gasped. His dark head bent to the task again and she fought the impulse to thread her own fingers into the thick, waving hair.

'You should wear a hat,' she scolded. 'You'll catch your death of cold.'

His answering grin as he helped her to her feet gave her a sudden glimpse of what he must have looked like as a boy, his bare head ruffled, his eyes sparkling with mischief. If they had lain together yesterday, then she might be carrying his child now. A son with his father's grey eyes.

'Nell?'

'Um? Oh, I'm sorry.' Her state of abstraction had carried her the few steps onto the ice without her realizing. 'Oh!' Her feet wanted to go in opposite directions. Nell grabbed the front of Marcus's coat and hung on. It was impossible to move.

'Stand up straight,' he said patiently, untangling her. 'And put your feet like this and hold my arm.'

Nell's feet shot out and she sat down with a thud. 'Ouch!'

'Up.' Marcus hauled her to her feet. 'Try again.'

After half an hour of skids, slides and inelegant landings on her bottom, Nell found she could stand up and move each foot forward in turn. 'Look! I'm skating!' Hal swooped past, laughing at her, and she grinned back. 'I wish I could go fast like that.'

'All right.' Marcus moved behind her, put his hands at her waist and pushed. 'Here we go, you move your feet too.'

And she was skating, laughing out loud, waving to Lord Narborough, who had Honoria on one arm and Verity on the other. Behind her, Marcus's body was strong and warm, sheltering her, supporting her, keeping her safe. She turned her head and smiled up at him. 'I love this!'

His eyes widened, his smooth pace faltered just a fraction and Nell lost her footing. Her feet shot out in front of her and she went down like a stone, landing virtually on Marcus's feet. There was a sharp crack, echoing around the valley. He stumbled, but she was too close for a recovery, and they ended up in a laughing heap on the ice.

In a moment they were surrounded by the other

skaters, helping them to their feet. 'What was that noise, just as we fell?' Marcus demanded, dusting ice powder off his coat. He looked around at the pond. 'It isn't breaking up, is it?'

Diana Price flew towards them from the far end of the little lake like a racer, her face white. 'A gunshot!' She came to a halt, her skates kicking up a shower of frozen fragments. 'I felt the bullet go past me, just as you went down. Someone is shooting from the woods.'

The men, without a word being exchanged, encircled the women, hurrying them off the ice. 'There!' Marcus, tearing off the bindings of his skates without looking, was scanning the woods. 'By that dead oak.'

'I see him.' Hal was already free of the encumbering blades and running hard for the carriage. Nell saw him pull a shotgun out from beneath the driver's box, slinging it over his shoulder on the run as Marcus joined him.

'Into the carriage, everyone.' Lord Narborough was snapping orders, shepherding the servants into their brake. 'Leave everything.'

Crammed into the carriage, they jostled together as the coachman whipped the horses into a skidding canter on the icy track. He pulled up as the carriage came out of the woods and Hal and Marcus jumped up, one on each step, clinging to the door frames on either side.

'Gone,' Marcus said through the open window. 'There were hoof prints, then he was into the deep wood. The ground's too hard and there is no snow in there. We lost him.'

Nell kept her eyes on Marcus as the carriage bounced and swayed its way back to the house. He looked grimly angry. She could imagine his frustration, chasing a ghost, his actions tied by the need to protect a houseful of women.

This campaign of persecution was moving beyond mere attempts to frighten and disturb. She had no idea whether that shot had missed on purpose or whether they had all been fortunate, but someone could have been killed.

As she went up the steps in the wake of Lady Narborough she realized, with a sort of calm fatalism, that she could keep her secret no longer.

'George,' Lady Narborough said as they stood in the drawing room, dripping onto the fine carpet. 'What is going on?'

Nell saw Marcus meet his father's eye and nod. Yes, the time had come. As his father began to explain, she touched Marcus's arm. 'I need to speak to you.'

'Now?'

'Yes,' she murmured, drawing him aside. 'Your father will tell the others what he feels they should know, will he not?'

'Very well.' He led her out of the drawing room, across the Great Hall to the small panelled room she remembered. 'What is it, Nell?' Marcus shut the door and leaned one shoulder against it. 'There is no need to be afraid; he cannot get us in here.'

'I am not afraid. Not of that.' She found she was standing almost to attention as though she were in the dock of a court. Her hands were trembling. Nell clasped them tightly, raised her chin. 'My real name is not Nell Latham. I was Lady Helena Wardale.'

He did not speak for a long moment, but he pushed away from the door and stood, quite still, staring at her across the six foot of space that separated them. Finally he said, 'Younger daughter of the Earl of Leybourne.'

'Yes.'

'You *knew* what that rope signified.' It was not a question.

'Yes.'

'You delivered it. You were in my father's room when someone broke into it to bring another rope—and yet you said nothing.' He sounded as coldly calm as a lawyer setting out the case for the prosecution, as though this meant nothing to him but an academic exercise in justice.

'Yes.'

'Is Salterton your lover?'

'No!'

'Your brother, then?'

'No. Nathan may be dead, for all I know.' *I will not cry*, she told herself fiercely, biting her lower lip in the hope the pain would steady her.

'You have every reason to hate my father, this family. You were the instrument of his heart attack, you shot me. You have lived under our roof for weeks. My mother and sisters treated you as a friend. And all the while we worried and speculated and you said nothing.'

'I never lied to you. Latham is the name I have used since I was a child. It is my name now.'

'And if we had known all along who you were—can't you see how important that could be?' His calm cracked suddenly in an explosion of movement that took him across the intervening space to stand before her. When she had first met him, she had thought him too big and too male to be close to. Now she fought the instinct to flinch away and he saw the fear in her eyes.

'I won't hit you, Nell. I'm not like your mysterious friend. I don't make war on women, even treacherous ones.'

'I am not a traitor!' she flared back at him. 'All I knew was that my mother brought me up to hate the name Carlow and now I have read my father's letters, her diary, I can see why. I did not know Lord Narborough's family name when I brought the parcel.

'Yes, I believe he betrayed my father, his friend, but now I have met your father I can see that he only acted out of conscience and he is suffering for it. He was wrong, so wrong, but he acted honestly and I forgive him.'

'That's magnanimous of you,' Marcus said, his eyes narrowed on her face. 'You can hardly take the moral high ground on this. Your father was a traitor and a murderer *and* an adulterer into the bargain.'

Nell slapped his face before she even knew she was going to do it. The blow jarred her wrist, the sound shocked her. He grabbed her wrists one-handed, the fragile bones shackled in one big fist. 'Let me go!' She kicked out and was jerked hard against his chest, then tried to bite as he took not the slightest notice of her boots cracking against his shins.

With his free hand he took her chin, pushing it up until she had to open her mouth and stop biting. 'You hell cat! Stop this, Nell. I don't want you to get hurt.'

'You are quite safe, I don't have my pistol,' she panted, twisting in his grip. But it was futile; he was too strong. Nell stopped struggling.

It took them both a minute to steady their breathing. Nell stood quiescent in Marcus's hold, wondering why all she could read in his eyes was grief. But that had to be wrong. After all, she had proved over and over that she did not understand him.

'If you had nothing to do with this, it is stretching co-incidence too far to think you were an accidental choice to deliver the rope,' he said at last, his voice flat. 'How do you explain that?'

'I cannot. Who hates both our families? It seems incredible, yet it is happening. But, Marcus, someone who is obsessed enough to be doing all this could have tracked me down, given time and money, if they knew the name we took after my father's death. I give you my word, I do not know why they are attacking your family. But I knew, once I discovered who you were and read Papa's letters, that you would never believe me. You wanted me to tell you my secrets, but I knew how it would be—listen to yourself.'

'Then why tell me now?' he demanded.

'Someone could have been killed on the lake today. I had to give you my pieces of the puzzle.'

'I wish I could believe that you know nothing.' There was sincerity in the deep voice, but she was hurting too much to credit it.

'Do you?' Nell jerked her hands again and this time he let his own drop away. 'Why should you care? All you want from me is to have me in your bed, under you—and at that just once, a notch on your bedpost.'

'No,' he said. 'No. Damn it, Nell, I love you.' And before she could stammer out a reply, Marcus dragged her into his arms, crushed his mouth down over hers and kissed her.

Chapter Sixteen

He loves me? Nell closed her lips against the demand of Marcus's mouth and twisted her head away, trying to look into his face. She had dreamed of him saying those words to her and now that he had, she was frightened, confused and angry. *He cannot mean it, so why is he saying it?*

'No!' She pushed at his chest and he let her go, his face as dark as it had been when he threw bitter accusations at her. 'You want me, you have brought me into the family home and now you have to convince yourself your motives were something other than desire,' she said, holding up one hand to ward him off.

'It has to be love to excuse your misjudgement, doesn't it? How strange you never thought to mention it before—in the folly, for example.' She could not afford, not for a moment, the weakness of believing him. Her heart would break.

'I didn't realize then, I only knew that I couldn't let you go, however much I mistrusted you.' He made no move to touch her again. 'I realized what it was when I saw you with Hal.'

'Two cock pheasants strutting their plumes in front of the female?' she jibed. 'That isn't love, Marcus. That is simple male possessiveness.'

'Damn it, do you think I want to fall in love with a milliner?' He took an angry pace away and stared at an old portrait hanging against the linen fold panelling as though he could not bear to look at her. 'Or the daughter of an attaindered earl, for that matter? I am a Carlow, damn it.'

'And I am a Wardale, and proud of it,' she flung back. 'You think I could love you, you arrogant, suspicious autocrat? You cannot even tell me you love me and look happy about it. Do you know what I want? What I *need?*' Marcus turned slowly to look at her and shook his head. 'I need love and laughter and tenderness and humour and trust. I do not need breeding or money or status. I do not need a man who has experience in bed, I just want one who cares about me.'

Nell was out of the door before he could stop her. She slammed it back in his face, spun round and ran straight into Lord Narborough, Hal and Diana Price.

There was no disguising the tears on her cheeks, no hiding the fact that her hair was half down and her face, she could feel, was as white as a sheet. The earl caught her as she stumbled to a halt and stared down into her face.

'*Catherine?*'

'Catherine Wardale was my mother,' Nell said, seeing the colour drain out of his face until it was waxy.

'*What?*' The sharp exclamation was Miss Price's, even as she hurried to take Lord Narborough's arm.

'Father.' Hal caught him as he swayed, supporting him to the nearest chair. Nell dragged at the bell pull then ran to help them. Behind her the door opened. 'What's happened? What have you done?'

'Resembled my mother,' Nell said bitterly, not looking at Marcus. 'Not, I believe, a crime. Give Lord Narborough some air. I have rung for help—he needs his drops.'

'I am all right.' George Carlow shrugged off Hal's arm and pulled himself upright in the big carved chair as the butler came in. 'My drops, Watson, in the study. And a tea tray for there and for the drawing room. Come.' He looked at the four clustered round his chair. 'The study and some explanations, I think.'

Marcus went to Nell's side as they settled around the hearth in the study. She turned her head away and stared into the fire, giving him her shoulder. He could hardly blame her. How could a declaration of love go so hideously wrong? How could he have told her *then,* on the heels of berating her about her secrets?

'Little Helena.' His father was shaking his head as he looked at her. 'You must have been four when I last saw you. The resemblance has been haunting me and then I saw it just now. It was Catherine's face when they took Will away.'

'She is dead now,' Nell said without turning. 'A congestion of the lungs four years ago. It seems a broken heart can take a long time to kill.'

'Oh, my dear. And Nathan and Rosalind?'

'Rosalind took a post as a companion to a lady— under a false name. We were never to write, or contact her, in case of discovery. She would always write to us.'

'And your brother?' demanded Miss Price.

'Nathan vanished, suddenly, as though he had been snatched out of thin air.' Nell's voice was flat, as if she were recounting some dull and trivial piece of gossip. Knowing her now, sensing every nuance in her voice, Marcus could read her pain and the effort such control was costing her. He wanted to hold her, make this all go away.

'There was no money, our landlord was…violent, and Mama was sick. I had to move us away. We lost contact with both of them. I tell myself Nathan is not dead and that Rosalind is safe.' Her composure cracked, and with it her voice. 'I cannot always believe it.'

Marcus put his hand on her arm and she froze. After a moment, he lifted it away and heard her sigh. 'Helena—'

'Nell,' she murmured.

'Nell says she did not know that the Earl of Narborough, to whom she was to deliver a parcel with unknown contents, was George Carlow,' he said to the others, determined to present the facts fairly in the midst of the emotion threatening to swap them all. 'All she knew about the scandal was that her mother hated the name Carlow.'

'Nell?' Hal asked.

'Mama never spoke of what had happened to Papa. I knew virtually nothing until I read her letters and diaries over the past two weeks. And I could not bring myself to do that until I came here and realized that I had to find out.'

Watson came in with the tea tray and placed it before Diana, but she got to her feet. 'If you will excuse me, I must help Lady Narborough. I will not say anything of this, of course.' The door clicked shut behind her, leaving the four of them in silence.

Without a word, Nell shifted in her seat so she could reach the tray. She passed the drops and a glass of water to Marcus's father, then began to pour tea with a steady hand as though this were a normal social tea party. Marcus watched, unable to believe she could appear so unaffected. Then, as she turned to hand him his cup, he saw her eyes, filled with a miserable anger and realized that she was holding on to her control with fierce determination.

'I give you my word I did not know who you were,' she said to Lord Narborough, the quiver of passion under the calm words more convincing than any display of extravagant emotion would have been. 'Once I knew, then I was afraid, both for you and for myself. I do not understand who is doing this, or why. But I knew that Marcus would not believe me if I told him that.'

That hurt, an unexpected thrust of pain in his chest, made worse because it was true—he had not let himself trust her.

'Perhaps his loyalties were divided,' his father said, surprising him. He looked sharply at the older man. There was a faint smile on his lips. *He knows. He knows I love her.*

'No,' Nell said. She stared into her cooling tea. 'Marcus knows where his loyalties lie. And that is right, after all. It would be wrong to place…desires before the safety of one's family, one's sense of honour.' She lifted her head and looked directly at Marcus, the tear tracks plain on her cheeks. He wanted to hold her, wipe them away, kiss away the memory of them. 'It is how *I* feel, after all.'

'Nell,' the earl said gently, 'it is possible, you know, that the people one loves may yet do things that are very wrong. Your father was involved with someone.'

'Amanda Hebden, Lady Framlingham, I know.' She nodded. 'It is in the letters. And Lord Framlingham was not treating her well. But why would they not duel? Why murder?'

'Because Kit Hebden was about to unmask your father as the spy—that is the only reason, the only possible way to explain it. Believe me, Nell, I tried to find another explanation, and in all these years I have failed.'

'I believe you tried,' she said, her voice flat. 'And I am sorry I did not tell you before who I was. That man, whoever he is, might have shot someone this morning.'

'But knowing who you are takes us no further forward,' Hal interjected.

'It does,' Marcus said, thinking aloud. 'It tells us that this is not some campaign against the Carlows alone. This is someone with a connection to that affair who, for some reason, is attacking both the child of the man who was executed and the family of the only survivor of the three friends.'

'You are right.' The earl sat up, alert. 'Hebden's family has all gone except his daughter—she lives with her mother's family. So, who does that leave?'

'The real traitor? The man who murdered Lord Framlingham?' Nell asked, defiance in her voice.

'Oh, my dear.' The earl shook his head. 'For your sake, I wish that were true.'

'I want to go home,' Nell said flatly. 'I should not be here.'

'But the danger,' the earl protested.

'You mean the man who shot Marcus who might know where I live? That man never existed. I shot him.'

'I know,' the earl confessed, and Marcus almost smiled at the gasp of surprise from Nell.

'It was an accident,' Marcus said, clarifying it for Hal. 'I was following her, frightened her. And then I used that as a weapon to make her come here.'

'So—' the earl frowned '—Nell is stalked by our mysterious enemy, who must have exerted some time and trouble to trace her. She is sent with the silken rope, thus making her appear to be part of the conspiracy, then hounded by you and blackmailed into coming here. Do I have that correctly?'

'Yes, sir.' Marcus held the grey eyes. 'I thought her in danger—and a danger to us. And you will both have to forgive me, but I put our family's safety first.'

'I forgive you,' his father said dryly. 'You will have to discuss absolution with Nell.'

'We have nothing to discuss.' She looked at him. 'Nothing at all. I quite understand Marcus's feelings.' The look she directed at him said quite plainly that she placed no value on his declaration of love. He could hardly blame her. 'Please, let me go home now.'

What would she do now, if he went down on one knee and proposed in front of his father and Hal? Would she believe him then? For a crazy moment Marcus considered it. But she was distressed and angry, and if she said 'no' now, he sensed it would be irrevocable.

'I offered to buy a business in a good area, something Nell could run. It would be a partnership,' he said instead, and felt her relax a trifle. Yes, she had been afraid he would make some kind of declaration.

'Would you like that?' his father asked her. 'I wanted to help your mother, but she vanished before I could try. It has always been a grief to me.'

'Thank you.' From somewhere, Nell found enough polite enthusiasm to reply. 'That would be wonderful.' And it would be. Comfort, respectability, control of her own destiny. A few weeks ago, she could have hoped for nothing better. It was the answer to her prayers.

And beside her sat the answer to her dreams, and he had said he loved her. He had said it still half-suspecting her. He had said it as though it had been dragged out of him, as though he was ashamed of himself for loving the child of a traitor and a murderer, a woman fallen so far below her true station in life. *Do you think I want to fall in love with a milliner?* he had demanded. Which meant both that it could well be true and that it was an impossible basis for a relationship.

Marcus could not marry her, even if he really did love her. The scandal would be terrible. She had no understanding of polite Society, of how the mills of gossip worked, but she could imagine the impact such a match would make.

She could never ask it of him, even if this fog of mystery and danger was no longer hanging over them. And she would not be his mistress, even though she ached for him, because to live every moment waiting for him to marry another, as he must, would be hell, pure and simple.

The men were talking, their voices a distant hum in her head. There was so much to come to terms with, so much to try to understand since that shot had rung out and shattered the fragile peace.

'Nell?'

She looked up and saw them all watching her. 'I am sorry. I was not attending.'

'Understandable,' Marcus said. 'We were agreeing that you cannot go back to London alone, not with this mystery still unsolved. Whoever is behind this does not bear you any goodwill, that is plain. At the very least, they do not care what happens to you.

'Come back with us when we return and we will decide on what kind of shop you want, set it up, employ staff, find you a maid. That will all take some time.'

'And if we never find who is behind all this?'

'Then your establishment will include a bodyguard,' Marcus said flatly. 'For as long as necessary.'

I don't want a bodyguard, I want you, she thought, folding her hands tightly together to stop herself touching him, clinging to his hand. 'What will you tell the others? Lady Narborough may not want me here when she knows who I am.'

'She played with you as a baby, she would not spurn you now,' the earl said, smiling at her. 'I will tell her, but not the girls. Just now I told them that someone from the past, when I was working for the government, has returned with a grudge against me. There is no need to rake up more of that old tragedy than we need. It is suf-ficient to put them on their guard.'

'I see,' Nell murmured. 'Thank you.' Their voices seemed to come from a long way away. She felt numb, cold, tired and knew that beneath the numbness lay deep sadness, like water rushing beneath thick ice. They got up, leaving her. She was aware of the movement, of the door opening and closing, but she stayed in her chair, watching the leaping flames in the gate.

'Nell?'

'Oh!' She spun round, heart in her mouth. 'I thought you had all gone.'

'No.' Marcus smiled a little and came to lean an elbow on the mantle, looking down at her. *At least he isn't frowning*, she thought vaguely, wondering why he was still there. 'I do not think that telling a lady that you love her in the midst of a blazing row is very...sensible.'

'No,' she agreed. 'It is not. Do you believe me now? Do you trust me?'

'Yes. I believe you and I trust you. And, Nell, I do love you.' She had never seen him so serious without that endearing frown. Almost, she could let herself believe him.

'And whatever you do about that—except ignore it— will cause a scandal,' she observed dispassionately, fighting the need to throw herself into his arms. 'You cannot marry me. That would be shocking, especially with two sisters on the Marriage Mart. And if you made me your mistress and anyone found out who I was, then that would be almost as bad. Your loyalty might be called into question—to the Crown and to your father.'

'Anyone questioning my loyalty will find themselves looking down the barrel of a pistol at dawn.' His right hand flexed as he said it, and Nell shivered.

'Wonderful, you will be killed because of me,' she said.

'I am an excellent shot,' he countered. 'What I aim at, I hit.'

'Oh well, that is all right then,' she retorted. 'Do I stay

behind to explain to your family why you have had to flee abroad having killed your man?'

'Has anyone told you how infuriating you can be?' Marcus demanded, coming upright in a sudden burst of temper.

'Yes, *you,*' Nell said, trying not to dwell on how magnificent he looked, towering over her, dark eyes blazing. 'And I am not being infuriating now, merely right. You, on the other hand, are unused to anyone gainsaying you and are not, I have to point out, taking it very well.'

'Then tell me how you feel, Nell.' Marcus dropped to one knee with a suddenness that startled her. 'Tell me how you feel about me. About us.' He caught her hands in his. In the strong grip, she could feel a pulse thudding. Hers or his, she could not tell.

I love you, I love you... She only had to say it and all her good resolutions would be for nothing. He would not let her go and the outcome—whatever it was— could not be happy. Not for them, not for his family.

'I desire you,' she said, making herself meet his eyes. 'I find, when you touch me, that morals and proper behaviour seem to count as nothing. You kiss me and I go up in flames—and that is wrong and cannot last. And you make me weak.' She laughed—shakily, it was true—but her amusement brought a flash of answering humour into his eyes.

'Good,' Marcus said, his voice husky, leaning in to her.

'Not weak like that.' Nell swayed back, away from his wicked, tempting mouth. 'I am an independent woman. I must stand by myself, not come to lean on a man. You are too big,' she complained, feeling suddenly tired and querulous. 'I just want to sit back and let you fight my battles, and that will not do.'

'Nell, you have agreed to let us help you,' Marcus began. He was stroking the soft skin on the inside of her wrist. Nell closed her eyes for a moment, imagining his mouth there.

'And I am very grateful and fully intend it to be a business relationship,' she said with as much firmness as she could manage. 'I cannot be a dependent.'

'I am not asking you to be a dependent, Nell, I am asking you to—'

'No! No,' she repeated, more gently. 'Do not say anything that we will surely regret as soon as it is said. I will stay with your family until I can set up my business, and I am so grateful for that, I cannot properly express it.'

Marcus sat back on his heels and shook his head at her, frowning. 'And then, every Quarter Day,' she persisted, 'I will meet with your man of business and we will discuss profit and loss. I hope to be able to return you a respectable sum for your investment. And when your friends lament the amount their mistresses cost them in millinery and haberdashery, you will tell them of an elegant establishment you know where, if not exactly dagger cheap, one may find a stylish bonnet at a keen price.'

'And you will be content?'

'Of course. I will be too busy for foolish daydreams about…passion. And so will you be.'

'I see.' Marcus got to his feet. 'How very practical you are, Nell. You pour a positive bucketful of cold water over heated dreams.'

'That is how it has to be.' Nell managed a smile. 'I cannot afford dreams.'

'I would give them to you if I could,' Marcus said, and for a moment the tenderness in his eyes was almost more than she could bear.

'I know,' she managed, the smile still intact.

He stooped and she did not try and avoid his mouth, or the gentle touch of his hand as he cradled the back of her head and held her for his kiss. It would be the last time, the last dream.

She would remember every detail, she told herself as his mouth moved over hers with possessive tenderness. The taste of him, the texture of his skin as she laid her palm against his cheek, the scent of him, the leashed power under her other hand where the muscles of his arm clenched with the effort he was making to hold back, the sweep of his eyelashes as she opened her own eyes to look into his face.

And then those thick dark lashes lifted and he broke the kiss.

'Wise Nell,' he murmured. And was gone.

Chapter Seventeen

For that day, and the next, a strange calm lay over Stanegate Court. Hal and Marcus rode out, deployed the keepers and the grounds staff on patrols and searches, and found nothing.

The Gypsies had moved, the keepers told him, only ashes and hoof marks to show where they had been. 'And wagon wheels,' Randall the head keeper reported. 'Not like their usual tilt carts, something bigger.' He shrugged. 'Gone now anyway, my lord.'

Marcus doubted it. Moved, certainly, but the Romany tribe was still around somewhere. 'A pity,' he said. 'They have sharp eyes; they might have seen someone.'

He was restless, urgent for action, frustrated by the dark man's ability to melt like a ghost into the woods. And Nell's presence in the house did not help. He wanted her more with each passing day and she, it seemed, might want his lovemaking, but not his love.

'Are you going to marry Nell?' Hal asked as they sat on their horses on Beacon Hill, scanning the hillsides for some betraying trickle of smoke.

'No.'

'Ah, the scandal,' his brother said. 'No doubt you are wise. You are the heir, after all.'

'I have not put it to the touch; she will not allow me to ask.'

Hal's gasp of astonishment would have been flattering if it was not followed by a snort of laughter. 'Sensible woman.'

'Indeed?'

'Don't poker up with me, Marc. She wants to be independent.'

'She was independent and on the edge of poverty. I fail to see the virtue of independence for a woman under those circumstances.'

'And now she will be independent and comfortable. Secure. And she does not have to listen to scandalmongers dragging her father's sins out to be picked over, or have you issuing challenges left right and centre whenever you think she's been slighted.' Hal turned up the collar of his caped coat against the wind. 'And she can take a lover if she wishes, when she is ready to.'

Corinth tossed his head as the bit jabbed his mouth. Marcus forced his hand to relax. 'I'll not bother with the challenge if you touch on that subject again,' he said flatly. 'I'll just knock your teeth out.'

'You can try,' Hal said, equally calmly. 'Just remember, I've been fighting for my life recently, not in Gentleman Jackson's boxing salon.'

'Believe me,' Marcus said, looking out over the bleak expanse of the snow-covered Vale of Aylesbury, 'I would kill for Nell. But not you, little brother.' He set his spurs to the big grey's sides and galloped off along the ridge, hearing the thunder of Hal's hunter behind him, trying to forget everything in the sting of the wind and the feel of the surging muscles under him.

Mid-morning on the second day, Nell found herself alone in the small drawing room with Diana Price. The companion was reading what looked very like a book of sermons, but put it to one side as Nell came in and sat on the other side of the fireplace. She was, Nell thought, almost supernaturally calm, collected and *proper*. Her energetic skating had been the nearest Nell had seen to her letting go and enjoying herself. It was a relief, somehow, to be curious about someone else and not be constantly staring inwards at her own preoccupations.

'Do you mind me asking,' she said, stretching out a hand to the fire, 'but how did you come to be a lady's companion? My sister was one—she may still be, for all I know—and I was thinking about her, wondering what the life is like.' Diana looked up sharply, and Nell hastened to add, 'I do not want you to say anything about your employers, naturally.'

'One's employers make all the difference,' Diana said dryly. 'With considerate, intelligent people such as the Carlows, the position is very congenial. With a stupid or tyrannical employer, it can be hell, I believe.' She bit her lip, as though undecided whether to say more; then, almost as if it were dragged out of her, she added, 'My father lost everything gambling. In one night he was, effectively, ruined by—' She broke off, staring into the flames.

'Please, say no more. It must be most distressing,' Nell said, feeling quite dreadful that her probing had touched such a raw nerve.

Diana shook her head as though trying to clear it, looked at Nell and seemed to reach a decision. 'He was ruined by a card sharp. A man so young, so innocent looking, my father had no idea of his danger. By morning he had lost everything—our house, his money…everything. Papa never recovered, his health was shattered. I thank God that Mama did not live to see it. He moved North and took what work he could. Somehow he managed to keep out of debtors' prison, but I had no option but to seek employment.'

'I am so sorry,' Nell said warmly. 'And I am so glad you found a happy position here.'

'We have one thing in common,' Diana said, her eyes fixed on Nell's face as though she was searching it. 'We have both been ruined by a feckless young man. You would not have been in the position you were, had your brother not deserted you.'

'Oh, no! Nathan did not desert us, I am sure of that.' Distressed, Nell got to her feet and began to pace. 'I do not know what happened to him—and I fear the worst—yet surely I would know if my own brother had died? He was getting into bad company, that I do know. Suddenly there was money—not regularly, but more than I could account for by him taking odd jobs of work. He would not tell us where it was coming from, yet when I challenged him he swore he was not stealing.'

Diana Price made a sound so like a snort of disbelief that Nell turned in surprise. The other woman was on her feet, gathering up her book and handkerchief. She gave Nell a thin smile. 'I like you, Miss…Wardale. Despite everything.'

The door closed behind her, leaving Nell puzzled and uneasy in the quiet room.

Nell watched Marcus, as she had throughout dinner. He was brooding, but not, she sensed, about her. As Lady Narborough rose after dinner, Marcus came to himself with a start, almost late on his feet as the women got up.

'Nell, Hal, Father—there is something I would like to discuss. Mama, can you spare Nell for half an hour?'

'If she does not object to your port,' his mother said with a smile.

'Thank you, Watson, that will be all.' The earl waited for the room to clear. 'Would you care for a glass of ratafia, my dear?'

'Might I try port?' Nell asked. 'I never have.' The room seemed suddenly overwhelmingly masculine with the silver and porcelain cleared, the white linen removed, just the glasses and the decanters and a bowl of nuts on the polished board.

'I have been trying to remember back,' Marcus said, cracking nuts in his fingers as his father poured the deep ruby liquid into her glass. 'I was nine years old, young enough for none of it to make much sense, old enough to be able to escape being whisked off to the nursery every time an adult conversation took place. I seem to recall a lot of time spent behind the curtains in the window seat.'

'I have told you all that occurred,' the earl said with a frown. 'What you recall as a child cannot add to that.'

'But this is something that has never been mentioned since. Not to me, at least. It sounds melodramatic, but was there something about a curse? I have this vague memory of a Gypsy's curse.'

Lord Narborough set down his wine glass with a snap. '*That* nonsense.'

'These woods are a haunt of Gypsies, yet they have suddenly vanished. Nell's dark man might be a Romany.' Nell looked from one man to the other. Hal appeared sceptical, the earl uncomfortable. Marcus caught her eye and held it, a silent conversation she could not, dare not, try to understand.

'There was something,' Lord Narborough said at length. 'Kit Hebden—Lord Framlingham—took a Gypsy woman as a lover, had a son by him. Amanda, his own wife, seemed barren, so he brought the baby home, forced her to rear it.'

'Tactless,' Hal remarked.

'Cruel,' Marcus countered. 'As good as saying he was potent and any lack of children was his wife's fault.'

'Poor little boy,' Nell said, moved. 'Just a pawn in his father's games.'

'Not at first. Lady Framlingham came to love the child, reared it as her own. And, as so often happens, once there was a baby in the house, she too began to increase. She had a daughter and a son and was expecting again when her husband was murdered. She lost that baby, and her own son shortly afterwards.'

'The love child must have been a comfort,' Nell said hopefully, remembering that Amanda Hebden, Lady Framlingham, had been her own father's mistress. What a hideous muddle.

'Not for long. After the murder, Amanda was in no fit state to dress herself, let alone look after children. Her family descended, took over—and sent the boy away.'

'Back to his Gypsy mother?'

'No, off to some foundling hospital up in the North. Yorkshire Moors, I think.'

'But how terrible,' Nell murmured.

'They were scandalised that Hebden had imposed the child on her and refused to take her own protests that she loved him into account. Then his true mother came. Her lover was dead, her child gone. She cursed us all— the Hebdens for betraying her, the Wardales for her lover's death, me for failing to stop it, for being part of, as she saw it, the conspiracy.' The earl sipped his port. 'Beautiful creature. Wild, exotic—and completely unhinged with grief.'

'What happened to her?' Nell asked.

'She killed herself, sealing the curse with her own blood. It made it more potent, so the Romany believe.'

'That is why Mama was wary of Gypsies,' Nell realized. 'She would cross the street rather than pass a harmless peg seller, or an old dame with heather to sell.'

'But the woman is dead, and Gypsies have been in these woods for ever, without doing us any harm,' Hal protested.

'But the child?' Marcus said. 'What about the child?'

'Veryan may know.' Lord Narborough filled his glass and pushed the decanter towards his elder son. 'I had a letter this morning—took two days; the mail is in a dreadful state with this weather. He is coming over tomorrow, bringing the papers from the old case.' Nell was not aware of moving or speaking, but he glanced sharply at her. 'I am sorry, my dear. This must all be very painful.'

'I just want to know the truth and for this persecution to stop,' she said, swallowing the last of the port in her glass. It sent a warm, rich glow through her, attacking the chill of what they were talking about. 'It seems tragedy heaps upon tragedy—that poor woman, her child.' She shivered, trying to imagine the depths of despair of Hebden's Gypsy lover.

'We will know more tomorrow,' Marcus said. 'Let us rejoin the others and speak of happier matters.'

But Marcus's optimism proved false. Lord Keddinton, stamping snow from his boots and moving gratefully to the heat of the fire in the study, could offer little except to slam the door on their latest theory.

'You think the Gypsy brat is behind this?' He curled his elegant fingers round the heat of a glass of punch and shook his head. 'Dead. I made it my business to find out what happened to him. They sent him to some place up in Yorkshire. A year later, there was a fire, the child perished in that. Imogen Hebden is the only offspring of Framlingham's still alive. A charming young woman, friend of my daughters. She isn't behind this, you may be sure of that.

'The Rom might be acting as agents for whoever it is, of course,' he added with a shrug.

'And the files, sir?' Hal asked.

'Here you are.' He handed a slim folder to the earl. 'I've looked at it and young Gregson hunted down every scrap he could find—getting quite obsessed with the case, poor devil.'

'What's wrong?' Marcus caught the fleeting expression of pain that crossed Veryan's face.

'Dead. Hit by a vehicle it seems, on his way home a week ago.'

'I am sorry to hear that.' The earl looked up from the file. 'A promising young man, I thought.'

'He was. I had high hopes of him.'

'Just coincidence that he was reviewing this case?' Marcus asked. Cold fingers were trailing up his spine. He told himself he was being fanciful, but the news made him uneasy.

'So I had believed,' Veryan said slowly. 'Now, I wonder.' He left them soon afterwards. Marcus returned from the hall, having waved him off on his cold journey home, to find his brother and father in fruitless speculation.

Marcus pulled the door to and began to pace. 'Never mind who he is or why he is doing this,' he said after a while. 'We need to get our hands on him.'

'Set a trap, you mean?'

At the sound of the earl's voice, Nell stopped in her tracks as she passed the study door. It was just ajar. With a guilty glance around, she tiptoed closer and gave it a slight push so the gap widened to an inch. She should not be eavesdropping, but if Marcus was planning something dangerous, she wanted to know.

'Yes.' Marcus sounded as though he were thinking aloud. 'We need to get him inside. There's too much space out there; he will always have the advantage.'

'We'll need to pull the patrols back,' Hal said. 'Concentrate them on, say, the stable block as though we were expecting an attack that way. It's an easier target, all that inflammable material, it would be logical if we thought it was a threat.'

'I bow to your military tactical experience,' Marcus

said sardonically. 'Then we patrol inside, taking care not to be seen?'

'It's a big house,' the earl observed. 'Rambling, several wings.'

'We would need to direct him somehow,' Marcus mused. 'But he's no fool; he'll suspect an open window.'

'I don't like it,' Lord Narborough said finally. 'Not with the women here.'

'One of you could take them up to town?' Hal suggested.

'We need the three of us here. No, Father is right, it is too risky.'

Nell moved softly away. With the men so protective of the women, the dark man had them just where he wanted them. Someone needed to carry the fight to him, confront him, discover whether there was some purpose behind this persecution or simply the vicious spite of a madman.

She had brought the first rope, her father was the man accused of treason and murder. She was at the heart of this, so she must do something. He would be watching; she was certain of that. Nell began to hurry. Down at the end of this corridor was the gun room and the men were occupied, if her luck held, until luncheon.

As she hoped, one of the baize-lined drawers held a number of handguns. Nell cautiously lifted the smallest out, not troubling to search for bullets. She had no idea how to load the thing and the thought of shooting anyone again—even the sinister Mr Salterton—turned her stomach. But he was not to know that.

With the weapon held under her heavy cloak, Nell walked boldly out of the front door, then took the path that led to the edge of the woods. It was only a few hundred yards to the paling fence that acted as a barrier to the deer. Beyond it the woods were deep and seemingly endless, the grey trunks of the beeches rising straight, their roots tucked into a thick quilt of golden leaves.

Nell began to stroll along the boundary path, trying to look like a woman taking a walk, interested only in the vivid flash of a jay overhead, peering into the woods in the hope of seeing a deer.

After fifteen minutes of toe-numbing dawdling through the snow, Nell was convinced she was alone. A dog-fox trotted out of cover, saw her, froze, then slid back into the brambles. Behind her was the flutter of wings as the pigeons she had disturbed returned to their roosts. She was the only human to alarm the wildlife.

With a sigh, she turned her back on the woods and leaned against the fence.

'Looking for me, Helena?' a soft, lilting voice said, just behind her.

Nell closed her eyes and sent up a silent prayer that she had some support; without the fence, she would have slid to the ground in shock.

'Yes, Mr Salterton,' she said, turning slowly to give herself time to compose her face.

And then it hit her: he had called her *Helena*. Not Nell, not Miss Latham, but Helena. *He knows who I am.*

The lithe figure stood a few feet back from the fence, poised like the fox between cover and the open, and something in his alertness, the fluid lines of his body, reminded her of the animal.

He wore a loose coat with a blue shirt under it, a black-and-white spotted kerchief tied around his neck, breeches and boots. Good boots, she noticed.

But his collar was turned up and the brim of his slouch hat down, and all she could see of his face was dark eyes in the shadow and the curve of a sensuous, mocking smile.

'A little rash of you, venturing out here alone,' he remarked. Nell stared at him, intent on gathering every detail. Black hair, olive skin, the flash of gold from one ear lobe, ungloved hands with long fingers.

'I think not,' she said, producing the pistol and pointing it at him.

'You can use that?' He seemed amused, the flexible, musical voice sending an answering quiver through her, as though in response to a plucked string.

'Of course. Lord Narborough insists all the ladies carry a pistol and we have been shown how to use them,' she lied. 'Why are you here? Why are you persecuting us?'

'Persecuting?' He was smiling, but his voice was suddenly colder than the air around her. 'What do you know of persecution?'

'A good deal,' Nell retorted tartly. 'Well? Have you a reason, or are you merely insane?'

'Oh, yes, murderer's daughter, I have a reason. I might even tell you about it. But not here, not with their lordships and that rake in uniform so close. You do not want them hurt, do you?'

'No. No, I do not want anyone hurt. Where? When?'

'You will know when. Come to the folly where your lover took you.'

Nell felt her face flame. 'How do you know about that?'

'I go where I like, I see what I like.' There was a flash of white teeth as he smiled. 'You have more passion than he deserves.'

'You…Peeping Tom!' Nell tried to recall how clear the glass had been in the window, feeling the blush flood from her toes to her hairline.

The dark man reached out and twitched the pistol from her lax grasp before she could react. 'I do not need to watch others in order to get my pleasure,' he observed calmly, checking the weapon and handing it back. 'Is your lord's weapon equally lacking in shot?'

Nell snatched it before their fingers could touch, wondering whether the snow was actually melting around her feet. 'I will be at the folly.'

'Of course you will,' he said, with a flash of those very white teeth. '*Kay zhala i suv shay zhala wi o thav.*'

'What does that mean?' Nell demanded. And what language had it been? But he had vanished back into the shadows, leaving only his footprints on the edge of the wood to show he had been there.

She walked back to the house, shivering a little with reaction and, she had to admit to herself, a little from the impact of Salterton's personality at close quarters.

He was dangerous to life and limb, she knew that. He was also dangerous to women; she was in love with Marcus, and yet something sensual and primal in that amused, lilting voice and the movement of the fit, sensuous body called to her.

By the time she had returned the pistol and was peeling off scarves and gloves in the hall, her cheeks were pink with confusion, cold and guilt and her pulse was hammering.

'Nell?'

'Ah!' She dropped her gloves and spun round. '*Marcus.* Oh, Marcus.' And then she was in his arms in the middle of the mercifully empty Great Hall, clinging as she might to a rescuer.

Oh, yes, this was who she wanted; this was the man she loved and desired. The dark man wove spells with his voice, but the magic vanished at the touch of reality. And Marcus was the reality and would be, she knew now, for the whole of her life.

'Nell? What is wrong?' His hand cupped her cheek, his eyes were dark as he looked down at her, and the warmth she saw in his expression was both sensual and gentle.

'I missed you,' she said without thinking, then realized it was the truth. 'I went out for a walk alone, and I missed you.'

'Why on earth did you go alone? It isn't safe out there, Nell.'

With a sickening swoop in her stomach, she realized she was going to have to lie to him. She had been angry because he had not trusted her and now, when he gave that trust, she was going to betray it. But if she told him, they would set a trap and someone was going to get hurt—and it could be Marcus.

'I needed to go out.' *Not a lie*, she consoled herself. 'I was in sight of the house all the time.' But her conscience could not be quiet.

'The man has a rifle.' Marcus pulled her tight to his body. 'I dare not risk losing you, Nell.'

But you will, and I will lose you. She clung without speaking, feeling the strength of him seep into her bones, sinking into the embrace. Safe and loved, all she had ever wanted, all she must give up.

'Marcus,' she said into the folds of his neckcloth, inhaling the scent of warm man and clean linen, a faint touch of cologne, a trace of wood smoke. 'Marcus.'

'Mmm?' he murmured into her hair.

'Will you come to my room tonight?'

'Why?'

She tipped her head back so she could look up at him and managed to smile at the expression on his face. Desire, affection, love, purely masculine bafflement.

'Because, just once, I want to know what it is to be loved by a man. I want to be with you. Just once.'

'Nell.' He set her back from him as though his touch would influence her. 'I should say *no*.' She held his gaze, her own steady until he smiled. 'But I cannot. Are you sure?'

'I have never been more sure of anything in my life,' she said, feeling the calm certainty flood through her. 'At midnight.'

Chapter Eighteen

As the clocks began to chime, Marcus stood outside Nell's chamber door, his palms flat on the panels, trying to think with his head, not his heart.

He loved her. She did not love him and perhaps what had happened to her had convinced her that she never could love. Her belief in her parents' happy marriage had been shaken by the discovery of her father's infidelity. Her first experience of sex had been ugly, brutal and forced. And he had thrown his declaration at her in anger, mired in mistrust.

She desired him; that was a start, surely? But if she returned his love, what then? He could not ask her to become his mistress. One day he must marry; it was his duty. Could he abandon Nell then? Of course not—nor could he betray the wife he must take. Bad enough that he would come to her without love to offer.

Marriage. Marcus took a long, shuddering breath. Marriage and scandal, just when his sisters were making their come-outs. Scandal thrown in his father's face every time anyone recalled who his daughter-in-law was. And Nell would fight every step of the way.

The door opened so suddenly that he had to throw up his hands and grip the door frame to stop himself falling. Nell stood on the other side, looking up at him quizzically.

'Are you going to stand there all night?' Her hair was down, her feet were bare and she was dressed only in a long, white nightgown, innocent of so much as a scrap of lace.

Marcus found his voice from wherever it had fled to. 'Possibly,' he said warily. 'How did you know I was here?'

'I could feel you thinking,' she said simply, as she turned and walked into the room. She stopped at the foot of the bed and faced him. 'Have you changed your mind?'

'I should,' he confessed, holding on to the wooden uprights as though to a lifeline. 'But I do not think I can.'

'Good,' she said and unfastened the three buttons at the neck of her nightgown.

'Nell!' Marcus almost threw himself through the doorway and shut the door behind him. 'We should talk about this first.'

'Why?' She stooped and took hold of the hem, lifting it as she straightened.

Marcus tore his eyes away from the sight of her slim ankles, the curve of her calves, fought the memory of how her skin had felt under his hands. 'Nell, I want you to marry me.'

She dropped the handful of cotton and gasped. 'Impossible.'

'Why is it?'

'Leaving aside any other considerations, the scandal makes it impossible. You must see that.'

'I see only a problem that I have not yet found the solution to,' he said, suddenly certain that this was right. Impossibly difficult, but right.

'You can make me love you?' she questioned, the smile on her lips denied by the sparkle of tears in her eyes.

'I can have a damn good try.' Marcus heeled off his evening pumps and began to take off his coat. 'And if I cannot do that, I will make you so dizzy with desire you will say *yes* anyway.'

Nell found she was smiling. There was something so recklessly confident about the way that Marcus spoke, something so far at odds with his usual thoughtful demeanour that she found herself believing him. It could be all right…somehow.

'Before, in the folly, you stopped. What will be different now?' she asked, watching in fascination as his waistcoat joined the coat on the floor and his neckcloth fell in a creased tangle on top.

'Before, I was not determined to marry you. I thought I could make you my mistress and then I realized I could not, in all conscience.'

She shook her head, afraid to believe it might be possible, that he really meant it.

Marcus stopped, his fingers halfway down the fastenings of his shirt. 'You don't believe me, do you? Well, let me be sensible, prosaic even. I will take care not to get you with child tonight and if, when, this is all over, you still will not have me, then you will have a respectable trade, a shop of your own. I will not be making a fallen woman out of you.' He broke off as she laughed. 'Now what have I said?'

'Nothing,' Nell said, stepping forward to help with the shirt buttons. 'Nothing at all. But you started frowning again because you were being sensible and prudent and thinking so much. I do adore your frown.' She reached up and rubbed the groove between his brows as he chuckled.

'I cannot imagine any other man feeling his heart leap for joy when his beloved said she adored his frown,' he mused, tossing aside his shirt. 'It is a start, I suppose. Nell, what are you doing?'

'Looking,' she said from behind him, laying her hands on his narrow waist just above the band of his thin silk evening breeches and smiling when he caught his breath. She ran her palms up his back, her thumbs dipping into the hollow of his spine, admiring the way his broad shoulders tapered to his waist, feeling the shifting muscle beneath the warm silk of his skin.

There was a light dressing over the bullet wound. Nell laid her hand over it carefully. 'Is that still painful?'

'Sore, if it chafes, but it is almost healed.' Marcus shifted but she dodged to keep behind him, laughing as he swore under his breath. Then he feinted with a swordsman's grace and caught her in his arms. 'Tease.'

'I am still looking,' Nell protested.

'You have seen my chest already.' He reached for her nightgown and Nell danced backwards.

'Take off your breeches.'

'Stockings first.' Marcus sat down on the bed and began to drag them off. 'There are few things more ludicrous than a naked man in stockings.' He stood up. 'Now your nightgown.'

Nell shook her head. 'I know what will happen the moment I take it off, and I want to look at you.'

There was colour on his high cheekbones. 'Why?' Marcus demanded, his fingers on the fastenings of the breeches. The thin knitted silk left very little to the imagination. He was finding this highly arousing, she could see, her pulse quickening.

'Because you are beautiful.' Nell bit her underlip and saw he was watching her mouth. She ran her tongue over the fullness just as his breeches dropped and he kicked them aside. 'Oh.'

Strongly muscled rider's legs, narrow hips, and between his thighs the dark tangle of hair and the weight of his erection, already proof of his arousal. Marcus appeared unembarrassed by her frank stare, standing with his fists on his hips, waiting for her.

'Hal is the beautiful one,' he said.

'He is too frivolous for beauty,' Nell pronounced, finding her feet could move after all. 'You have gravitas. Amongst other things.' She came to stand just in front of him.

'I don't feel very grave now,' Marcus said as he bent to catch the hem of her nightgown and pulled it up and over her head. There was a long silence while he looked at her.

Nell could feel herself blushing under the steady regard. Then she saw the physical effect it was having on him and her eyes widened.

'You are very lovely, Nell. Do you doubt how much I desire you?'

'Not at all,' she said frankly. 'I can well believe the evidence of my own eyes.'

'Are you frightened?' He reached for her, pulling her against his body so she could no longer see, only feel. She wriggled, loving the heat of him, loving the blatant pressure against her belly and the liquid, heavy feeling that was beginning, low down.

'No. Not at all,' she said honestly, managing to slide a hand between their bodies and curl her fingers around him. 'Impatient.'

'*Impatient* is my word, you wicked woman, and if you don't stop that I am going to be too impatient to do this occasion justice.'

Nell opened her fingers and let them sift through the coarse hair, teasing up over his flat belly. With a growl, Marcus swung her off her feet and laid her on the bed. 'There are definite advantages of doing this in the warm,' he remarked, looking down at her.

'On such a soft bed as well.' Nell wriggled into the downy covers, wondering what he was waiting for. 'Oh!' Marcus leaned over, grasped her hips and pulled her to the edge of the bed. 'What are you doing?'

He did not answer, but went to his knees, parting her thighs as he did so. Nell gasped as the dark head bent, rearing up on her elbows in alarm. 'No! You can't, that's indecent!'

He looked up, laughter crinkling the corners of his eyes. 'Tell me to stop, then.'

'Stop! Ah…no, don't stop.' Nell fell back, limp and gasping, unable to do anything but endure the delicious onslaught of tongue and lips as he worked his ruthless, wicked magic. Her body was burning, melting, twisting like metal in the forge and he was the alchemist, transforming her into liquid gold, into…*exploding starlight*.

Nell came to herself to find her head on the pillow and her body pressed into the bed by the hard weight of Marcus. Tiny aftershocks still quivered through her body and she arched up, instinct pressing her against him so the quivering became a new, demanding ache as he shifted, poised to take her.

His face was stark as he looked down, predatory even, but she saw the tenderness in his eyes and smiled, curving her arms up around his neck to pull his head lower for a kiss.

'Are you certain, Nell?' Marcus asked, and she felt the strain in his muscles as he held himself back, knew that if she shook her head he would leave her despite his need for her.

'Love me, Marc,' she whispered.

'Always.' His lips brushed hers then he lifted his head again, their eyes locked as he surged slowly into her. Deep in the back of her mind, she had feared her body would resist him, that the terror of the past would sweep back and take over, but those ghosts had gone, exorcised by his tenderness, and she opened to him, revelling in the knowledge that he was filling her, completing her. They were one and, whatever happened after this night, they always would be.

'Marc?' he queried, his voice almost harsh with the effort he was using to keep himself still now he was within her.

'Yes, *Marc*,' she murmured, a little dazed, lifting her head to kiss the corner of his mouth. 'My Marc.'

'Ah, Nell.' His eyes were almost black as they watched her, holding her as he began to move and she found the rhythm and went with him, drove him and was driven, gasped and clung and was lifted higher and higher until it all unravelled and she was crying out against his mouth and she felt him shudder and pull away, leaving her, and she was lost in the darkness with just his voice to cling to. 'Nell, oh my God, Nell…'

Nell woke to find herself wrapped around something hot and large. She blinked for a moment, confused, trying to wake up from the dream of ecstasy and Marc. *Marc*. She had let go, allowed herself to think of him like that, dreamt of him taking her, loving her.

The pillow against her cheek moved and she blinked again, trying to focus.

'That tickles. You have indecently long eyelashes, Nell.'

'Marc?'

'Who else did you expect, might I ask?' He sounded more amused than affronted, his voice rumbling in his chest under her ear.

'I thought you were a dream.' She pushed herself up on one elbow and looked down at him. The lamps were still burning and in their light she could see he was lying on his back, as relaxed as a big cat, his hair tousled on the pillow, one arm flung out above his head, the sheet clinging, like a sculptor's attempt at decency, to his hip bones.

'I am solid reality,' he protested, laughing at her.

'I recall parts being extremely solid,' she said naughtily, sliding her hand under the sheet, revelling in his gasp as her questing fingers found him, already more than half aroused.

'Nell, that is disgraceful behaviour. Can you not see I am quite exhausted?' Marc's attempt at severity was deeply unconvincing. Her fingers tightened at the root and began to pull upwards. 'Even if that is not!'

'Oh, dear. I am wide awake,' she said with a pout that made him gasp with laughter. 'Whatever is to be done?'

'Why, you will have to do all the work.' He shifted across the bed a little and lay back watching her from under heavily lidded eyes. 'Ride me, Nell.'

It seemed outrageous. She pulled away the sheet and straddled his narrow hips, tightening her thighs along his flanks then lowered herself, inch by inch as he groaned, his eyes closing. The feeling of power was overwhelming. Nell inched lower, her hands splayed on his chest, his nipples hard under her fingertips as she teased them out of pure instinct. Then she was lodged securely, the whole hard silken length of him tight within her.

There were muscles she did not know she had that she could tighten, she discovered by accident as she hung, breathless above him, tiny movements that wrenched a groan from his throat. 'Nell, this it *torture*.' His voice belied the word. This is *bliss,* it said.

But she could not resist any longer. Nell began to move, slow at first, then faster, driving them both up, up, while his fingers tightened on her hips and his body bucked under hers and then as the whirlwind caught her again he spun her over, so he was on top for two hard thrusts before he pulled free and her cry was lost in his shout of triumph and the world spun out of control again.

The next time she woke, she knew where she was and who she was with and every glorious thing that had happened since she had opened the door to find Marc there, his hands gripping the door frame. Those hands were drifting across her body now, tracing the swell of her belly, tickling up her ribs, playing with her nipples, which tightened into hard knots of exquisite—

'Marc! Are you in there?' The shout was accompanied by a thud on the door from a clenched fist.

Nell opened her eyes with a small shriek. Beside her, Marcus threw back the sheet and vaulted out of bed, stark naked, strode across the floor and unlocked the door.

'What the devil?'

Nell's second shriek was muffled as she slid down under the covers at the sight of Hal, snow melting on his coat as he shouldered into the room past Marcus. 'We've got him, as near as damn it. One of the keepers saw him at the back of the stables and he took off towards the Aylesbury Road—not the woods. His tracks are plain if we can get on them before they are filled with drifting snow again. Get dressed—you can't go chasing after him stark boll—'

There was a muffled sound that Nell had no trouble interpreting as Hal receiving a cuff round the ear from his older brother.

'Er, sorry, stark naked.'

'Well, get out of here and find the guns and I'll be right down,' Marcus growled. 'Can't you show a bit more discretion, damn it? This is a lady's bedchamber, not a cavalry barracks.'

'Quite, of course. Only you weren't in your room so I assumed…'

'Hal!'

'Sorry, Nell.' The door closed with a discreet click.

Nell peered cautiously over the top of the sheet. Marcus was pulling on his breeches and looking remarkably cheerful.

'You'll have to marry me now.'

'Nonsense. Hal is hardly likely to be gossiping about this.' Nell slid out of bed with a harassed glance at the clock—just past six—and began to pick up scattered clothing. She straightened to find Marcus looking at her with an expression that sent goosebumps scuttling up and down her spine. 'Stop that!' she protested, diving into the comfortingly chaste nightgown.

'Well, don't bend over dressed in nothing but your very delightful skin if you do not want me transfixed,' he said mildly, picking up the bundle of clothes. 'I can hardly believe our friend is so foolish as to be seen in broad daylight and then to leave plain tracks… He must be getting desperate.'

'Oh God.' Nell sat down with a bump on the edge of the bed. *You will know when*, the dark man had said. This was a decoy and now she must go, warm from sharing her bed with Marc, and deceive him while he and Hal hunted their enemy in the wrong direction.

'Marc—'

'Don't worry. We'll find him, deal with him. And then I'll come back and we will talk, Nell.' There was a wealth of meaning in his voice and a tenderness as he stroked her cheek in farewell that had her choking back tears. He would not feel like that when he discovered what she had done after all her protestations that he could trust her.

'Be careful,' she said, covering his hand with hers for a moment. 'Come back safe.'

But he *would* be safe, that was her one consolation. The danger would be at her side and it was up to her now to convince Salterton that this persecution must stop.

Whatever her father had, or had not done, she was the only Wardale able to deal with the consequences now. Nell scrambled into her warmest clothes, praying that Marcus would believe she was acting for the best. But even if he did not, she thought, it would make no difference. She could not marry him. Somehow that was not much comfort.

Chapter Nineteen

'Another rope.' Hal held it up, dark with moisture, a sordid threat dripping limply in his hand.

'He's damned arrogant, I'll say that for him.' Marcus swung up into the saddle, scanning the meadow behind the stable block. 'Look at this trail.'

'He wasn't expecting to be surprised and thought the snow would soon blow in to fill the tracks,' Hal countered, stuffing the rope into his saddlebag. 'And it will, if we don't get a move on.'

'This isn't a cavalry charge.' Marcus caught up with him, then held Corinth to a steady canter. 'Look out for an ambush.'

'Speaking of which.' Hal sent him a quizzical look. 'Are you walking into parson's mousetrap?'

'I hope so. If she'll have me.'

'You think Nell might refuse you? She'd be mad to.'

'You said she was sensible not to have me when we last spoke of this.'

'That was before I had seen you together, and before I knew you were lovers.'

Marcus tightened his lips and rode in silence for a while. It was against his instincts to discuss Nell with anyone and yet, this was his brother and for once Hal looked serious. 'She doesn't love me and she can see all too clearly the scandal there would be.'

'Doesn't love you?' Hal sounded incredulous. 'Then what are you doing in her bed? She's a good girl, I can tell that. If she's there, it's because she loves you.' He veered off to put his raking bay gelding at a fallen tree trunk.

'Do I need to tell you, of all people, that women experience sexual desire?' Marcus enquired as his brother drew level again. 'It doesn't occur to you that she may desire me? If she loves me, why not marry me?'

'*Because* she loves you, you clodpoll,' Hal snapped. 'Do you need it pointed out that some women have as strong a sense of honour as a man does? Nell fears the scandal. Not for herself, I imagine—she can always duck back into obscurity—but for you, for us.' When Marcus did not answer he added, 'The two of you are like April and May, even Father's noticed it, for Heaven's sake!'

'He's noticed what I feel, probably,' Marcus conceded, still reeling from the novelty of Hal lecturing him. The possibility that he might be right and that Nell really loved him was too important a thought to be explored now.

'He's noticed both of you, believe me.'

'And how is he going to feel about it? He seems to like her.'

'Pleased?' Hal ventured. 'Heal the rift and so forth?'

'I hope so. But it all depends on her saying *yes*, which I doubt. She's damn stubborn.' Marcus put Corinth to a five-barred gate, then wheeled round to scan the field they had just landed in. The hoof prints ran clear as a blaze diagonally across.

'Well, that makes two of you.'

Half an hour later Hal stood in his stirrups. 'Something happened over there, look.' They cantered up to the area of churned snow in the corner of the high, tangled hedge. Marcus dismounted and squatted down to look.

'Two horses, one tethered—waiting perhaps? They pushed through the hedge here.' He clambered through cursing the quickthorn as it pulled at his coat. 'Two sets of tracks here, heading in different directions. I can't tell if they've both got riders.'

'We'll have to split up. Wait there.' Marcus stood while Hal brought the horses through the gate lower down. His gut instinct was telling him something was wrong. They'd been drawn from the house—both of them—on what he was increasingly certain was a feint.

'I don't like this,' he said, remounting. 'I think we're being decoyed away. We've certainly been led round in a big loop. One lot of tracks are going up into the woods—on this hard ground and with no snow in there, they could double back towards the house.'

'You take that way, then,' Hal said. 'I'll take this— it looks as though it's heading for the turnpike.' He pulled the rifle from its holster and slung it over his shoulder. His eyes, slitted against the snow dazzle, swung from a contemplation of the ground ahead back to Marcus. 'Watch your back.'

'And you,' Marcus called after him as Hal spurred the gelding into a gallop.

As he guessed, Marcus lost the tracks a few yards

into the woods. Something was still nagging at him. *Nell.* Corinth, with his head turned towards home, needed no urging. They passed the point where the way branched off up to the folly, the big hunter eating up the hard ground as the track descended towards the park.

Marcus made for the front door. Then out of the corner of his eye, he saw a mark across the white expanse that covered the lawns. Corinth turned at a touch of the reins, leapt neatly over the skeletal rose border and cantered across to the tracks. Marcus jumped down and set his own booted foot against the clear, fresh footprints. They were unmistakeably a woman's prints, the marks where her cloak had brushed the snow clear on either side as they headed for the edge of the woods.

Nell. And she had more than an hour's start. Was she running from—or to—her dark man? Marcus stood, trying to listen to his instincts. All his life, it seemed, he had relied on his intellect to tell him what the right thing was. Now, with Nell, he no longer knew. Was he besotted and his judgement hopelessly awry, or should he listen to the still certainty within him that she was true?

Corinth bent his neck round to butt Marcus on the forearm and he looked up. 'You know,' he said to the big horse who pricked his ears and snorted, 'I had no idea love was going to be like this. I thought, fool that I am, that it was going to be easy.'

He swung up into the saddle and rode hard for the house.

'We can't find Nell,' his mother said as he strode into the Great Hall. She looked concerned, catching his mood.

'I know. She's been lured out. Watson! Get all the footmen in here and the keepers and the grooms. Open the gun cases. I am going to end this,' he said grimly as his father emerged from his study, 'and then I am going to marry Nell.'

Nell stood at the door of the folly and shivered. She was cold and frightened, she admitted to herself as she scanned the empty clearing. But she was also angry, burningly angry. This man, Salterton, was raking up her family's tragedy for his own reasons. And it was not just what had happened to the Wardales. A man had been murdered and Lord Narborough had lived under a cloud of rumour and guilt ever since.

Salterton had put her in the position where she must try Marcus's trust to the limit and that, somehow, felt worse than anything else. She put her hand on the cold iron ring of the handle and it opened onto the shadows of the room.

'Come in, Helena.' He was another shadow, standing by the cold hearth, his long, caped coat brushing his booted heels, his eyes glinting as they caught the light.

'You have been reading too many Gothic novels, Mr Salterton,' Nell said, pitching her voice down a little to keep it steady. 'Really, all this drama! Can you not just say plainly why you are doing this?'

'What, and have you run screaming out of the door?' he asked, amused. 'Empty your pockets, if you please.'

Nell pulled out the linings. 'One pocket handkerchief. I have no pistol, you have my word on that.'

'Then we will be on our way. Turn around, Helena.'

She thought of correcting him, telling him her name was Nell now. But his use of that long-ago name distanced him, made this less real. 'Where are we going? I thought you wanted to talk.'

'No, *you* wanted to talk. Turn around,' he repeated. 'I am sure you would much prefer to walk than be slung over my shoulder.'

'Very well.' Nell stepped outside. 'Which way?'

'Go around to the back of the folly and you will see a narrow path. Follow that. Do not look around.'

'Very well.' She could not hear him behind her as she threaded her way along the path, hardly more than the passage forced by deer through the bracken and brambles. 'What did you say to me yesterday? That foreign language?' She was less interested in the meaning than in judging how close he was; the man moved like a ghost.

'Hmm? Ah, yes. I said, *Where the needle goes, surely the thread will follow.*'

'A Romany proverb?' she guessed. 'You are a Gypsy?'

'A Rom?'

Ah, she thought, *he corrects me. This is something he is sensitive about.*

'I am what I chose to be, when I chose,' he said, very close. 'Turn down the hill—'

There was the thunder of hooves. A big horse, ridden fast. *Marc and Corinth,* Nell thought as Salterton's hand came over her mouth and she was pulled back hard against him.

'Stand still, Helena,' he murmured. Through the trees there was a flash of grey as the horse passed, then the woods were silent again. Salterton continued to hold her. 'You smell good, Helena,' he said, his breath feathering her cold ear.

She bit down, hard, and wrenched at his imprisoning arm. Foolishly it had never occurred to her that she might be in that sort of danger.

'You have spirit.' He released her and gave her a little forward push. 'There is no cause to fear, I do not force women. I have no need,' he added a moment later as her pulse rate began to slow a little.

'Your arrogance is astonishing,' Nell said, concentrating on walking steadily. She refused to let him see he was frightening her.

'It is only arrogance if it is unjustified.' The chuckle from behind had her gritting her teeth. 'Carlow has fallen in love with you. He will be so very unhappy to have lost you.'

'Lost me?' The slope was steeper now, Nell told herself. That was why she stumbled, had to put out a hand to steady herself.

'Calm yourself, I do not kill women either,' Salterton said. 'He will not want you back, that English aristocrat, after you have lain with me.'

'You think you can seduce me? *You?*' Nell put every ounce of contempt she could manage into her voice. 'You can force me, no doubt. But *seduce* me?'

'Oh, yes. It may take a little time, but I am a patient man. A very patient man.'

'Why are you doing this?' Nell demanded. She was breathing heavily now, despite her best efforts at control. Her breath was making clouds in the freezing air and her throat was raw.

'I owe the Carlows nothing but misery and death,' he said simply, so simply that at first she thought she had misheard him. 'It is a long story and an old one, but then, as I said, I am a patient man and I do not forget.'

'Or forgive, apparently,' Nell said tartly and heard him laugh softly. 'And why involve me?'

'Why, you are a part of the thread too—you and your brother and your sister.'

'They are alive?' She stumbled again, badly this time, and he caught her by the shoulders, holding her so she could not turn to face him.

'Don't you know, Helena?'

'No. No, I do not,' she admitted. 'Nathan vanished—did you kill him?'

'Perhaps.'

Nell stifled a sob and pulled free, walking on ahead. *He is not going to make me cry. He is tormenting me. Nathan is safe, Nathan is alive; they both are.*

'You should ask Miss Price,' he said. 'She has secrets too.'

He was trying to unsettle her, torment her. Diana Price could know nothing of Nathan. After a moment, when she regained her composure, she said, 'This thread you speak of is silken, I presume, and makes a rope to hang a peer with?' She heard a grunt of assent. 'And the rosemary is for remembrance?'

'What rosemary?'

'You did not send a sprig of it? To Lord Narborough?'

'No,' he said, and for the first time she thought she had unsettled him, just a little, but he said nothing more.

Almost at the bottom of the slope now, she could see meadows through the trees and guessed they must be downstream of the lake where the party had skated. Where was he taking her? Should she try and escape, or should she stay passive and hope to learn more?

'Here, turn to the right.' There was a hut of some kind nestled in the edge of the wood. A shepherd's night shelter perhaps, for when the flocks were brought down to the water meadows to graze. 'Go in. It is not locked.'

Nell pushed open the door. It was snug enough, although dark, without a window. The thick planks overlapped to keep the worst of the draughts out, and a pallet heaped with blankets lay against one wall. Nell eyed it nervously.

'Sit down on the stool and put your hands behind you.'

With a sigh of relief she did as she was told, sinking down on the three-legged stool in front of a small hearth. She had hardly settled when her wrists were lashed together, not brutally, but with a ruthless efficiency— and what felt like a soft cord. Salterton had left the door open for light while he knelt to strike a flame and touch it to the pile of dry kindling on the hearthstone.

'It is very dry,' he remarked as though reading her thoughts. 'There will be no smoke to guide your gallant lover here.'

'He will find you,' she swore, looking down at the sweeping brim of the slouch hat.

'I doubt it. When the time comes, I will find him. I will find all of them.' Salterton got to his feet and shut the door, leaving the interior of the hut lit only by the flickering flames. He sank down on his haunches beside the hearth and tossed his hat onto the pallet. In the firelight his face was a mask with dark, glittering eyes, the lines made harsher by the shadows.

But he was, she could tell, a disturbingly handsome man with a feral grace about him and the edge of wild danger in every movement. It was a strange contrast with the calm irony of his voice. It would not do, Nell told herself, to underestimate his intelligence.

'Why will you find them?'

'To deliver an old foretelling,' he said, and it seemed to her that a nerve jumped on one of the beautiful high cheekbones as though he was in pain. He lifted a hand and touched his forehead for a moment.

'What? What is foretold?'

'You will find out. All of you. The children will pay for the sins of their fathers. It has been seen and it has been said.'

Nell told herself that the thin trickle of ice down her spine was a draught from the door, not the effect of the lilting voice speaking its prophesy.

'I will leave you here. Just for a little, Helena, while I make sure the coast is clear. And then you will come with me and learn how to please me.' The dark man's voice dropped into a caress like velvet on her skin, and he came up onto his knees beside her, one long brown finger tracing the line of her cheek as his lips just brushed her own. 'Wait for me, Helena,' he said as she recoiled. 'Wait and think of your lover's suffering when he imagines what will pass between us.'

Nell strained her ears as the door closed behind him, listening. Even in the deep snow around the hut he made no sound. She counted in her head—one minute, two, three—then stood up, her arms awkwardly behind her, and knelt down on the pallet with its thin covering of blankets. Somehow she had to get her hands in front of her.

For what seemed like an hour, but was probably only fifteen minutes, Nell rolled and twisted and swore, hampered by her heavy coat and thick skirts. Finally, at the cost of wrenched shoulders and sore wrists, she managed to get her arms under her bottom and thread her legs through.

She sat on the pallet panting for a moment, then used her fingertips to pull out the knife she had concealed in the side of her half-boot. It had seemed wildly melodramatic when she had selected the sharp little fruit knife and slid it into its hiding place; now she was grateful for the impulse. It was far more useful than any pistol would have been; with it wedged between her feet she sawed through the bonds easily.

It was not until she looked more carefully at the loops still tied around her wrists that she realized it was more of the silken rope, spun this time into a thin cord. Nell started to tug at the knots, then realized she was wasting time. She had to get back to the house, tell Marc what Salterton had said, and hope he and Lord Narborough and Hal could make some sense of it.

All I have to do is elude him, she thought ruefully as she opened the door and peered out. Salterton's tracks led back behind the hut—he had gone into the woods. Nell took a moment to get her bearings, then set off along the edge of the trees, hugging the hedge line. It was at least a mile back to the house, more likely a mile and a half by this route.

Nell ran and walked alternately, stumbling as she kept turning to check around her for pursuit. How long would he take on his errand before he returned for her? Where was Marc?

Then out of the corner of her eye, in the distance, she saw movement. Nell stopped, squinting against the dazzle of sun on the snow, and realized it was the top of a carriage—and with this snow, the only route a carriage could take was the turnpike road. If she cut across the meadows, across the frozen river and up the other side, then there was a good chance she would find another carriage, a cottage, a farm. Refuge.

But it meant leaving cover and going into the open. Nell hesitated, then turned her back on the woods and ran, the snow kicking up behind her, her throat raw with the cold air. For a moment she thought she had done it, then a dark figure burst from the woods by the hut, threw off its hampering greatcoat and began to run diagonally across the meadow to intercept her.

He had farther to run but he was stronger, his legs longer, and she was battling her clinging skirts. Nell wrenched off her bonnet and struggled with buttons as she ran, gasping with relief as she left hat and coat behind her. But the advantage was not enough; as she reached the river and launched herself across its treacherous slippery surface, she could hear Salterton behind her.

Sheer terror took her across the ice as though on skates but her very speed betrayed her. At the far bank Nell tripped, tried to stop, felt herself falling and was jerked upright.

'You spurn my hospitality, Helena?' The dark man pulled her round to face him. He hardly seemed to have exerted himself at all, his breathing calm compared to her panting breaths.

'Oh! I am going to be sick!' She doubled up as though retching and he freed her arm. Frantic, Nell's groping fingers found the knife in her boot again and she straightened with it held out in front of her. 'Let me go or I swear I will use this,' she gasped, meaning it.

Salterton moved so fast his hand seemed to blur. Nell screamed in fear and fury and slashed at him, but he caught her wrist with one hand and wrenched the knife from her with the other.

'Hellcat,' he snarled, all his control gone, and she stood there transfixed, the blood from his slashed hand dripping onto the frozen river as the knife pressed against her throat.

Chapter Twenty

'**Y**ou said you did not kill women,' Nell said, the blade moving against her windpipe as she spoke. With her mind she tried to reach out to Marc. *I'm sorry, so sorry, I love you…*

'I do not.' Slowly Salterton lowered the blade. 'Not even wildcats like you.' The knife vanished, the grip on her arms changed as he pulled her back towards the centre of the river. Under their feet the ice gave an ominous creak. It was deep water here, Nell remembered, the outflow from the dammed millpond.

'Back across to the woods, and this time, if you try anything, I'll knock you out and carry—'

The shot was explosive in the cold air. Salterton spun round, Nell held before him like a shield, to face the horsemen galloping towards them. It was all three of the Carlow men, she realized, both Marc and Hal riding with rifles in their hands.

Nell blinked back tears and smiled through trembling lips. *He has come for me.* The horses skidded to a halt on the bank in the flurry of snow, and the three riders held them back, their faces set.

'He's armed,' she called. 'He has a knife.' And it was in Salterton's hand again, the hand that was not clasping her in front of him in a cruel parody of the way Marc had held her when they skated together. The blade lay against her breast.

'Nell, are you all right?' Marc's voice was calm, but under it she could hear the killing rage.

'Yes, yes, I'm fine.'

'Let her go,' Lord Narborough said, his face set in lines of fury. 'What sort of coward hides behind a woman?'

'One who has some sense,' the dark man retorted, apparently amused by the older man's anger. 'And besides, I haven't finished with her yet. She is a woman of spirit this one. I shall enjoy having her in my bed.'

There was a snarl, and Hal flung out an arm and seized the barrel of Marc's rifle. The brothers exchanged a long look, then Hal released his grip and Marcus lowered the gun.

'Let her go, come here and I will fight you, man to man, with a damned knife if that is your weapon.'

'Why should I?' Salterton was edging Nell closer to midstream, perhaps eight feet from the bank. Under their feet the creaking became cracking. 'She's mine. You won't touch me while I hold her—you think I care for your foolish notions of duels and honour?'

'No, it is plain you do not,' Marc said, his voice contemptuous. 'You are no gentleman.'

'But I have the woman,' the dark man pointed out. 'You will not attack me while I hold her, and soon, very soon, she will be where you will never find her, enjoying a man who is just that—a man, not some aristocratic parasite hiding behind his valet and his butler.' He pulled Nell back as he spoke and rubbed his cheek possessively against hers. 'Mine, you see?'

Nell jerked away as far as his hold would let her, and the long barrel of Marcus's rifle came up, unwavering. She stared at the tiny black hole of the muzzle.

'I'm sorry, Nell, I cannot let that happen,' Marc said.

Nell gasped. He was going to shoot her rather than let Salterton ravish her? She wanted to shout out, but her voice was dry in her throat.

Beside her the dark man chuckled. 'Bloody fool, with his gentlemanly dramatics. He thinks you would rather be dead than dishonoured? You have not changed at all, Marcus.'

'I love you, Nell,' Marc said, his deep voice projecting across the still air. 'Remember how I held you on the ice when we skated? Remember that, how it ended?'

The skating? What on earth? Nell stared back at the rifle and realized what he meant. She let her feet slide out in front of her and dropped like a stone through Salterton's clutching arm to land heavily at his feet.

And as she fell she heard the shot, its sharp report mingling with the sound of the ice. Above her there was a sobbing gasp. She scrabbled with hands and feet, seeing the long cracks beginning to radiate outwards, and Salterton fell, landing even more heavily than she had, and the cracks opened, the world tilted and she slid down, hitting icy water that knocked the breath from her lungs.

Beside her, Salterton thrashed, twisted, and got one brown hand up and onto the edge of the ice and the other locked into her hair. There was blood in the water and his face was distorted in a rictus of pain and effort as he fought the current that was dragging them both under, away from the hole.

'Nell!' And Marcus plunged in; his hands supported her as he fought to lift her. She felt her hair freed, then the other man had his hand under her armpit and was pushing, working *with* Marcus, and she was lifted towards the surface and Hal's reaching hands as he lay on the ice.

Marcus kicked against the pull of the river, his boots filling with water, his coat a dead weight around his shoulders. But Nell was half out now; he glimpsed his father kneeling beside Hal, reaching for her.

'Together,' a voice rasped, and he realized it was the dark man. With a great effort he lifted, and Nell slid out onto the ice. Hal pushed her towards their father, then leaned in again, his hand closing over Marcus's wrist.

'Here, hold the edge, we'll get you out.' Marcus turned in the water, reaching for the other man with his free hand.

Like a gaffed fish, the dark man twisted away, his face stark with rejection.

'Don't be a fool, you'll drown.' But he had gone, swept away under the ice into the green gloom.

'Can you get out or am I going to have to come in and get you?' Hal demanded through gritted teeth. 'My bloody arm is half out of its socket.'

Marcus took the other hand held out to him, kicked, and was hauled out onto the ice. 'The damn fool wouldn't let me save him,' he gasped, sprawled on his belly, coughing up water.

'That's an economy then,' Hal said, his tone at odds

with the urgency with which he was dragging Marcus's coat off him and wrapping him in his own. 'No trial and no hanging.'

'Nell?' Marcus turned to find her cradled in his father's arms, his greatcoat round her as the earl chaffed her hands.

'She's fainted,' he said. 'We need to get her back, now.'

'We all need to get back,' Marcus said, finding his feet and limping towards the horses. 'Hal, can you lift her up to me?' he asked as he got up onto Corinth. He wasn't sure how he kept going, but he was damned if anyone other than himself was taking Nell home.

She came to as he snuggled her against himself, one arm around her, one hand for the reins. 'Marcus? I knew you'd come. I'm very sorry. I thought I could find out...'

'And I thought I'd lost you,' he said gruffly.

'Not when you can shoot like that,' she murmured against his sodden shirt front. 'He's gone, hasn't he? Under the ice?' she asked, her voice stronger as she turned to face the river.

Marcus saw his father and brother looking at him, their eyes reflecting the hope—and the doubt—that he knew was in his. 'Yes, he's gone,' he said firmly, with a shake of his head to the other two to keep them silent, and sent Corinth into a smooth canter towards home.

'Where am I?' Nell asked, confused. She was in a room that was not her own, surrounded by a babble of voices and bundled up so tight in a cocoon of blankets that she could not move or see properly.

'In my room,' Marcus said beside her. 'Will everyone please go?' he added, raising his voice to somewhere just short of a parade ground bellow.

'Marcus, my dear, it is hardly seemly. Nell should be in her own room and Miss Price and I will see to her.' Lady Narborough sounded uncharacteristically flustered.

'Go and look after Father, Mama,' Marcus said firmly. 'He got cold and has probably overexerted himself.'

'Oh, yes, of course. But Miss Price—' Nell heard her voice die away down the corridor, still protesting faintly.

'Thank you, Diana, if you could just take the staff with you. The fire is lit, the tub is filled.' With ruthless efficiency, Marcus cleared the room and came back to Nell. 'Now then, let's get you out of those wet clothes.' He started to peel back the blankets.

'And you,' Nell protested, trying to pull herself together and be practical and sensible, and just feeling as though all she wanted was to melt into Marc's arms and never to let go. 'You must change.'

'I have,' he said, throwing the last damp blanket aside, and she saw he was wearing a heavy silk dressing gown over loose trousers and a shirt.

'Now, out of these clothes.' He swore under his breath as the sodden fastenings refused to cooperate, picked up some scissors from a side table and ruthlessly cut everything off her.

'Marcus!'

'My God, you are cold right through,' he said, ignoring her flustered efforts to shield her white, goose-pimpled body. 'Into the bath with you.'

'Marcus,' she tried again as he lowered her into the warm water. 'Your mother, Miss Price—everyone knows I am in here with you! Oh, oh that is wonderful.' The blissful warmth distracted her for a moment. 'What are they going to think?'

He rolled up his sleeves, knelt by the tub and began to wash her, his big hands sure and gentle. 'They will think that I love you and don't want anyone else looking after you.'

'Yes, but Lady Narborough—'

'Hush.' He silenced her by the simple expedient of kissing her, his mouth gentling over hers until she stopped trying to talk and simply relaxed back against the towel he had draped around the rim of the tub.

'Sleepy,' she heard herself murmur as he freed her lips. 'So sleepy.'

'You are warm now, it is safe to sleep. To bed with you, Nell.'

She was vaguely aware of being lifted, of the embrace of soft linen and strong arms, then sound and feeling faded away and she slept, knowing only that she was safe.

Nell woke slowly in a strange bed. The room was unlit except for the cool wash of moonlight turning everything stark black and silver. In the grate the fire burned low, a dull, deep red that told her she had slept for hours. The curtains must be open, she reasoned, blinking her eyes into focus as she turned her cheek on the pillow. *Marcus.* She could smell his cologne, that faint tang of citrus, and beneath it the scent of his skin. She was in his bed. Now she recognised the room from that night when she had slept there chastely in his arms.

Her reaching hand found no other body in the bed, only a dip in the mattress beside her and a faint residual warmth. He had been there, she thought, looking after her through the night. She lay still for a while, letting the events of the day wash over her, absorbing them, hearing again Marc's voice. *I love you,* he had said as he had fired the shot that freed her, his aim as true as his heart, she thought, her own heart catching in her breast.

She sat up, and found she was wearing a nightgown, even though she had no recollection of putting one on. 'Marc?' He was standing by the window looking out.

'Are you all right?' He turned and strode to the bedside, dropping whatever he had been holding onto the covers. 'Were you dreaming? A nightmare?'

'No.' She let him take her hands, cupping them in his as though to reassure himself that she was warm. 'I was thinking of you, how you saved me.'

'I have never been more afraid in my life,' he admitted, sitting down beside her. 'I saw the knife at your throat, the blood—'

'His blood, my knife,' Nell said, daring to boast a little. 'But you shot true.'

'One of the few things Hal will admit I do better than he can,' he confessed. 'Why did you do it, Nell? Why did you go out alone to meet him?'

'Because I felt responsible. I am sorry. I know I deceived you, I know I asked for your trust and then betrayed it.'

'No, never that. I never thought that, Nell. I was angry that you had put yourself in danger, but my trust in you never failed.'

Comforted, immeasurably relieved, she pushed the pillows up and sat so they were shoulder to shoulder, Marc's body a comforting bulwark. 'I brought the first rope to you. I am my father's daughter. I had to go.'

'And I am my father's son,' Marc said dryly. 'But you

are no more responsible for your father's actions than I am for mine, Nell.'

'I know. And you know I understand why your father did what he did. But if Papa *was* innocent, then there is still a murderer and a traitor at large.'

'Nell, it is history now.' He put an arm around her shoulders and held her tight.

'It is not. How can it be? Salterton, or whoever he was, said that he was the agent of an old foretelling. He called me *Helena*. I asked him what he meant and he said, *You will find out. All of you. The children will pay for the sins of their fathers. It has been seen and it has been said.* And he knows you—did you hear him say you have not changed?'

'I don't know *him,* it is more of his tricks. He has gone, Nell, and the threat with him.'

She knew every tone of his voice, the feel of his body, and something did not ring true. 'You don't believe that, do you? You do not truly believe he is dead.'

'He should be. I hit him square in the shoulder, the water was deep and fast and bitter cold.' Marcus paused, then said, 'I'll not lie to you, Nell. I will not be sure until I see his dead body.'

'Then we must take precautions,' she said, trying to sound matter-of-fact. 'I will need a large footman-body-guard at my new shop.'

Marcus got up abruptly and began to light candles until the room was ablaze with light.

'Marcus?'

'I want to see your face, Nell. Look.' He held out the thing he had been holding by the window, a cut and frayed length of silken cord. 'I took this off your wrists. I faced what it would have felt like to lose you and I cannot bear that again. I love you, Nell, you know that. Marry me.'

'Your parents,' she said hopelessly. 'The scandal.'

'My father adores you, my mother enquired tartly when I was going to make an honest woman of you, commenting that I did not deserve you.'

'Oh.' Unable to look at him, Nell picked at the frayed ends of the cord. It had dried and the intertwining colours showed vividly: deep rose-red, periwinkle-blue, golden yellow. 'But—'

'The scandal. I would say to hell with it and what anyone says, but I'll not have anyone hurt you, Nell. We will go away for a long honeymoon, visit Longrigg, the Carlow estate in Northumberland. It will be a nine-day wonder, for those who recall who Helena Wardale is. When we come back there will be other scandals, you will see, and what there is we will face down together.'

'Truly?' she questioned. 'Marcus, the past—'

'The past is gone into history. We must build a new life, new memories.'

Something very like hope stirred. *We*, he had said. *We*. 'Marcus, do you truly want to marry me?'

'I love you, Nell.' He stood by the bed looking down at her, smiling ruefully. 'I will love you always, whether you'll have me or not. But say *yes*. You like me a little, I have it on good authority that you love my frown. You seem to enjoy my lovemaking. Could you learn to love me just a little too, Nell?'

'Learn?' Her voice was all over the place. She very much feared she was going to cry. 'I love you already, you idiot man. I've loved you for weeks. But I thought it would be wrong, I thought it would hurt you, Marcus.

Marc, darling—don't look like that…' The smile had faded as she spoke, his eyes had darkened, he looked as though he was in shock.

'Don't I look like a man who has just been given his heart's desire?' he asked after a moment that seemed to stretch for ever. 'Like a man who is realising that he has found his soulmate and that, by some miracle, she feels the same way? I'm not sure quite how to contain so much happiness, what to do with it, Nell.'

'We could make love,' she suggested, realising that tears were trickling down her face and that she did not care, she was so happy. 'Would that make it better?'

'That would make the end of the world better, Nell,' he said, smiling at her.

'And you won't need to be careful?' she suggested as he bent to unbutton the long row of bone buttons on the chaste nightgown.

'No, I won't need to be careful,' he agreed, his voice husky. 'You know, Nell, that night after Salterton broke in here, when I saw your robe with its careful darns, I swore I was going to buy you something pretty and frivolous from Bond Street. Just think what fun we can have shopping,' he murmured, bowing his head to take her right nipple into his mouth, his teeth and his tongue together making her gasp as it hardened and peaked.

'We would come back, laden with bandboxes.' He released it and leant over to tease the other one. 'And you would try everything on for me.' His tongue trailed lower as his hands pushed the nightgown apart.

'And then I would take it all off again?' Nell managed to gasp as his tongue circled lazily in her navel.

'Oh, yes. Very, very, slowly. Of course, you've got

these nightgowns already and it would be extravagant to replace them while there's wear in them.' Marcus gripped the sides and tore. 'Damn, look at that. Quite unwearable.'

'I do love you,' Nell said, a laugh escaping her despite the utter havoc Marcus was causing to her internal equilibrium. He was managing to simultaneously shed his dressing gown and kiss his way along her hipbones. 'But, Marc, please, I don't think I can bear this. I want you, now, this moment.'

'You've got me,' he said, his eyes bright in the candlelight.

'Inside me,' she said, and felt herself blushing.

He knelt between her parted thighs, looking down at her, and she blushed more intensely as she saw the heat in his eyes, the intent. 'I cannot think of anywhere I would rather be,' he said, lowering himself over her, taking just enough weight on his elbows that she was conscious of every hard-muscled inch of his body.

'Love me,' she whispered as he eased into her, inch by aching inch.

'Always,' he said against her lips as she curled her legs around his hips to take him as deep as she could. 'Always.'

And when he brought her to the peak of delight he stayed with her, driving her higher and higher until she was sobbing his name as he lost all control, lost in her body, lost in her love.

'Sweetheart?' Marcus stirred drowsily, reaching out a long arm to pull Nell down against his body. 'What is the time?'

'Nine.'

'Nine?' He sat bolt upright, blinking in the morning light. 'Aren't you hungry?'

'No.' Nell shook her head, sat up too and carried on carefully pulling threads out of the remnants of the silken cord and sorting them by colour on the white bedspread.

'What are you doing?'

She turned her head and smiled at him. His hair was rumpled, his chin deeply shadowed with his morning beard and his grey eyes were heavy lidded from a night when they had taken little time for sleep. He was beautiful and he was going to be her husband.

'We are going to make a new family out of the pain of two old ones,' she said, hoping she could explain, hoping he would understand. 'Perhaps one day I will find Nathan and Rosalind, but…' An image of Nathan's face as she had last seen it, sharp with intelligence and sinful secrets, seemed to shimmer before her and was gone.

'We will create a new love to heal the wounds,' Marc murmured, lifting her hair to kiss the hollow under her collarbone.

Yes, he understands. 'These are so lovely.' Nell held up the vivid threads that clung to her hand with a life of their own. 'I am going to embroider my wedding veil with them. Hearts and flowers, not pain and death.'

'You would make something beautiful out of all that hate and fear,' Marc murmured, turning her face for his kiss.

'I don't remember ever being this happy.' The silken threads fell from her fingers as she held him to her heart.

'I swear,' Marc said against her lips, 'that, if you will trust me with your heart, you will say that every day of your life.'

'I trust you,' Nell said. 'With my life, with my heart and with my love. We have made a new foretelling, one that will come true, one that will last for our children's children.'

'In that case,' Marcus said, kissing his way down to where her heart beat so strongly for him, 'we had better make a start on the first of those children, don't you think?'

'Oh, yes,' Nell murmured, and it was the last coherent thing she said for quite a while.

* * * * *

COMING NEXT MONTH FROM

HARLEQUIN®
HISTORICAL

Available June 29, 2010

- **ALASKA BRIDE ON THE RUN**
  by **Kate Bridges**
  (Western)

- **PAYING THE VIRGIN'S PRICE**
  by **Christine Merrill**
  (Regency)
  Book 2 in the *Silk & Scandal* miniseries

- **UNTAMED ROGUE, SCANDALOUS MISTRESS**
  by **Bronwyn Scott**
  (1830s)

- **THE MERCENARY'S BRIDE**
  by **Terri Brisbin**
  (Medieval)
  Book 2 in the *Knights of Brittany* trilogy

HARLEQUIN®

A Romance

FOR EVERY MOOD™

Spotlight on
Heart & Home

Heartwarming romances
where love can happen
right when you least expect it.

See the next page to enjoy a sneak peek
from Silhouette Special Edition®,
a Heart and Home series.

Introducing MCFARLANE'S PERFECT BRIDE
by USA TODAY *bestselling author Christine Rimmer,*
from Silhouette Special Edition®.

Entranced. Captivated. Enchanted.

Connor sat across the table from Tori Jones and couldn't help thinking that those words exactly described what effect the small-town schoolteacher had on him. He might as well stop trying to tell himself he wasn't interested. He was powerfully drawn to her.

Clearly, he should have dated more when he was younger.

There had been a couple of other women since Jennifer had walked out on him. But he had never been entranced. Or captivated. Or enchanted.

Until now.

He wanted her—*her,* Tori Jones, in particular. Not just someone suitably attractive and well-bred, as Jennifer had been. Not just someone sophisticated, sexually exciting and discreet, which pretty much described the two women he'd dated after his marriage crashed and burned.

It came to him that he...he *liked* this woman. And that was new to him. He liked her quick wit, her wisdom and her big heart. He liked the passion in her voice when she talked about things she believed in.

He liked *her.* And suddenly it mattered all out of proportion that she might like him, too.

Was he losing it? He couldn't help but wonder. Was he cracking under the strain—of the soured economy, the McFarlane House setbacks, his divorce, the scary changes in his son? Of the changes he'd decided he needed to make in his life and himself?

Strangely, right then, on his first date with Tori Jones, he didn't care if he just might be going over the edge. He was having a great time—having *fun*, of all things—and he didn't want it to end.

*Is Connor finally able to admit his feelings to Tori,
and are they reciprocated?*
Find out in McFARLANE'S PERFECT BRIDE
by USA TODAY bestselling author Christine Rimmer.
Available July 2010,
only from Silhouette Special Edition®.

Introducing

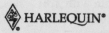